KRISTIN ROUSE

IF IT'S BROKE

BOOK ONE

I0527479

CITY OWL
PRESS

THE FIX
If It's Broke, Book 1

CITY OWL PRESS
www.cityowlpress.com

Cover Design by Olivia at MiblArt. All stock photos licensed appropriately.

Edited by Mary Cain.

For information on subsidiary rights, please contact the publisher at info@cityowlpress.com.

Print Edition ISBN: 978-1-944728-37-3

Digital Edition ISBN: 978-1-944728-38-0

Printed in the United States of America

For the kind, brave souls who unflinchingly told me their stories of

addiction and triumph as I was creating Ezra's—

I hope I've done you proud.

CHAPTER ONE

For not liking me very much, Mac's cat seems awfully invested in where I am at any given moment. I've been on my porch for all of two minutes, just long enough to puff down a third of my cigarette, and already she's butting her face against the screen and scraping at it with her clawless paw. She mewls pathetically at me. If I didn't know her better, I'd try picking her up. But walking around Anja's wedding with the little shit's bite marks all over my arms isn't high on my agenda.

It's possible she's trying to get me to pay attention to the fact that I'm starting a fire inside my kitchen. Shit.

I stub my cigarette out in an old coffee can, make it through the screen without the cat darting past my legs, and fling open the waffle iron in time to see a plume of smoke and a charred, black pastry.

Fucking hell, Mackenzie. Can't you do anything right?

You know you can't.

This is what I know: my name is Ezra Mackenzie. I'll be twenty-six in just under a month, although half the time I feel like I'm still a sixteen-year-old idiot, and the other half I feel like I'm pushing forty. And that's because I'm an alcoholic six months into recovery. Right now, though, if I don't get the fucking lead out, I'm going to be seriously late to my sponsor's wedding rehearsal brunch.

For the sake of clarity, let's just get it out of the way here and now that there is no "I used to be an alcoholic." I am an alcoholic—I just don't drink anymore. You're either an alcoholic or you're not. You can handle your liquor, or you can't. I have plenty of friends who can handle their liquor just fine. I can't. I never could. Booze was my most consistent, most reliable partner for my entire adult life. There are a lot of things about being in recovery that suck, just like there are a lot of things that are freeing and about a million times better. But for the moment, that stuff is kind of beside the point. I'm about to be so, so fucking late, and Anja *will* kill me.

It's not entirely my fault. The damn cinnamon rolls I tried making never rose, and I had to improvise. Unfortunately, I only have one waffle maker—an ancient yellow Cuisinart model Mac used nearly to death before he handed it down to me—so the process has been sort of slow going. At least I have something to offer like I promised.

The cat, another bequeathment, is now stalking up and down the high, narrow counter separating my kitchen from my living room. I've been trying to get her to knock off doing that. Mac had her trained, but damned if I can figure out how. I hiss at her, which makes her skitter across the counter and knock my wallet, keys, and cigarettes onto the floor in her retreat under the futon. The little light on the waffle maker finally clicks off, thank God. I pull the cookie sheet the other successful waffles are resting on out of the oven, flip a couple of switches, and cover the sheet with a dishtowel.

I press another cigarette between my lips once I'm behind the wheel of my car. I debate stopping for coffee, but I remember Anja said her future sister-in-law is bringing home coffee especially for this morning straight from Brazil. It's probably rude in some way to decline coffee that has been smuggled through customs specifically for one brunch, as caffeine-deprived as I am at the moment. I pacify myself with chain-smoking, since I didn't get my adequate nicotine fix earlier. I'm crumpling up a now-empty pack by the time I pull up to Mama A's house. I balance the sheet of waffles in one hand and use the other to pop my trunk and haul out the collared shirt I trade my jacket for, then spritz myself down with some essential oils diluted in water to mask the cigarette stench. Deep under the layers of eucalyptus and orange, there's a faint trace of the alcohol that's yielded from the pressing process. I know the scent of booze anywhere, even if this application is toxic as shit. Still, I don't want to be smoky-Joe in the corner who no one but the Almeida family knows.

I'm halfway up the walk to the front door when Anja bursts through it, looking at me wide-eyed and frantic. She's normally so put-together—hair perfect, eyebrows sharp and pointed, a wide smile on her face, her clothing never mussed. Playing bride has worn down her penchant for perfection and this morning she's anything but put-together. I wonder if she slept at all the night before.

"You're *late*," she snaps, her face contorted and eyebrows as high on her forehead as I've ever seen in all my years of knowing her.

"I'm sorry," I say, trying to sound contrite so she won't actually try to strangle me. Which she is more than capable of. "The cinnamon rolls were a major bust. I brought waffles instead, but they took forever."

She rolls her eyes, but the look on her face softens a little. She has a real screw-up for a best friend, but she loves me in spite of it. "Mama made more food than any twenty people could ever eat. And they're all going to be here any minute."

She yanks me through the front door, takes the sheet pan from me, and marches us through the foyer. Before we turn the corner to the kitchen, I drop my voice and nudge her. "Are your parents among those twenty people?"

Her face falls. "No. They said they had plans they couldn't get out of."

"Ah, kid. I'm sorry they're still being such assholes."

She tosses her long blond hair over her shoulder with a flick of her head, and twirls her engagement ring around on her finger. We both have our nervous, post-addiction habits—I chew my nails. She twirls her ring. We both smoke like chimneys. She and I know that they serve to mask our cravings when the compulsion starts coming on too strong.

"It's fine," she says, but I'm not convinced for a second. Bad blood in the MacCullor family runs deep and Anja has never been their favored child. Under-age drinking charges and DUIs tend to reflect poorly on politicians and make the child who earns them something of a black sheep.

"It's not fine that they're treating you like shit," I say.

"I don't want them here if they're going to be like they are. You're here. Mattias's family is here. That's all that matters to me."

"If you insist," I say, even though I don't entirely believe her.

She peeks around the corner and swallows hard. "I wanted to warn you—Mattias and Lukas went out last night with their sister. They tend to go a little over-the-top when they get together. Mattias slept on the couch so he wouldn't bother me when he got in last night, but... Well, they're all sort of detoxing this morning."

When you're only six months into your recovery, you tend to be a little sensitive about certain things. I can smell a whiskey bottle opening from a room over. And I can definitely smell the residual alcohol leaching out of someone's pores the morning after a big night out. I feel a massive pang of jealousy—of course, I wouldn't have been invited out to whatever bar they celebrated at, but mostly, I wonder what they drank. How many they had. Microbrews or rum and cokes, whatever—I want it. I'm achingly jealous that they got to drink last night and I didn't.

"Right. Thanks for the heads up," I say.

"Are you going to be okay around them?" Anja's my sponsor. It's her job to ask me things like that.

"Sure."

"Liar."

"I'll be fine," I say emphatically, although it's a vicious lie. "I have to get used to this sort of thing, don't I?"

"Yes, you do. I'd just prefer it wasn't today that you have to do it."

"Is there ever going to be a better day?"

She shakes her head. Before we turn into the kitchen, she peeks under the dishtowels to survey my offering. "Hey… Well done, Mackenzie. You didn't even burn them."

"It's been years since I set my kitchen on fire, thank you very much." I refuse to admit I almost did set my kitchen on fire today. Anja knows what not even my landlord knows about that kitchen fire—that it was a drunken accident. It's a wonder my eyebrows grew back in properly. And it's a damn good thing, plastered as I was, that I figured out how to use my fire extinguisher. Thinking on it now, I'm not sure why I don't smoke in my apartment. It's not like I'm ever going to get my security deposit back after that.

We turn the corner and enter the kitchen. As I expected, Mattias, Anja's fiancé, and Lukas, Mattias's brother, are hunched over steaming cups of coffee and hiding their eyes from the light streaming in through the windows. An extra-large bottle of Aleve sits between them, and Lukas's now-empty Gatorade bottle has tipped over on the counter in front of him. Mama A—I think her real name is Claudia, but I couldn't say for sure, she insists on being called 'Mama A'—

shrieks when she sees me, puts her hands on the side of my stubbly cheeks, and kisses my forehead. I kiss her cheek in return, and she coos over the sheet of waffles Anja shows her before pointing me towards Mattias, who's supposed to be folding napkins around silverware and is slacking on the job.

"What you guys probably want is straight water," I mutter as I reach for a stack of napkins myself and roll one around a bundle of cutlery, but that's just because I can't stand sports drinks. Already I can smell the morning-after booze stench coming off both of them. It's every bit as difficult to have it rubbed in my face as Anja suspected it might be.

"There is not enough water in the world for this hangover, man," he says. From the way he's squinting in the kitchen light and the sallow look to his skin, I almost believe him. I have had many of those hangovers myself. I almost miss those hangovers—*almost*.

Mama A barks something formidable in Portuguese— there's little about Mama A that isn't formidable, even with her diminutive stature and permanent laugh-lines—the only word of which I understand is a name. *Juliana*. The one Almeida I don't know yet, save for pictures of a pretty brunette scattered around the house.

The owner of the name turns, pulls a dry cloth from the back pocket of her low-slung pajama pants, and dries the hands that had been plunged in a sink full of murky water. I'd been so distracted by Mattias and Lukas I hadn't even realized she was standing there. "I'm going, Mama, I'm going." Her husky voice draws my attention, but that's not what keeps it. Her clingy tank top is speckled with water and her navel peeks out between the hem of her top and the waistband of her pants. My eyes travel up her body, surveying her bronze skin, her long neck, the messy heap of ebony hair piled on top of her head. Her barely-conscious expression and sleep-filled eyes the only mar on her beyond-lovely face.

The pictures on the mantelpiece do not do this girl justice.

Anja nudges my shoulder. "Ezra, you haven't met Juliana, my new sister-in-law. Jules, this my... Ezra."

"Anja's Ezra? I've heard a bit about Anja's Ezra. Nice to meet you," Juliana says with a smile.

It takes me less than a millisecond to notice her dimples, deep-set in both cheeks, and the way her lips rub together like she's rubbing in invisible lip gloss after she speaks. She reaches out to shake my hand, and her fingers are pruney against my palm. As I grip it, a jolt ripples through my arm and courses its way up to my chest. I'm sure it's just me, because the next second, she's swatting at her mother and leaving the room, presumably to change into something other than her damp pajamas.

I feel something foreign, something I haven't felt in a long time, and certainly not since I sobered up. It feels like the beginning of a problem I shouldn't mind having. Problems of any kind aren't exactly welcome these days—even ones that look like Juliana Almeida.

***

I take Anja up on a piece of nicotine gum for the rehearsal later that day. I don't chew my nicotine typically, but I'll make an exception today. The tingle of it against my cheek is handy for distraction—it keeps me from paying attention to curves, to the intoxicating scent of her subtle, citrusy perfume. Or at least, I try to pretend it distracts me, even though I'm having no further luck banishing the image at the back of my mind of the girl I met in wet pajamas voraciously eating the waffles I'd made. Or the way we seemed to keep catching one another's eye through the crowd of people at brunch. But the thing that's really making all this stewing, all this pining all the more difficult is that the girl in question is on my arm right now. I am Juliana's escort down the aisle.

It's a small wedding party—just me, Lukas, Juliana, and

Anja's younger sister, Amanda. Juliana and I keep getting sent back to "give the walk in another try." According to the wedding planner, I walk down the aisle like Lurch from *The Addams Family*. I don't think I'm that terrifying, but I'm not the one being paid an ungodly amount of money to make sure everything runs smoothly.

"I'm know I'm no winning conversationalist when I'm hung over, but are you all right?" Juliana asks as we line back up in the Clock Tower wings. She's been so quiet since we started that I startle when she speaks. I'm sure this does not comfort her at all. She must think I'm either a huge asshole or utterly antisocial. I don't fancy myself either, but I'm trying not to let this beautiful woman on my arm affect me too much. I can't remember the last time I felt like this, to the point I'm not even sure what 'this' is. I'd heard from her mother and her brothers that Juliana is a special sort of person, the sort of person people just like right away, but I didn't expect to feel it so acutely. That's part of the problem of spending the last five years at the bottom of a bottle—I feel *everything* now.

"What? Oh. Yeah. Fine. Sorry," I say, trying not to sound like a total moron. "I, ah, just… I've never been in a wedding before. And my tux came with these crazy shiny shoes that I think have as much polish on the bottom as they do on the top and let's just say that grace has never been my strong suit."

She laughs. I made her laugh. Shit, that's awesome. I didn't know I was capable of making a girl laugh without us both being plastered. "Well, even in the insane heels Anja picked out for us, I'm incredibly steady on my feet. I promise to catch you if you start to fall."

Here's the thing about being in recovery—I can't really pick up on things sober the way I used to when I drank. If Juliana and I were drinking right now, I'd swear that was an innuendo of some kind. But sober, I have no idea. I'm probably just imagining it, because I'm a sucker for brown eyes and dimples.

And hips. But I'm pretty sure the more I listen to her talk, and definitely the more I hear her laugh, the less I'm going to only be attracted to these physical features.

"I'll hold you to that," I tell her, and I mean it. Clearly the maintenance staff at the Clock Tower buffed the floors recently. I wonder if they thrive on the comedic value of an entire wedding party slipping and sliding as Pachebel's *Canon* mocks them.

"Surely they'd skip the second coat of wax on a wedding weekend," Juliana says, echoing my thoughts perfectly.

"Anja said they were trying to convince her to book for today instead because it's not being used at all, other than this," I mention.

"I bet they did. The extra money she and Mat would have shelled out for a Saturday wedding versus a Sunday wedding I'm sure wasn't a mitigating factor in the slightest." Sarcasm suits this girl.

I can see the appeal of the Clock Tower as a wedding venue—the panoramic view of downtown Denver and the Rockies off to the west can't be beat. But weddings in general make me nervous. I don't have a lot of good memories involving them, and hardly any sober ones. I really wanted to tell Anja no when she asked me to be one of Mattias's groomsmen, but I owe Anja big. I owe her everything.

The wedding coordinator beckons us all to line up again, and shoots me a dirty look, as if defying me to walk like a monster again this run. I studied movement in massage school, and my gait is perfectly normal, thank you very much.

"If it makes you feel any better, no one really looks at the guys in the processional—unless you're the groom. They look at the groom, and the bridesmaids, and definitely the bride, but the guys? Not so much. You're basically my arm candy." She nudges my shoulder with hers. She winks at me, or tries to— her left eyelid shuts completely and her right does almost as much. It's probably just a quirk of her musculature, but the way her eyelashes flutter against her cheeks sends that pang through my gut all over again.

Damn.

Damn, damn, *damn.*

We manage to go through another run of the rehearsal without the coordinator complaining about my walk, and the officiant actually gets a chance to run through the ceremony. Poised where I am, I get a great view of Anja's face as she smiles through the jokes Mattias makes, and Lukas's insistence that he isn't *really* going to pretend to lose the rings when prompted for them. It's good to see her smiling. If anyone in the world deserves to smile like she is, it's Anja, who's been repeatedly saving my ass for the last six months. She had the same smile in her eyes even when I was screaming at her during the darkest of my detox days. She smiled at me when I told her to *stop* smiling at me, because nothing about how I was feeling was something to smile about. She wisely told me I was right, but that she had to smile so she wouldn't sob for me instead. And really, when it came to sobbing, I was doing more than enough of that my own pathetic self.

The officiant's throat clears, and I realize I've lost myself in my thoughts so completely that I haven't noticed Lukas and Amanda following Anja and Mattias up the aisle. Juliana has her eyebrows raised at me. I fake a chuckle that isn't 90% nerves and offer her my arm. Well, sort of my arm—I hold out my hand expecting she'll loop her arm through the bend in mine, which she does, but not before her palm grazes mine. It's almost reflex to close my fingers around hers before our elbows link.

There's a shot of disappointment surging through me—I would have *loved* to hold her hand. I wonder how her fingers would feel laced through mine. Then I remind myself I shouldn't be thinking like that. I really, really shouldn't be thinking like that.

So why fucking me? Why her? And most importantly—why fucking now?

CHAPTER TWO

I wake up the next morning absolutely freezing. I hear the cat meowing in some hidden away corner, pathetic as ever, and tug my covers around me. I shouldn't have slept with the window open last night, but it's just habit by now unless it's below freezing when I go to bed. I force my eyes open and hunt for the clock to check the time. First, however, I see the view out my window, and my stomach drops. Snow had not been in the forecast, and yet....

My phone begins to trill and Mattias's name comes up on the caller ID.

"Hey, Ez. You up yet?" He sounds exhausted.

"Just woke up," I tell him. "How's the weather over at your mom's?"

"White and fluffy. It'd be nice if I hadn't woken up to sixty text messages from Anja about it. That's what I'm calling about: I know you, me, and Lukas are supposed to meet up here at Mama's but I think Anja needs another person around her this morning. I guess Amanda is being passive-aggressive on behalf of their parents and Jules said Anja's sort of losing it. I don't think it's bad enough that she'd, you know—"

Yeah. I do. "No problem. Um, my tux is at your place."

"Hey, as long as you show up to the Clock Tower shaved and showered, it shouldn't take more than ten minutes to put that on. I just... if anyone can get my girl down the aisle in one piece, it's probably you."

Mattias and Anja have this funny way of giving me way more credit than I'm worth. But for everything I owe my sponsor, making sure she gets through the morning is the least I can do for her.

"No problem. You said Juliana is already there, right?"

Mattias laughs. "*Jules*. Mama calls her Juliana when she's in trouble. But yeah, she's there, holding Anja together best she can. I think they'll need a lift to the salon. Couldn't tell you the last time Jules drove in weather like this."

"Got it. Anything else?"

Mattias breathes a relieved sigh. "No, this is above and beyond the call, Ez. Thank you."

"Anytime," I say.

I slam the window shut and blast the heat while I get ready. I punch in a quick text to Anja telling her I'll be heading over there as soon as I get out of the shower. A response is almost automatic. It clearly wasn't typed by Anja.

Anja: Good man. She needs you something fierce. Also, coffee? ;)

I normally hate emoticons in text messages. But surmising that came from Juliana, I find it damn endearing.

I spend my entire shower thinking about how I'll be spending the wedding ceremony and reception breathing in Juliana Almeida's perfume—it shouldn't be what I'm focused on, but it is. Which, of course, is fucking terrible.

It probably seems dramatic, how wrapped up I am in not wanting to be as attracted as Juliana as I clearly am. If I were a normal person, I'd just take it at face value as a simple crush and let it flit on by. One day out of my life, and really, it's not like it should be a problem to spend it with a pretty, funny, alarmingly smart woman. Most groomsmen should be so lucky as to have someone like Juliana on their arm for an evening. But not all groomsmen are six months into a recovery from an addiction that ended because he couldn't keep his damn fly zipped around a woman he shouldn't have been attracted to.

I have to remind myself that this day isn't about me and my lack of self-control. This day is about Anja and Mattias, who probably never should have taken me in as part of their family, but did anyway because they're that sort of wonderful people. They deserve to have me level-headed and not distracted for a few hours so Anja can cope with shitty parents and a bratty sister, and walk down the aisle with a smile on her face, because she and Mattias belong together. They fought hard for one another. My demons have no place in their day.

I pull a hoodie on, grab a couple of packs of cigarettes from the carton stashed in the freezer, and toss a handful of food into the cat's dish. I realize I'll need my winter coat, and root around in the back of my closet for it. The fabric smells a little musty, and it occurs to me that I haven't worn it since last March. Last time I'd needed it, I had a flask in the breast pocket, necessary for getting through the shitty-beyond-shitty day that was Mac's funeral.

Never mind all that, I tell myself. *It's not important.* I dig in the pockets for my gloves, happy that they're all I find, and head out the door. I watch the snow fall for just a second. I breathe in the frigid air, which prickles my throat and lungs. Thirty seconds—that's all the time I give myself to think of Mac and what he'd think of me today, of what I'm doing, of *how* I'm doing— andthen I head down the cement stairs, wondering if my ice-scraper made it through last winter and my perpetually messy backseat.

***

It's Juliana who opens the door to Anja and Mattias's

apartment. She and Amanda slept here last night while Mattias crashed in his old room at Mama A's so the girls could start all their preparations for the day together. It doesn't escape my notice that Amanda is nowhere to be seen. Juliana looks about how I met her yesterday—pajama-clad and sleepy-eyed. I hand over the Box o' Joe I picked up on my way.

Her eyes light up as she takes it from me and goes as far as clutching it to her chest as though I've given her something far more valuable than crappy drive-thru coffee.

"You have no idea how badly I needed this. Thank you. Anja's in the bedroom. Mat's gonna kill her when he figures out she was smoking in there, but I wasn't gonna tell her no," Juliana says.

I set down my car keys and cell phone on the kitchen counter. "What happened?" I ask in a hushed voice.

"I'm out of the loop about the exact issues her family has with mine, but I heard a lot of 'not good enough' and 'disappointment' thrown around between the two of them first thing this morning. Do you know any of those details?"

I know enough to know that it isn't the Almeidas that Anja's parents have the big problem with—it's Anja. You'd think two years of sobriety, a stable job, and a fiancé from a good family would be enough to placate her incredibly demanding family. You'd be wrong unless you knew the MacCullors.

"It's... complicated. And maybe not my place to say anything," I say. "I don't hear screaming. Is Amanda still here?"

"Nope. Anja suggested she take a hike and she seemed all-too glad to. Haven't seen her in over an hour."

"Well, I guess that solves that dilemma. What time are you supposed to be at the salon and all the other, you know, girly places?"

"We've got a little time, but I think she still needs to shower. Were the roads bad?"

"Nah, nothing CDOT can't sort of handle. You know, in the way CDOT handles anything."She laughs, and my heart almost leaps out of my chest. *Dammit.* I really shouldn't feel my heart race every time this girl laughs. "I haven't lived here in five years, so I really don't."

"Right. I knew that," I say as I fix myself and Anja cups of coffee. "Have you checked in on her at all?"

"Mat told me it might be best to wait for you and make myself scarce. If she's not going to shower, I am. Crack a window if she's still smoking, will you? She might not beat you if you reach over her."

"She'll *absolutely* beat me, are you kidding?"

She laughs, my heart gallops, and she turns on her heel to head for the guest bathroom. It's everything I have not to watch her go. Not only do I have to escort this girl during the wedding with a straight face and no condemning bulges, I have to look her in the eye all morning.

When I let myself into the bedroom to see Anja, I barely miss the pillow she throws at my head and succeed in spilling half a cup of coffee down my hoodie.

"Excuse you," I say, and hold up the coffee mugs in offering, hoping she'll see them before she starts throwing things again. "All I'm doing is bringing you coffee."

Her hands fly to her face, a cigarette dangling from between the fingers of her right hand. "I'm sorry! I heard the door and thought Amanda had come back."

"I think you're safely stuck with just me and Juliana for the time being."

Anja nods and puffs away at the stump of cigarette. "Mattias filled you in?"

"Sort of. Juliana told me she heard you and Amanda fighting."

"Same old bullshit," Anja says. "Don't put it past my father to lord around that his daughter married into a Latino family next election cycle, but far be it from him to actually attend my wedding with anything less than a scowl on his face."

"Would it really be the worst thing in the world if they didn't come?" I ask her, cracking the window before I plop down next to her, my own cigarette in hand.

"Oh, and how would *that* look if it ever got out? No, they'll be there. And Amanda will too, but not before putting me out $300 for hair and makeup she's not going to sit through because she 'can't handle me when I get like this.' Like *I'm* the one being irrational when she's the one being a piece of shit to me on my wedding day. This is all so fucking stupid… I should have eloped."

"I think it's a little late for that now. It's one day. I know it'll be impossible to not think about, but maybe focus on what you can control? You're welcome to boss me around all day, if it'll help at all."

She sniffles and wipes her fingers under her eyes. Her irises are even more vibrantly blue, rimmed with red as they are. "I shouldn't be dumping any of this stuff on you, it's not particularly sponsorly of me…."

"Stop it. I don't mind. It helps keep me distracted, remember?"

She nods, her bottom lip firmly tucked between her front teeth. I can handle girls crying fine, but there's something infinitely sad about a bride crying the morning of her wedding about anything other than nerves.

"And they wonder why I drank," she says thickly, and I pull her into my side. "It's always, always been a little bit like this."

"I know it," I tell her, and give her another squeeze.

When we were in high school, we'd sneak out past the football field and sneak sips from a flask of cheap vodka and cigarettes or the occasional joint. When we did, we'd perch together as small as we could get, her arm looped through mine and her head on my shoulder. People thought we were dating the whole of our senior year, but it was never like that. She plops her head against my shoulder now and it feels a little bit like we're still a couple of kids who haven't quite fucked everything up yet, but are ever on the verge of it.

"Look, don't focus on them," I remind her, and rub her back softly. "Focus on you. You can control you. This is your day. You still need to shower, right?"

She nods against my shoulder.

"Juliana beat you to it for now, but I bet after you drink this coffee and finish that cigarette, she'll be done. What do you need for the day? More smokes? Patches? A cliff to drive off?"

"Can you stop the snow so I can still have my wedding pictures outside on the roof?"

"Alas, that I could. I'll tell you this, though: it's not actually all that cold. No wind. And think of how pretty the city will look with snow falling in the background. Steal Mattias's tux jacket from him and you're all set."

I know inherently that what she wants more than anything right now is a stiff drink. She was a white wine drinker in her day. I've heard women down mimosas and Bloody Marys in excess on the morning of their weddings. She must be missing out on the idea of that. Women usually have supportive sisters on their sides, too. Maybe that makes missing out on the former even worse for her. I light another cigarette and hand it to her.

"Look, I need to clean out the backseat of my car so there's enough room for dresses and whatever else we need to cart around. Finish your coffee and shower, and I'll go take care of that and get it running so you're hopping into a nice, warm car. We'll just one-step-at-a-time it, all right?"

She nods and throws back a sizable gulp of her coffee. I give her another hug, a kiss on the crown of her head, and a big, cheesy grin before I head out of the bedroom.

I feel a set of eyes on me as I head towards the front door.

I resist the urge to turn around, but I see Juliana's face reflected in a wall mirror. She slips into the guest room before I can look closer, although the last thing I need today is a visual of her in a towel or clingy, wet pajamas.

Still, I can't help but wonder why on Earth she'd be spying on me.

***

"You're adorable if you think I'm going to go scuba-diving," Anja says as she and Juliana are getting primped and fawned over by the ladies at the salon.

"It's not scuba-diving, it's *snubaing*," Juliana says with that infectious, slaying laugh of hers.

"Now you're just making words up," Anja says.

"It's a thing! I swear, it's a blast. You cannot go to San Pedro and not go. As your new older sister, I command it."

"You're, like, *six months* older than I am. And I am petrified of dark water. It's not going to happen."

I want to tell Juliana she's wasting her time—Anja can barely be convinced to get into a shallow, unlit swimming pool at night, let alone submerge herself in the ocean to look at coral and fish and WWII-downed airplanes. But Juliana is doing her damnedest to keep Anja laughing and distracted, while about all I've done since getting the pair of them out of Anja's parking lot without fishtailing is finish a book on my phone and smoke the better part of a pack of cigarettes. I've only had to light about two for Anja, and that means whatever Juliana is saying, it's working. I can tell from the way Anja's shoulders have finally unwound from up near her ears that she's more relaxed now than I've seen her in a couple of weeks. I sneak outside again, there being nothing better for me to do in the salon than try not to keep sneaking glances at Juliana until they're fully styled. We're out of there by noon, which leaves us us more than enough time to swing by a drive-thru for the greasy fried chicken Anja's been craving for three months and hasn't dared eating so she'll be able to zip up her dress.

I carry their dresses up the spiral staircase to the the bridal
suite at the Clock Tower while Juliana waltzes up and down the
aisle with Anja, trying to keep her laughing as they check in on
the workers prepping the space. When Anja is made up and
ready to get into her dress an hour later, she's got as big a smile
on her face as any bride could hope to. She and Juliana are
sipping lattes and laughing, so I decide it's a good time to sneak
out and get dressed myself. Maybe she's got a supportive sister
around her after all.

I duck out so they can change, smoke a couple of cigarettes,
then hunt down a nervous Mattias and slightly-buzzed Lukas. I
try not to be too jealous of Lukas.

"How is she holding up?" Mattias asks. He, like me, chews
his fingernails when he's nervous. I make a mental note about
slipping him the nail file I always carry around before pictures
are taken of their hands with their new wedding bands. Look,
my hands are basically my business card—I may chew my nails,
but I know my way around a file.

I whip out my phone and show him the picture I slyly
snapped of Anja getting her hair pinned up in her elaborate up-
do at the salon. She's grinning into the mirror, her face the very
definition of a happy bride. I swear, I see the guy fall for her all
over again.

Lukas peeks over his brother's shoulder. "She's a pretty
gorgeous bride, brother," he says, elbowing Mattias in the ribs.

I let Mattias hold onto my phone while I change into my
tux. After, he reluctantly hands it back and says, "Much as it
pisses me off you get to see her before I do, can you go back
up and make sure she's still all right? She'll need a friendly face
when Amanda finally deigns to show up."

"'Course," I say, and clap him on the shoulder. I haven't
known Mattias as long as I've known Anja, but I know he's not
the sort of guy to get all choked up. I can't help but wonder if

he's trying to get rid of me so only Lukas can lord it over him later that he's totally about to start crying. I'm a long way from married, of course, but that seems about right.

Amanda arrived while I was gone, but Anja is doing a great job ignoring her while Juliana hooks her into the long row of buttons down the back of her ivory gown. She spies me in the long mirror and gives me a little wave. Juliana peeks over her shoulder, grins broadly, and then twirls Anja around with a flourish.

Years from now, when I think of Anja's wedding day, I'll remember how she giggled when her new sister-in-law spun her, and how somehow that made her that much more of gorgeous bride. Then she looks at me, imploring, her head tilted and shoulders tensed until I step forward, hold out my hands, and beam at her. Her dress is that sort of crinkly, sheer-over-solid material that looks like it'll never wrinkle, which is good, because every one of her eighty-odd guests is going to want to hug her as much as I do.

"You've never looked more gorgeous, kid," I tell her, and yeah, my voice is a little scratchy with emotion. "Mattias is gonna lose it when he sees you."

She's leaning against me like a buoy for a long while, and I keep my arms firmly around her until she stops trembling. I pull away to make sure I didn't muss her hair. The last of her tension seems to unwind before my very eyes.

"You're still missing something," Juliana says, tugging her away and coaxing her to sit so she can clip the short bunch of mesh that is her veil over her eyes. That's when I finally get a good look at Juliana. She's in the same burgundy, floor-length dress that Amanda, scowling at us from the corner, wears. But on Juliana, the material hugs her curves and falls daintily while Amanda looks uncomfortable and even mussed. The color is perfect with Juliana's dark skin. Unlike Anja's, up in curls at the back of her head, Juliana's long hair falls in waves down the

right side of her neck, held in place with a matching ribbon.
Juliana swipes it down her shoulders and back with her fingers
when she straightens from fitting Anja's veil; the brown tresses
brush the neckline of her strapless dress in a satiny wave I can't
help but be mesmerized by. Anja is every inch the blushing,
vibrant bride who'll take everyone's breath away as soon as she
walks down the aisle. But I can't help but feel as if *I'm* going to
end up being the lucky bastard who's going to have the
prettiest girl in the room on my arm. I try to memorize the
dimpled smile she and Anja share in the mirror, but before I
can, the wedding coordinator bustles up the stairs and tells us
everyone's arrived and seated. Amanda skulks off down the
stairs after the woman, but Juliana links arms with Anja and I
fall in step on her other side. Anja clings to both of us for
relief, and, together, Juliana and I get her to the threshold.

Anja's father isn't escorting her down the aisle. Despite her
iron grasp on our arms, Juliana and I still have to be at the head
of the procession. As the music is piped in over the speakers
and the coordinator gets us in our spot, Juliana slips her arm in
the crook of my elbow and jabs me playfully in the side.

"You clean up pretty nice," she says to me. "I like this look
better than the coffee-stained hoodie you've been sporting all
day."

"Thanks." I keep the clenching of my gut in check by
focusing on the music as we start down the aisle. I'm
remarkably composed, and it's possible she doesn't notice just
how nervous she makes me. She cracks a joke through her
smile-exposed teeth as we stride along and the photographer
snaps our picture. It's nearly impossible not to laugh out
loud—it's not every day I find someone who detests
Pachelbel's *Canon* as much as I do.

I keep quiet because I have to, of course. A minute later,
Lukas brings down a faux-faced beaming Amanda.

And then, when the music changes, Anja steals the show.

***

Juliana is back on my arm the moment Mattias and Anja say "I do" and march triumphantly back down the aisle. I know that it was supposed to be this way for the ceremony, but for all this time at the reception, too? And yet here she is, cracking jokes and snarking in my ear.

After our part of the pictures are taken care of, we're allowed into the reception area by the wedding consultant, Anja having declined a formal announcement for the wedding party lest Amanda do something catty. It's not a sit-down dinner reception, so Juliana isn't even obligated to be near me. Yet everywhere I turn, she's there. She insists we get appetizers from one of the stacked high tables. And then, in a move that sets my stomach roiling, she declares it's high time to get drunk already, and forces me with her to the bar.

It's cash-only, on account of Anja, something Juliana wrinkles her nose at.

"First round's on me?" she offers.

I shake my head, my skin already pebbling from nerves. "I've got to drive."

"We won't be going anywhere for hours. First one's on me, come on...."

Lukas dives in at the exact right moment. I swear, I could kiss him. "You're buying drinks, sis, you can buy for me. I'll drink Ez's share."

The knowing wink he gives me behind Juliana's shoulder communicates two things: first, that Anja must have asked him to keep an eye on me around the booze, since she'd be too busy glad-handing her guests to do it herself. Second—and I couldn't tell you why it disconcerts me—that Juliana clearly has no idea I'm in recovery. I've known her two days, and I can already tell for certain she's not the sort who'd be insensitive enough to shove a drink in an alcoholic's hand. Juliana orders them two dirty martinis with extra olives. I ask for a glass of straight soda water to soothe the bartender and watch as Juliana convinces her brother to join her in a shot. Lukas shoots me another contrite look, but gladly accepts the shot of whiskey the bartender sets in front of them. I try not to envy the burn in their throats as the alcohol works its way down, but the longing is there. It's as niggling now as it was six months ago. I've got to get the hell away from this bar.

I want to cry in relief when the DJ announces the arrival of Mr. and Mrs. Mattias Almeida. It's impossible to not be drawn in by the blissful looks on Mattias's and Anja's faces. They opt to make the rounds of their guests before the dancing starts, which gives me just enough time to sneak downstairs for a cigarette. I have to suck down two before my hands stop shaking and the overwhelming craving that'd crested over me abates.

"You're missing their first dance!" a voice calls out. Juliana slips out the side door, having stolen Lukas's tuxedo jacket.

All the same, she bounces on her heels as a gust of frigid air blows down the long corridor that makes up 16th Street Mall.

"They're done saying hello to everyone already?" I ask, agape.

Her face contorts, like she's biting something nasty. "Her parents requested they get things moving," she says. "It sounds like they have somewhere else to be. What the fuck is with them?"

"They've been this way forever," I say, and my heart aches for Anja. Mac would never have pulled something so shitty. "Whatever you might think it has to do with your family, I can promise you it doesn't. Anja never stood a chance of being their favorite. And over the last few years...."

Juliana nods, like she knows what I'm going to say. Of course she knows all about it.

"Still, it's adorable that Mat can't dance, so stub out your cancer stick and come up. It's a long song. And you realize it's your duty to dance with me, right?" She says the last part with that strange sort of wink of hers. It's more like she's batting her eyelashes at me. It makes me feel something significant and dangerous.

"I can almost guarantee you that Mattias looks like a pro-ballroom dancer in comparison to me," I say as we board the elevator.

"Ah, but he's dancing with a white girl," she says with a smirk. "You'll be dancing with a Brazilian girl with amazing rhythm. Me and my hips can make anyone look good." Her hips *are* pretty amazing.

We make it back upstairs in time to see Mattias try and fail to dip Anja, though at least he doesn't drop her. They kiss passionately to much fanfare, and the DJ puts on something more up-tempo. She pulls me toward the dance floor, her hips already swaying with the beat.

"Seriously, I'll step on your toes and scuff your shoes. Or tear your dress. Or...."

She spins in place, her hair billowing out like the hem of her dress. "We'll be fine."

"Juliana—"

"Ezra," she teases back.

It's everything I can do then and there to not kiss her senseless.

"I just really—" I begin, but she presses her fingers to my lips and winks at me, again with that hybrid wink/bat thing.

"Stop thinking so much," she says, her voice sultry. "It's not a competition. It's your best friend's wedding. And I promise, you have an incredible dance partner who's been deprived of a dance floor for way too long. Just dance with me, Ezra."

Thirty seconds into the song, I realize what it is about her that I find so terrifying about Juliana. The girl is like a cigarette: she's addictive, and for me, that's dangerous.

***

The cat growls at me when I get home. I roll my eyes at her and toe off the rented tux shoes that were so not made for all the dancing I'd just done—but I find it almost impossible to be too irritated at her.

What no one told me about being in a wedding is that your evening does not end when the DJ plays the bride and groom off to Marvin Gaye's "Let's Get It On"—it's only just begun. Even with the paid cleaning crew, there were still wedding presents to collect and pile in the back of Mama A's car, centerpieces and favors left on the high-top tables, flowers that needed to be handled carefully so they'd last a few extra days, and an alarming amount of stuff in both the bride's and groom's suites that couldn't be left behind. With Amanda disappearing around the time her parents did, it fell to me, Mama A, Lukas, and Juliana. I actually took the emergency stairs one trip just to keep the momentum up without waiting for the elevator. Even before that, though, I was exhausted— Juliana really is an incredible dancer. And she's impossible to say no to.

When I finally was sent off by Mama A with copious kisses to the cheeks and a promise to come by for dinner even with Anja and Mattias off on their honeymoon, I navigated the confusing downtown streets to dodge construction traffic on the highway. Now, the cat's hissing is about the last thing I wanted to deal with, but at least my apartment is intact. We have something of an understanding, the cat and I—I keep her in kibble, water, and fresh litter, and she doesn't tear up all of my shit. I've never been a cat person. If not for my loyalty to Mac, I wouldn't have an animal at all.

For the second time tonight, I find myself craving a stiff drink. It's the exhaustion. I always kicked back after a long day with a scotch and soda or a microbrew, and six months sober does little to take the edge off that habit. I take the little scraps of aluminum that are my recovery chips out of their place folded into my wallet and rub them between my thumb and forefingers. The oldest two—my 24-hour and one month—are already a little smoothed out for how often I've done this while my most recent, an azure blue, is still shiny and new. A little calmer, I shirk off the dress shirt and slacks and change into a pair of sweatpants before hunting around in my cupboards for something that'll do as an ashtray. I crack the balcony door and light up. The nicotine surging through me levels my head. I search my discarded slacks for my cell phone and come up with nothing. It must have fallen out in my car, but it's far too cold to go out and fetch it.

Something mindless on Netflix is lulling me into a half-sleep when there's a knock at my front door. I haven't had the occasion to have late night guests since I quit drinking. It's not entirely uncommon for some guest of one of my neighbors to knock on my door by accident because of how terribly our building numbers are marked. I wait for a beat to see if whoever it is will leave on their own, but they knock again.

Even through a peephole, Juliana has the same sort of effect on me that I've been trying to ignore all evening. Of all the possible late-night guests I could have, she's the sort I should be most wary of. That doesn't stop me from opening the door for her.

"Forget something?" she says, a wide smile on her pretty face as she holds up my cell phone. Clearly, my car was not where I'd dropped it.

"Oh, damn… Thanks," I say, and take it from her. The air nipping at my nose is bitingly cold, and I can't help but notice she's still only wearing the tux jacket she stole from Lukas.

She explains before I get a chance to invite her in out of the cold. "Mama found it on top of one of the bins of stuff from the bridal suite and Luk realized it was yours. I was more sober to drive it over, so he gave me your address."

"This is a life-saver," I say. "About the last thing I've got extra cash for these days is a new phone."

"I was also sent with a message about laundry. Specifically—Mama wants to know if you're coming Wednesday to do yours."

I haven't trusted the laundry in my building since one of the dryers destroyed a set of my sheets last year. I'd been a pretty steady patron of a laundromat nearby that has functional machines and is kept pretty clean. Its initial draw had been its proximity to my favorite microbrewery, and I quickly adopted a habit of drinking myself stupid during the spin cycle. After I'd sobered up, Anja had offered up Mama A's house on Wednesdays, one of my days off, to avoid the temptation.

"Ah, yeah, I figured I would. Um, is that a problem for her because I can—"

"Oh, no, she'll be thrilled. It does mean she's going to conscript you to take me to the airport that afternoon, though."

Of course Juliana would be staying with her mother while she's in town, but part of the appeal of using Mama A's washer in the middle of the day is the solitude of it. And after an evening of trying to deny I'd want something more if Juliana offered it, I'd resigned myself over the past hour since I left her that it was just tonight. I only had to cope with one night of burgeoning feelings and wondering if I was deluding myself that maybe she was flirting with me, and then that'd be it. She'd be back in Brazil. I'd be back to living day-to-day without a drink. There wasn't ever going to be anything other than that. Spending another day with her wasn't in the cards.

"I have to get back to Sao Paolo sooner than Mama was expecting, so she didn't take Wednesday off. I know DIA is far and annoying, so you can totally say no," she says, almost like she can sense my reluctance. "I'll take an Uber or a shuttle or something and you can just tell Mama you took me."

"No," I say a little too quickly. "I don't mind. What time?"

"Really, Ezra, I can…."

"I usually come over around ten. I'll be happy to, Juliana."

What the hell am I saying?

She smiles, and it slays me. Utterly, utterly slays me. How is her makeup still perfect? I sweated like a pig while she sashayed around me. How is her hair not a frizzy mess? How the hell is it possible she still smells so damn good?

"Anja was exactly right about you," she says, her smile growing wider. "You're incredible. I'll fill your gas tank for the trouble, all right?"

I smile back and hope I'm not blushing or anything that would mark me as an idiot. "I'd be happier with a pot of that Brazilian coffee."

Another wink/bat of her eyelashes. If she were a different sort of girl, I might suppose this was more flirting. But flirting seems so ridiculous—girls as incredible as her do *not* flirt with guys like me.

"Ready and waiting for you. See you then."

I never get the chance to ask her inside to warm up. She waves, turns toe, and strides with purpose and grace down the stairs. Four-inch heels and almost a foot of snow can't keep her from practically floating. How the hell she does that, I haven't a clue. But she has me watching her all the way to the parking lot, where she slides behind the wheel of Mama A's car and, I swear, winks at me again before she drives away.

I'm deluding myself. I'm overly tired and I'm seeing things. But more importantly, I'm about to spend another day with her that I didn't think I'd get. And that is thrilling.

CHAPTER THREE

Once, and only once, I tried going back to my old laundromat after I sobered up. I made it through the better part of the wash cycle, but I picked a dud dryer with a burned-out heater for a batch of my work uniforms and ended up there for way longer than I should have been. The temptation of Comrade Brewery, one of my old haunts, was too much for my two-month sobriety and I ended up ditching my stuff, jogging home, and calling Anja to beg her or Mattias to pick my clothes up for me. They both had to sit with me for hours afterwards so I wouldn't do something stupid. Anja made me promise not to go anywhere near there again. Not my finest moment. Then again, this entire year has been one long series of "not Ezra Mackenzie's finest moments."

That's how Mama A's came about. Being a kindergarten teacher, Anja was already out of school for the summer and could let me in and hang out with me. It was those summer afternoons, with her keeping me distracted from the thought of open liquor bottles in a strange house, that our friendship rekindled into something functional and healthy. From the time we were dumbass teenagers, we used to drink together to glorious excess—we honestly didn't know what to do around one another unless there were drinks in our hands. Sober, we had to find new things to do with our hands, things to say that didn't spark one of us to want a drink. We had to figure out how to be friends again. Thankfully, so thankfully, we figured it out. I know I'd never be at six months clean without her.

After she went back to school, I kept up doing laundry there because I knew Mama A didn't keep liquor in the house day-to-day. It's safe ground to read, to think, to stew sometimes about what a mess my life feels like most days even though I'm arguably better now than I was this time last year. But I'll be honest—if Mama A *did* keep liquor in the house, I'm not sure I could trust myself alone there and not go bottle hunting.

I think that's why this infatuation with Juliana feels like such a bad thing. Alcoholics in recovery are not fun to be around. The word 'prick' comes to mind. I have my moments where I honestly wonder how anyone can be around me for *any* period of time, long or short. My job as a massage therapist helps me compartmentalize—it helps to focus on something external, something I can manipulate and control, even if it is just a housewife's tight shoulder muscles. Sometimes I'm mid-session when a craving hits, and have to pretend that I don't hate my client for taking up my time when I could be out getting absolutely hammered. This actually helps, too—depending on how long my session might be scheduled for, the craving might pass by the time I'm wrapping up and itching to call Anja and grab my chips and a cigarette. Sometimes, on really bad days, it gets stronger.

No one, especially not a terrific woman like Juliana, should be exposed to someone as volatile and temperamental as a recovering alcoholic. It's only by reminding myself that I'm literally putting her on a plane to another country this afternoon, and that I may never even see her again, that I've steeled myself to leave my apartment. Because seeing her, reminding myself that she is off-limits, and then seeing her off, is going to suck. Enough things in my life suck these days—she shouldn't be one of them. In my car, a half-pack of cigarettes gone on the four-mile drive to Mama A's, I try to convince myself that this really isn't that big a deal. It's just laundry and coffee and a ride to the airport. I've never been the greatest liar. Strange for an alcoholic, right? Yeah, I don't get it either.

I've had a key for months, but since Juliana is there, I ring the bell and wait for her to answer. I will my palms not to sweat as I wait for her to pull the door open. By the time she pulls the door open, though, they're slick and I almost drop my laundry basket, full of two weeks' worth of dirty underwear and scrubs, right at her feet. If she notices, she doesn't say anything. She waves me in, a smile in her eyes and on her lips. After a night of dancing, am I supposed to hug her? Shake her hand and let her feel how clammy my palm is? I cling to the basket, which acts as a convenient barrier for both.

I'm dressed predictably schlubby, as one should when doing laundry, and for some reason, I expected she might be as well. She is, after all, about to get on a ridiculously long flight—don't people wear comfy clothes on long flights? She's not exactly glammed out, but her jeans fit her hips like they were tailored for her, and her clingy shirt dips low into her cleavage. She's polished and put together, and, in comparison, I look like I just ran a half-marathon. At least I don't smell like it, although I am conscious of my still-damp hair from my shower and lingering cigarette smoke. And since I'm not made of stone, I'm grateful my pants are baggy, because she's showing exactly enough skin that maintaining eye contact is more than a little tough.

I wonder if we exhausted everything we had to say to one another at the wedding. Our greeting is stilted, and she feels compelled to show me to the laundry room. She lingers in the doorway for just a second more than is comfortable, then says she'll leave me to it and disappears. Grateful, I start a load and sort through two more while I collect myself. I'd spent hours with this girl just the other day—what's different now? Deciding nothing has to be, that I can be friendly without being overbearing or awkward, I head into the living room. She's balancing a cup of coffee on her knee and a book in her other hand. She jerks her head toward the kitchen, a more placid smile on her face.

"Coffee, as promised. There's half-and-half and sugar out; milk's in the fridge."

"Thanks," I say. I doctor my cup how I like it and settle back in the living room with her, wishing I'd brought a book of my own. I scan the shelves around the TV, wondering if I could pluck one up so I'm not staring at her while she reads. I'm about to hoist myself up to grab the first title I find that I've already read when she shuts her book and takes a deep gulp from her cup.

"The other night was a blast, by the way. I don't think I said that when we said goodbye. You're not as bad a dancer as you claimed to be."

"Flatterer," I say. "You know I'm terrible. But, ah, yeah. It was a lot of fun."

There's something poised on her lips, something she clearly wants to say but doesn't. She tugs on a bit of chapped skin on her lips with her front teeth. Compelled to break the silence, I stammer out, "So, ah… what's Brazil like?"

"Hot, mostly. But beautiful. Sao Paolo is enormous and crowded, but I like it. I'm never bored. Although that might have something to do with my job and the variability of ten- and sixteen-hour days."

Anja had mentioned in passing that Juliana is an environmental engineer for some major international firm trying to save the planet. She's working specifically with teams in Brazil trying to preserve the rainforest. She's doing the sort of work that gets people straight into heaven when they die, while I'm giving backrubs. Even if this girl didn't live on another continent, she'd be so ridiculously out of my league we wouldn't even be playing the same sport.

"How long have you been down there?"

"Two years. I got lucky and landed an internship out of grad school and it turned permanent. Already speaking the language gave me a boost."

I'd heard her speaking in Portuguese to her mother and brothers. It's a pretty language on its own. It's downright gorgeous coming out of her mouth.

"Hey, can I...." She leans forward and sets her coffee cup on the table between us. "Can I ask something? And you can tell me to fuck off if it's personal and none of my business."

I've never heard this girl flustered. I lean forward similarly, propping my elbows on my knees and nod at her. "Shoot."

"I know about Anja. About her drinking."

I know exactly where this is going. More than ever I'm sure that Anja hasn't sold me out to Juliana. I appreciate that of my sponsor, of course, but it doesn't make this conversation promise to be any less crappy. Especially not with someone as terrific as she is.

"I love Anja," Juliana continues, "I think she's fantastic and she makes Mat so, so happy. I don't care about her drinking, or what she's done in the past because it's all the past, you know? The most important thing is that Mat is happy and, you know, that they're happy together...."

"Can I just point out you're rambling a little?" I say. It's a little cocky of me to say, sure. But her rambling is charming.

She laughs at herself and studies her coffee cup. "I do that sometimes. I just wanted to clarify that because I'm not sure if I'm in the right here, and if I'm wrong then I'm so sorry and I'll shut my trap and we can watch TV and pretend I'm not awkward. But... you and Anja. You have a lot in common, don't you?"

It's an interesting way to think of it. I could simply tell her she's right, but instead I pull out my wallet and turn it over in my hand until my chips fall into my palm.

"Anja gave this to me on April 13th of this past year. It's a 24-hour recovery chip," I say. "And, every month since then, she's given me all of these." I place my chips one by one down in front of her. "We do have a lot in common. I'm a recovering alcoholic. And yeah, Anja is my sponsor."

"So offering to buy you a drink at the wedding and nattering on at you while I was downing shots was probably— shit, Ezra, I'm sorry. That was terrible and insensitive of me."

Vulnerable and contrite look good on her, too. As if she could possibly be more attractive.

"You didn't know. And I didn't tell you, so how would you? Can I just ask—what tipped you off?"

She smiles. "The toasts. The waiter handed you a glass of champagne, and you kept raising it but you never sipped it. And then you gave it back as soon as my mom was done blubbering into the mic."

That had been a nearly Herculean effort on my part. I should have given it back as soon as the waiter handed it out, but Mac always said toasting with water was bad luck. There wasn't anything else available, so I held that glass and pretended it was full of warm piss to keep it away from my lips. It helped that we were in front of the entire throng of guests and Anja was about four feet from me. Every time a speech ended, I saw her staring me and my glass down. I kept thinking warm piss, and finally, Mama A finished her toast and I got rid of the glass. The music had started back up and Juliana, newly filled with champagne, wanted to dance again. Anja had looked at me like she approved of my willpower, but really, my hands shook for a good ten minutes after we started dancing again. I decide not to say the words "warm piss" to Juliana, even though I suspect they might make her laugh.

Juliana runs the tip of her finger around the rim of her mug. If it were crystal, she'd set my skin on fire with the shrill noise. "Can I ask something else? How you can be diagnosed as an alcoholic when you're as young as you and Anja are?"

I purse my lips. It's not an entirely unfair question. I wonder, for a second, exactly how honest I can be here. They encourage honesty in AA, encourage you to share your story and let people know how far you've come. I hate opening my mouth in meetings as a general rule, and in this moment, I dread letting this amazing, perfect girl know how fucked up I am. But there's a bit of freedom in knowing I'm putting her on a plane in a few hours, that even if she decides (rightly) that I'm a total loser, I won't have to see her again if I don't want to. It emboldens me.

"Did your brothers ever tell you how they met me?" I ask.

She shakes her head. "Maybe they mentioned it, but not really in great detail."

"You know Anja and I went to high school together? Mackenzie," I say, holding my hand up, "and MacCullor. We usually got paired up in classes on account of our last names. Friends out of necessity, at first, you know? Then friends for real. I've known her longer than anyone I'm not related to.

"Anyway. We kept in touch after graduation since we both still lived around here, and as it turned out, we liked drinking together. Around the time Anja started dating Mattias, we were probably hanging out a couple of times a week, bouncing between happy hours we knew were cheap and within easy walking distance of one another. Mattias started coming with us, and then Lukas so I wasn't the third wheel. And we got to expand our haunts, because lo and behold, we suddenly had people we could count on to DD us."

The thing I don't tell her is how, at first, Mattias wasn't so much invited out with us to hang out—he was invited because

Anja knew he wouldn't drink. It wasn't using him, in the strictest sense of the word, because she wanted to be with him anyway. She and I just wanted to get plastered way more.

"I guess you can say the pair of them got kind of sick of it," I tell her. "And one time, they got so sick of it, they bailed on us."

Her mouth turns into a little circle of acknowledgment, and I know that if nothing else, she's likely heard the story of how we'd forced them out with us at one of our favorite places, and got so drunk we didn't realize when they got up, paid their tabs, and left. When Anja tried calling Mattias, he didn't answer. When I texted Lukas, I got the number for a cab company as a reply. We were both pretty pissed, because the money we were banking on paying our tabs with was suddenly going to have to go towards a cab halfway across town instead.

"That was when Anja and Mat broke up for a while," Juliana says, her voice low.

That was two years ago. It wasn't just for Mattias that Anja cleaned up—but being sober and stable enough to prove herself worthy of a second chance was a huge motivating factor. She stopped hanging out with me after that, because I wasn't the sort of person she wanted to be around while she was trying to clean up. Not to mention that I wasn't exactly Mattias and Lukas's favorite person at the moment.

I was pretty lucky when they took me back in six months ago, all told.

"It probably sounds like something people do when they're young and stupid," I say. "And maybe it is. But normal people can blow off steam with a drink or two at Happy Hour, sober up, and get themselves home safely. Most people don't drive home questionably fucked up, and then keep drinking when they do get home. And drink more to ward off the hangover the next morning. That's not how *you* drink, I'll bet."

She shakes her head.

"That is how Anja and I drink. It's how we would drink if we weren't trying to do better. That's how we know we're alcoholics. It's a disease, not a bad habit. And it really sucks to try to shake.

"It's been sort of an insane year for me," I say with finality and pick my chips back up. "Anja's been a big help. Your whole family has been, actually. I guess I'm a little surprised that you didn't know about me being their charity case."

Her jaw drops. "They'd never consider you that, Ezra. My mother adopts every one of our friends into our family. She's still in touch with more of my friends from high school than I am."

If I'm not careful, I could fall for this girl. Only a few more hours and she'll be on a plane back to Brazil. Surely, I can go a few more hours.

"Well, I'm really impressed by you and Anja. The first couple of times I met her, I worried, you know? I worried she was going to drag my brother down, and that thought killed me. I hate to say it, but I was glad they broke up, because watching her when she got really bad was killing him. But I see how much better she is now, I see how amazing she is, and I can't imagine my family without her.

"But what I really can't imagine is how hard it must be for you guys. I have a lot of respect for you both." The smile on her face shows that she's honest, and not just saying something nice she thinks I'd want to hear. This girl is genuine through and through. *Another* thing I find irresistibly charming.

"Thanks. It's nice hearing that." The three quick beeps of the washer indicate the end of its cycle, and I excuse myself to change loads. I look over my shoulder as I walk past her on the couch, and I see her smile at me. It's a real smile, one of respect and acceptance. Then she wink-blinks at me.

And here I thought I had a couple of hours left to not fall for her. My mistake.

***

I'm both relieved and crushed when Juliana disappears into her old bedroom to grab her suitcase a couple of hours later. My last load of clothes is in the dryer and by the time I get back from dropping her at the airport, it'll be ready to fold, and I'll continue on about my day like I didn't do something insanely stupid, like fall for my sponsor's new sister-in-law. She comes back down with a suitcase in one hand and a garment bag slung over her shoulder. I offer to take something, but she shrugs me off.

"The suitcase is crazy-light. That's how much coffee I brought up. And I have to take the garment bag on the plane with me so I can change before we land, so I might as well get used to carrying it."

"Change?" I ask.

We head out to my car and I get to at least open the back hatch and the passenger side door for her. After the embarrassment of to-go containers and empty cigarette packs littering the back seat of my car on the wedding day, I made a real effort to have it clean today.

"I'm connecting through Dallas and then the flight to Sao Paolo runs overnight. I'll have to go straight to work when I land."

"Sounds like a long couple of days."

"Oh, I'm gonna be a wreck. Thankfully my coworkers are pretty used to me failing at basic girliness—except for my shoes, of course," she says with a smirk, holding up her heeled foot. "A rumpled suit and bags under my eyes will be the least of what they've seen from me."

As I start my car and steer us toward the airport highway, I try to shirk away the nagging in me that I should ask her when she's coming back home next. I should offer to keep in touch. She's witty and smart and has interesting opinions about interesting things. Forget the fact that she's completely stunning; she's one of the most fascinating people I've ever met. Then I remind myself again and again that she lives thousands of miles away, and that even if she came home every couple of months, that wouldn't be enough for me. And anyway, Juliana Almeida does not need a perennial fuck up like Ezra Mackenzie dragging her down.

My jaw clenches with the sight of the airport looming in the distance, because how did we get out here so fast? Where was the traffic that always slows the drive into an interminable commute? Juliana is shuffling around, making sure she has her passport and cell phone charger, and I have no choice but to drive forward. I know as soon as I drop her at the terminal and say goodbye, that's it. I'll go home and"""" try to forget this incredible girl that had me wrapped around her finger from the very first sight of her in rumpled, dishwater-soaked pajamas. It's for the best, even though my heart feels like it's sinking from my chest to my gut.

"So, I'll be around for Christmas," Juliana says, causal as can be, without even looking up from rummaging through her purse.

In front of me, some asshole is trying to cut me off and I have to brake hard to avoid tearing off his bumper. I'm amazed I even noticed the car, given how her comment has infiltrated my ears and filled my head with foolish possibility. I square my shoulders to focus on the road, and just say a casual, "Oh?"

"I assume Mama has already made you promise to come to the big Christmas blowout she hosts every year?"

"Um. I, uh…." I stammer. Shit. Get it together, Mackenzie. She can't really read your mind; it's a coincidence. "Yeah, I'll definitely be stopping by. I don't get a ton of time off around the holidays, and I'll need to spend some time with my fam— my mother."

"Good. I'm glad this isn't the last I'll be seeing you, then," she says. I know without even looking at her she's done that hybrid wink/batting eyelashes thing. But it's all in my head. It has to be.

At the departures terminal, I pull up to the curb and leave the engine idling while I get out with her. I get to her suitcase first and set it at her feet. She's got something in her hand I think for a second might be gas money, probably at the insistence of Mama A. I'm ready to shrug her off until I see it's much smaller.

"It's sort of cliché, but this is my card. My cell number is there, and my personal email address is on the back. I, ah….." She bites her lip, like she's debating what to say.

Holy shit.

"I really enjoyed hanging out with you, Ezra. Don't be a stranger?"

I take the card and hold it gingerly. If I don't, I'll end up clutching it to my heart like I'm swooning. "It was good to meet you. And yeah. For sure."

"Thanks for schlepping out here. It was really sweet of you. I'll see you in a couple of months, huh?"

When she leans forward to wrap her arms around my neck, I try to keep my body from shaking the way my brain is. She smells amazing, and it's hard not to notice that her body sort of perfectly curves into mine. For a hug, it's shockingly intimate.

She pulls away and, I swear, I hear her sigh. "Thanks again, dance partner."

There's that wink again.

"Have a good trip." She waves at me over her shoulder and then disappears behind the sliding glass doors. I have to jar myself in order to round my car and get behind the wheel. I linger long enough that a security agent taps on my window to remind me it's a no-waiting zone.

I'm pulling away and back onto the highway before the significance of the card in my pocket registers. I glance at myself in the rearview mirror and shake my head, because surely, that didn't just happen. Surely, Juliana didn't just give me her number and email address. Surely, this crush of mine is still very much one-sided and a bad idea.

Even if it's not, there's nothing I *should* do about it. I'm not in the sort of place where I can muck up the life someone else has pieced together when I'm so thoroughly flailing. And that sucks even more than saying goodbye to her.

CHAPTER FOUR

I reluctantly throw my car into park in front of the house way out on the west side of town and sigh. It's Thanksgiving, and I'm expected inside my mother's house in approximately... now. I drove all the way out here, so the least I can do is go in. But I haven't spent a holiday with my mother in about fifteen years. In fact, I've barely even *seen* my mother in fifteen years.

I come by my alcoholism honestly, or at least I do if you accept the theory that addiction has a genetic component. Constance was one of the meanest drunks you'd ever meet. She wasn't physically abusive, but she had a short fuse and the sort of voice that carried. Mac told me once that before her drinking got out of control, she used to be gregarious and fun to be around when she had had a few. By the time it was finally bad enough that uber-forgiving, bright-side-of-everything-seeking Mac had to throw in the towel and leave her, they had ten years of turbulent marriage and and a set of twin sons in common.

I don't remember the version of Constance Mac must have first fallen in love with. What I recall from age of earliest remembrance to age ten is taking out the trash and listening to the wine bottles clinking together at the bottom, hoping and praying I'd make it to the trash can before the bag ripped from the excess weight. I remember dodging her line of sight so I wouldn't get a nasty earful of whatever her particular poison was on any given day as I came home from school, because she was in a foul mood more often than she was a pleasant one. I remember a lot of sitting at the top of the stairs with Dylan while she screamed at Mac and he tried to calm her down so she wouldn't "wake the boys." What I remember the clearest was the day Mac made us pack up our rooms and we left Constance for good, and how Mac promised us the entire ride to our new house that nothing much would change, except for all the yelling our mom did. As it turned out, the yelling stopped, and so did seeing her.

Mac passed on a pair of letters to Dylan and me a few years ago. Mac had read his, but hadn't told us what was in it. Dylan told me he burned his without ever opening it. I tucked mine in a random book and didn't look at it until well after Mac died and I was sober a couple of months. When you hit a certain point in a twelve-step recovery program, you make amends to people you've wronged, and that old, yellowed letter was Constance's amends for a decade of terrible mothering and another decade of abandonment. I tortured myself over it for a while after I got sober, but I finally got around to dialing the number she'd written at the bottom a couple of months ago, around the time I realized I'd be needing to make amends of my own and would be hoping for the same sort of forgiveness I never extended to her. I might have only forgiven her because she's about all the biological family I have left. We talked for a long time that first call, mostly about how she can't forgive herself for passing on her addiction to me. At least it skipped Dylan. It's too soon to tell about Gemma, though. By the way, being told at twenty-five you have a half-sister in kindergarten is a good solid mind-fuck, if that isn't an experience you've ever had.

Though not for lack of trying, I haven't seen Constance more than once or twice since that first phone call. She's about as far northwest as I am southeast in the metro area. My job has me working strange hours, and having a six-year-old she's raising on her own isn't conducive to odd hours. But when Thanksgiving was mentioned, I at least knew I wouldn't be exposed to open, flowing bottles of wine. Although, sweet Jesus, am I ever not used to being sober on feasting holidays— I mean, isn't that half the point? And to hear Constance say it, she owes me a few birthday celebrations as well. When we talk of everything owed, I'm going to be diplomatic enough to not charge emotional interest, lest I bankrupt her. Or myself.

The problem with not having a mother for a decade, and then suddenly having one you can only feel comfortable calling by her first name is that there seems to be little else to talk about. Gemma, my half-sister, is sweet and chatty enough to draw attention to herself the way little kids are pros at, but by the time she bunks off to watch an ancient Charlie Brown special, Constance and I are left alone to put together dinner in thick, awkward silence. There's a bunch of people from one of her AA meetings coming soon, so at least they'll diffuse this a little. But they haven't arrived yet, and son of a bitch, would this ever be easier with a drink or two. I'm sure the irony is not lost here.

"So… How did that wedding you were in go? All right?" she asks, her voice a little higher than normal. She catches my eye and smiles at me as if we're a normal, functional family, but it must feel as strange on her face as it feels to my eye, because she drops her gaze again and goes back to peeling sweet potatoes.

"Fine. Yeah, good," I reply, because this really is how I talk to my mother.

"Any fun stories? Did you catch the garter?"

"Ah, no. They skipped that tradition, and the bouquet

toss."

"Oh. That's too bad."

"Is it? They're sort of played out, don't you think?"

"I think they're charming."

"They aren't a super-traditional couple."

"Did you at least get to dance with the prettiest bridesmaid?"

I must flush or stutter or something, because before I even realize it, Constance has pulled a long string of convoluted sentences about Juliana out of me. To tell the truth, I haven't stopped thinking about her since I dropped her off at the airport.

It must be whatever is left of her maternal instincts when she tells me, in all earnestness, "That's dangerous, you know."

"Which part?" I ask.

"The different country part, for starters. But even if she lived down the street, relationships and recovery—they're very complicated things."

"Yeah. I've gleaned that." I don't mean to sass her. Well, not entirely.

She pokes her head into the living room, satisfied that Gemma is engrossed enough with Snoopy to talk about her. "Giving you advice this late in the game is laughable, I realize, but I met Gemma's father when I was trying to get sober the first time." *Not the first time*, I correct silently. There was a shining six months or so when I was nine that she put the bottle down, and we were a happy, functional family. Until something happened that made her drink again. Maybe nothing happened to make her drink again, I'm not sure—I just know we were gone by the following Christmas.

"It was fantastic, at first. He was supportive and sweet, and I thought—hoped—that I'd redeemed myself enough to be worthy of a good man, like I never was for Mac." She cringes, like she's worried that even saying my father's name will send me running for a liquor store. I very stoically continue chopping up potatoes. "But it was too much for him, in the end. We're civil now, for Gem's sake, but it took a while to get there."

I'd love to rub her face in how different she and I are. That I got my shit together and sobered up young, that I don't have a history of destroying marriages and abandoning sons I treated badly, and that Juliana is neither Mac nor Gemma's father, whom I haven't met and have no real interest in knowing. But, in all harsh, cold reality, I look just like Mac and, so far, I've acted just like Constance. I got his ruddy complexion, his long build, his poor eyesight but perfect teeth. And I got Constance's disease. Mac turned to a hanging punching bag in our garage to vent his frustration, started building ships in bottles to calm his nerves, researched the Scottish Mackenzies we descend from when he needed distraction. I drank, I drank, and I drank.

And that's how, in one awkward evening with my birth mother I can't remember ever loving, a baby half-sister I can't find common ground with past a coloring book, and a bunch of hardened, chain-smoking alcoholics I don't ever want to become, I decide for certain that Juliana's card will continue to go unused. At the end of the day, I know Juliana isn't Mac, but I'm too afraid that I'm just enough like Constance to fuck her up.

***

Since the wedding, Wednesdays have become family dinner night at Mama A's house, and according to Mama A, I'm very much part of that family. I linger around long after my laundry is folded and help Mama A in the kitchen. I find I don't have to talk on nights I'm not feeling up to it because Lukas and Mattias talk more than any ten people could, so it doesn't matter. Anja and I share packs of cigarettes on the back porch. It's nice, but mostly it's consistent, which I desperately need in my life. With the Almeidas, it almost feels like I have a family like I did before Mac up and died on me. It's on the first night of this after Thanksgiving that I realize with a guy like Mattias in my life, it feels an awful lot like I have a functional relationship with a brother—even and especially when said brother is currently railing on me for being what he terms 'an asshole to his sister.'

Right? It threw me for a loop, too.

To Mattias, it seems, it sort of doesn't matter that Juliana lives on another continent and I'm not even nine months sober—the polite thing to do, I'm told very forcefully, is to, at the very least, be in touch, and to make it clear things can't go beyond friendship until my life is a little more stable. And I'll own up that emailing her would have been the more polite thing to do, of course, but why the fuck would someone like Juliana Almeida ultimately care that someone like me never emailed her?

That's when Mattias hits me with, "You messed with her head, man."

"I… I have no idea how. We just talked."

"That's not how she saw it at all. She figured it meant something else. You're not the sort of guy to lead a girl on, Ez, at least I'm pretty sure you're not. So what the hell gives?"

Holy shit.

"I didn't mean to lead her on, Mat, I swear. I… Wait. Does she…?"

"Like you? Yeah. She told me she told you as much when she said goodbye to you at the airport."

Apparently getting sober has done very little for my comprehension of girl-speak. Drunk or sober, the phrase "I enjoyed spending time with you" does not equate, in my head, to "I'm interested in you." And why the ever-loving-hell would she be? I'm a fucking disaster.

"I… I really don't know what to say."

He snorts. "Clearly not."

"Mattias!" Anja hisses.

"I didn't mean it that way, Ez. Just... She's my *sister*, man."

When we're smoking together, I tend to light and hand cigarettes to Anja. I fumble this at the moment because all this about Juliana has me baffled and confused. It makes no sense. But if I suspend my disbelief for just a minute or two and actually consider what Mattias has said—

Holy shit.

"He shouldn't have cornered you like that." Anja says when Mattias ducks back in the house, leaving us polluting our lungs just like he found us.

"I'm so confused," I admit.

Anja bounces up and down for a minute while she thinks, then blows out a long puff of smoke. "Juliana isn't the sort of girl to beat around the bush about what she wants. She's pretty on top of her shit. I'm sort of amazed she didn't make it more obvious that she was interested. She mentioned it to me, but I didn't think it was my place to say anything."

My head is nearly spinning in place. "She said something? I... What did she say?"

"That you're good-looking, that you have a good personality. Both of which are true. I was a little too preoccupied to play matchmaker at the time, though. And I'm not sure I would have even if I hadn't been."

She doesn't have to elaborate for me to understand what she means. Constance is right: addiction and recovery and relationships are hard enough all on their own. Combining them can be a nightmare. One tends to destroy the others. Just ask my parents.

"I don't think I'm completely oblivious," I say. "She seemed kinda flirty, but I... I figured I was just seeing what I wanted to see, not what was actually there."

"It was easy to see that you liked her. But I don't know if

dating should really be on your radar with everything you have going on," she says.

"It's not. Believe me, it's not. It was just a crush. I never thought she'd… you know…."

"Reciprocate?"

"Yes! But Jesus, Anja, I'm a fucking train wreck."

Anja blows a smoke ring with a flourish. "Mat and Luk are incredibly protective of Jules. It's just how they are. But she's also a big girl, and she'll understand if you tell her you're not interested in all that right now. Just, you know, sack up and tell her."

This whole thing seems wildly incongruous. I should not be the one in this situation who's being lectured about clarifying our relationship. *She's* the beautiful, funny, massively intelligent woman who's completely out of *my* league. Surely *she* should be the one letting *me* down easy.

I say as much to Anja, who shakes her head. "She is not out of your league. Addiction aside, Ezra, you're a total catch."

I glare at her. "Don't humor me. We've known each other too long for that crap."

"It's not flattery. Honestly, another time and place, the two of you would make kind of an adorable couple."

I roll my eyes. "Well, I don't really think that's much of an issue now, do you? There's long distance, and then there's ridiculous distance."

"I think you're right about that. Just do the guys a favor? Explain that to her? She's super-cool and she'll understand as long as she knows where your head is at. But as a fellow girl, I can attest that being strung along sucks."

It's my turn to cough nervously, and Anja even whacks me on the back a few times to help me clear my pipes. Never in a million years would I ever guess that a guy like me could possibly "string along" a girl like Juliana. I figured it could only ever work the other way around.

"Guess you learn something new every day," I mutter to myself.

***

I've been on the receiving end of rejection before, but rejecting someone else is entirely new to me. And I've certainly never rejected someone like Juliana. Truth be told, I don't want to close the door to her. So as shitty as I know it makes me, my email to her reads:

> *Sorry I haven't been in touch—I hope you're doing all right. And I'm looking forward to seeing you in a couple of weeks when you get here, if you still want to hang out with me. You know... as friends.*

It's such a pansy-assed move. But apparently it's just enough to work, because within an hour, I get back:

> *It's all right—life gets hectic sometimes. And I definitely want to hang out. As friends. I'll see you soon.*
>
> *Julianna*

I don't realize at the time this'll start a month-long cycle of daily emails between us. Every message she sends, short, long, or anything in between, I find myself replying to within minutes. It's easy because, as friends, I don't have to torment myself over what I'm saying to her.

Yeah, right.

Just friends or no, I realize full well that I'm playing with fire here. That appeals to my addictive personality way more than it should.

CHAPTER FIVE

Juliana: I know they're terrible for the environment, and it's literally my job to care about that—but oh my God, I love Post-Its so much.

Me: Post-Its?

Juliana: Post-Its. They're magical. Don't you think they're magical?

Me: I don't think I have nearly the occasion to use them as you clearly do.

Juliana: Watch. Now you're going to use them all the time because I've told you why they're wonderful. I could write poetry about Post-Its. And I don't even like poetry.

Me: I don't like poetry, either. I'd read your poems, though.

Juliana: I'd read yours, too.

I don't have the sort of job where I sit at a computer all day, and I've been pretty thankful for it—I like moving around and being on my feet, and, frankly, I get headaches when I stare at a screen for too long. I've done a pretty good job in my adult life of avoiding an obsession with my phone. Maybe because I spent so much time being obsessed with booze. Other than Anja, Mattias, and Lukas, I barely even text. Now, however, I'm finding my phone to be an extension of my hand when I don't have my hands on bodies at work, because Juliana's job definitely involves sitting in front of a computer. And ever since asking her to see her 'as a friend,' I see her name a lot more than I ever expected I would.

Me: It won't freaking stop snowing here. My ice scraper actually snapped in half this morning. This winter shit is for the birds.

Juliana: I'm going to be truly magnanimous and not tell you that I went to the beach yesterday. Oops.

Me: You're killing me.

Juliana: You were the guy who was convincing Anja all day that the snow would make her wedding pictures prettier. And they did! Why bitch about the snow now?

Me: Because my ice scraper snapped in half this morning. Pay attention.

Juliana: I can't. I'm too busy sunbathing.

Me: I thought we were supposed to be friends.

Juliana: We are.

Me: So why are you trying to kill me?

Juliana: Oh… Is it working? ;)

Me: Sorry. I couldn't answer because I'm dead.

Juliana: I'm looking forward to seeing all this snow that's chapping your ass so much. I miss it, sometimes.

Me: I miss the sunshine. Bring the sunshine with you,

please. And hurry.

Juliana: I'll do my best. Anything else I should bring?

Me: No, you and the sunshine are more than adequate.

Juliana: Me?

Me: …yeah, you.

Juliana: No coffee?

Me: No, the coffee goes without saying.

I become that person habitually checking my phone between sessions at work, scrolling through message chains on my break while I puff down cigarettes in my car, holding up traffic at red lights because her name has just flashed over my screen, and I can't wait until I pull up to my destination to figure out what charming thing she might have typed into an email or text message. I have the traffic ticket to prove this one—I've gotten better since then, as much as seeing her name on my screen still thrills me.

Me: So should I get you Post-Its for Christmas? Anja says they make recycled paper ones now.

Juliana: I know they do. I'll never say no to them. Are you sure you don't want to give me a massage for Christmas?

Me: I told you… I don't work on people I know. It's a boundary thing for me.

Juliana: You wouldn't make a tiny exception for me?

Me: Sorry.

Juliana: Mean. I just want to know what all the fuss is about.

Me: You'll have to come up with something else for me to get you.

Juliana: I'm sure I'll think of something.

I find myself wishing I sat at a desk, double computer monitors in front of me, a tablet in my lap, my phone ever at the ready, because then I'd be able to respond as quickly as she does to my own rambling messages.

Juliana: But just to clarify—you're looking forward to seeing me?

Me: Pretty sure I've told you as much before.

Juliana: Interesting. Since you're seeing me as a friend.

Me: What? It's interesting that I don't have many friends?

Juliana: That isn't what I said.

Me: What, pray tell, did you say?

Juliana: Nothing, friend. I'm looking forward to seeing you, too.

***

That must be how I end up picking her up at the airport two weeks later. I'd like to say she suckered me into it with pretty words and promises in our emails, but I was the one who offered. Mama A mentioned that she'd pulled a shift when Juliana was due in, and I volunteered so quickly I think I made Mama dizzy. She didn't mention it to Mattias or Lukas, but she smirked at me in this funny way of hers. I might be dense, but I'm definitely not transparent.

Since I don't mention it to Mattias, Anja has no way of knowing. I feel pretty bad keeping something like this from my sponsor. I try to tell myself it's just not that big a deal, and that it really doesn't mean anything. But I'm pretty sure I'm wrong and have no interest in being right.

I chain-smoke out to the airport, and decide to park and go inside and meet her on the other side of customs. I tell myself it's better for the atmosphere to park and kill the engine than sit in the cell phone lot with it idling in freezing temperatures. She's an environmental engineer, so that makes a difference to her, right?

I'm humoring myself and I know it. Really, I'm just eager to see her. I'm hoping for another hug like that last time, where she melted against me. I want a few extra minutes to see if the emails we've exchanged actually mean something, or if she's really as content with 'just friends' as I claim to be. Try as I might, I don't *want* to think of Juliana as a friend.

I know I'm totally screwed when it comes to this girl. At least I didn't bring flowers or anything. Shit. *Should* I have brought flowers?

I don't really do waiting well. It gives me too much time to think, and when I think, I think about drinking. More immediately, I think about drinking and about what I'm going to do when I see Juliana come through the customs gate.

I try to tell myself again that my feelings were situational. It was a while ago that I saw her, and it was all under very highly charged emotional activity. It was a wedding, for crying out loud—aren't people supposed to feel all mushy and romantic during weddings? Maybe I was just reacting to that part of the weekend, and the little crush I developed was nothing more than that. Of course, that explanation doesn't settle the pounding in my chest that I feel every time her name pops up on my phone or email box, never mind the thudding my heart is doing right now as I wait.

I start pacing for lack of anything better to do. Maybe this is too personal, too much like something a boyfriend would do. Do I have time to run back out to my car, pay for the obligatory hour, and circle around like I was waiting in the cell phone lot the whole time?

But I don't—she's right there. And whatever I felt two months ago at the wedding wasn't a fleeting crush. Seeing her stepping out of the customs double doors brings everything back that I've been trying to ignore since the last time I saw her, everything I've been trying to ignore with every typed exchange between us since. I'd nearly succeeded, too, but she's too much goodness for me to ever really shake her. I'm already realizing that I don't want to.

There's no time to debate with myself further about how precarious this situation I've gotten myself into is before she's right in front of me. She smiles, and her dimples gut me like they did that first morning. My arms open and she steps into them. She fits like she did before. That isn't normal, right? A girl isn't supposed to fit into your arms until you know her, until you've proclaimed something and have a shot in hell of being anything other than two people in a glorious mess.

She steps back, and I notice for the first time her lips are glossy, like she's trying to draw attention to them. Kissing her is out of the question. It *has* to be out of the question. This moment and a handful of others over the next ten days is all we're going to be allowed. Getting attached would be almost as bad as walking into a bar.

Since I have to do something, I lean forward and peck to her cheek. I'm close enough to smell cherries or raspberries latent in her lip gloss. When I pull away again, her smile is a little less enthusiastic, but no less lovely.

"Hey, Ezra," she says, brushing the back of her hand against mine.

"Hi, Jules. Good flight?"

"Fine. But I'm glad to have landed."

Yeah, I think. I'm glad you did, too.

***

I'm wickedly glad that it'll be hours before anyone else will be off work. I want as much time alone with Juliana as I can get. I'm glad to get it before she becomes completely preoccupied with her family and I have to bow out and pretend I'm not a puppy following behind her, hoping for affection and attention.

It's different, though. I don't know if it's the emails or it's us picking up from where we left off. She's still good-natured and easy to talk to, but there's something to say for proximity—and now we have it. When we go for coffee to keep her awake after the lengthy flight, she leans across the table and looks straight into my eyes. When we get back to Mama A's, we sit together on the couch, our knees scant inches from one another. It sends a dangerous sort of thrill through me knowing I can reach out and touch her whenever I want to. So I do. I look for excuses to brush her hand or wipe an eyelash off her cheek. She doesn't stop me, not once.

Then there's this: I've realized when I'm with Juliana I don't want a drink the way I usually do. I still crave regularly at work. I get shaky and short-tempered with my coworkers between sessions, I silently mock and make faces at the back of some of my more demanding client's heads, and I need cigarettes or a rub of my chips to calm me down. As soon as I leave her, though, I can tell there is a massive difference in how I felt when I was sitting on the couch talking about anything and nothing with her, and how I feel after. It's Wednesday, and I'll be expected back for dinner. By then I imagine Juliana will have told Anja how she got home, and I'll have some explaining to do. I take a few minutes for myself at home to think about what I'll say and what everything means. But mostly I think about how, for three whole hours, I didn't think about drinking, not even once.

Anja catches me outside before I even come in. She's got a cigarette pack in her hand and her coat buttoned up to her throat, so I know we'll be having A Talk.

"I thought you said you were telling her you weren't interested?" Anja says, a sharp eyebrow nearly hitting her hairline. This is her 'significant look,' and when it's directed at me, I feel about as small as one of her kindergartners.

"I wasn't going to tell her that because it isn't true. We've just been talking, and it helped Mama A out to pick her up. That's it."

"Really? That's not the impression I get," Anja says. She lets me light up for us, then blows smoke out of her nostrils in a huff.

"I just figured spending a little more time with her wouldn't really hurt anything. You know—as friends."

Anja rolls her head from side to side. "Ezra, getting attached to someone like this might not be the best idea."

"You think I don't know that?" I definitely don't mean to sound as defensive as I do. "I recognize this is crap timing. But addiction aside, I am a big boy. And besides, when was the last time I told you I was thinking of drinking? Ages, right? Before the wedding, maybe. That's progress, isn't it?"

"It is. Of *course* it is. I can't tell you what to do. But I'm your friend and she's my sister-in-law. I don't want to see either of you hurt if it doesn't work out."

"There's nothing there to 'work out.' It's just... *time.* Together."

We finish our cigarettes in silence, but I'm quick to light us seconds.

"I won't fuck anything up on purpose, I promise," I whisper. "She deserves better than that."

"You *both* deserve better than that." She says it like she's exasperated she has to. I have a hard time accepting that I deserve anything good at all. But it's sort of Anja's job to say those kinds of things.

Juliana pokes her head out the door the next second. "You done polluting your lungs yet, sis—? Oh. Hey, Ezra."

Anja scans back and forth between the two of us, her large eyes saying everything she either can't or won't.

"Yeah, I'm all finished," she says, tossing the tail end of her cigarette in the ashtray. When she looks at me, I'm not sure if she's expecting me to do the same thing or not.

"I've got a few drags still," I say, holding up my own.

"Well hurry it up. Dinner's ready and it smells amazing." Juliana stands aside so Anja can slip past her, and the door closes again behind them both. I feel a little disappointed that Juliana didn't stay out here with me, didn't come near enough for a hug or even a kiss on the cheek. Maybe I shouldn't expect things like that with us yet. Or at all.

We're seated next to one another at dinner. All I want to do is grab her hand under the table like a middle school kid at lunchtime. I wonder if I did if she'd grab it back.

CHAPTER SIX

I don't see Juliana much after that first day until closer to Christmas, nor did I really expect to. Alcoholics might be vapid narcissists, but I hold no delusions that she came here to see me and me alone. So I mush on about my life—work, AA, home. Lather, rinse, repeat—and try not to think too hard about Juliana sleeping in a bed a few miles from my own. Mama A will be hosting her annual Christmas party a few days before the holiday. I decide not to hold out too much hope of spending much time with her then, either, as I've been told the party is basically a reunion of every person the Almeidas have ever met. And besides, I'll likely stick close to Anja out of both preference and necessity. There will be booze at the party—she and I can't be expected to change that—and the temptation for both of us will be huge. For the two of us, it's hang together or risk self-destruction.

I'm half-asleep in a comfortable, awkward position on my futon, lucidly dreaming about Juliana in place of the female protagonist in the Netflix show on my TV when a knock on my door wakes me. I glance at the clock on my stove when I go to answer, and register that it's nearly midnight. It's been a long time since I've had unexpected late-night visitors. When I see Juliana through the peephole, I press down the panic of late-night disturbances, though I gape at the general mess that is my apartment. Still, I can't just not answer. It's *her*.

"Hey, is everything okay?" I ask her as I shield my messy apartment from her view.

Her face brightens when she sees me. I swear I'm not just seeing things, it really happens. "Everything's fine. I know it's crazy-late, but Mama has been driving me crazy all day and I just... Oh God, were you asleep?"

"No!" I say, too quickly. "Just dozing. I work until closing on Tuesdays so I don't really settle in until late."

"Good" she says, and there's an almost wicked smile on her face. She bends and picks up a large bag at her feet. "Because I managed to find a Chinese place that stays open later than ten, which is impressive and terrifying all at once. You like Chinese, right?"

"Yeah, I love it, but...." I chance a glance behind me and try to decide how to best explain how my apartment looks. There are dishes in the sink, but I'd at least rinsed them before leaving them. The litter box is fine and the trash is relatively empty, but things are definitely messy. I apparently also need to pay better attention to the potted plants I keep on my windowsill.

"I really want to invite you in, Jules, but my place is kind of...."

She mock-gasps and covers her mouth with her hand. "Do you mean to tell me that you don't live in pristine conditions at all times? Are you trying to imply I might see an overturned shoe or stray sock? However will my delicate sensibilities handle such a thing?"

She grins, and there's that wink/bat thing again. I laugh in spite of myself, then rub my jaw and sort of half-hang my head. "It's definitely worse than that."

"I really don't mind, Ezra. I know I'm popping by unannounced. I just really needed to get out of my house for a while. But if you're not up to company and it's too late, I can just…."

The last thing I do is want her to leave. "Come in. I'm really sorry about the mess."

I take the take-out bag from her and send her straight into the living room, hoping she'll bypass looking at the kitchen altogether. She walks straight past my laundry baskets piled near the coffee table and plops down on the one part of the couch not covered by pillows or blankets (or my coat, or hell, even my mail). "It's not that terrible," she says. "Do you not celebrate Christmas?"

"No, I do."

"You don't have a tree up."

"I haven't really gotten around to it."

"It's in five days."

"Yeah… I figured I'll be other places or at work, so it's not like I'll be doing any celebrating here." I open the containers one after another. It's pungent, spice-scented music to my nose after three days of cold cereal and toast.

"Get me a scoop of everything, will you?" she says before I even ask. "You don't get a lot of good Chinese food in Sao Paolo, so I went a little nuts. Make as big oa plate for yourself as you want, if you're hungry."

I spoon two heaping plates and bring them to the couch. I move to set hers down on the coffee table when the cat jumps up onto it and mewls at her pathetically.

"Oh, I didn't know you had a cat," she says with a gasp.

"You're not allergic, are you?"

"No, not at all," she says, then leans forward and rubs her fingers together. The cat stalks towards her and allows Juliana to rub between her ears for a few seconds before scampering off to hide.

"She's pretty skittish. Want anything to drink?"

"Whatever you're having."

I set my plate down while she tucks in and head back to the kitchen. My kettle is the quick-boiling kind, so I'm back in the living room, a mug of peppermint and chamomile tea in either hand, before she's even half of the way through her plate.

She smiles as she chews, and holds her hand over her mouth to talk. "It's not half bad. Better than you can get in Brazil. Hence why I'm making a pig of myself."

I want to tell her it's quite charming, and even kind of sexy, to see a woman who enjoys eating. I think again of how I snuck peeks at her that first brunch, at the reception, the other night at dinner, and studied her lips and jaw as they moved. I don't say as much, because that's probably creepy at best. "I have a brother who played football in high school. If I didn't eat fast, he'd steal stuff off my plate. You're positively delicate in comparison."

"Mat and Luk, too!" She laughs and takes the peppermint tea. "Cheers. Thanks for letting me escape here, despite the hour."

"Anytime," I say before shoving my fork in my mouth.

She looks around between bites. "So is this a studio, or…."

"No, my bedroom is through there. Work has been sort of tiring the last week or so, so I've been crashing out here where there's a TV, falling asleep to Netflix."

"I do the same thing. I've got this big, plush chair I got at IKEA a few years ago, and I think I sleep in it as much as I do my own bed." She swallows another big mouthful. "So is Christmas busy in the spa world?"

"Massage therapist," I correct. "That's an antiquated term they used to use for, well, prostitutes."

"Does that mean I can't make happy ending jokes?"

"I guarantee you I won't find them the slightest bit amusing."

"Oh, I'm sorry," she says.

"It's all right."

"No, that's shitty of me to joke about. Although I can't say as I know the difference between what goes on in a legit massage and a sketchy one. I've never had either kind."

"Really? Any reason?"

"No time, I guess? It just never seemed like a priority to me."

She finishes her plate and before I can stop her, she's in my kitchen getting more. "I really don't care if you have dishes in the sink, Ezra," she says, sensing whatever my protest would have been. "I didn't crash your place late at night expecting to find it spotless."

I can't stop the words tumbling out of my mouth. "Why *did* you come here? I mean, you could have gone and hung out with Anja and Mattias or someone else you know…."

She looks at me like I've just asked the dumbest question on the planet. "I figured it'd be obvious."

I sip the still-scalding tea while I try to process her words. She comes back to sit, but spends more time pushing her food around than eating it.

"Jules, look… I think you're really great."

"Good," she says. "I think you're pretty great, too."

"I'm really not," I say with a sigh. "I'm sort of a mess."

"And I just told you—I don't mind a mess."

She sets her fork down and slides a little closer to me. She's gnawing her bottom lip and the friction of her teeth scraping over the skin pinks up the flesh. My mug is still cupped between my hands when her knee bumps against mine.

"I really don't get it," I confess, because I don't. What does a girl like her want with a guy like me? What could I possibly ever have to offer her?

"I don't think there's anything to get. I like you, Ezra. I just… wanted to see you. That's all. I figured if you didn't want to see me, you'd have told me to leave when I showed up."

"Of course I wanted to see you."

"So what's the problem?"

"This just doesn't seem like something friends do."

"Yeah, well… Maybe it isn't."

I wonder if the half-blinking, half-winking thing is more of a nervous tick for her than a purposeful gesture. I could ask her if I wanted to admit just how much I've been studying her face since we met. I could ask her if it'd be all right to kiss her, like I so badly want to. Or, I suppose, I could put down my tea cup, put my hands on her cheeks, and do it.

Before I get the chance, she leans over the small space between us on the couch, tilts my chin with the knuckles of her left hand, and brushes her lips over mine.

"Neither is that," she says.

I must gape at her. I try and recall the last time in my adult life a woman has kissed me before I've kissed her. I come up with nothing. 'My heart 'won't stop pounding in my ears, my mouth has gone dry, and probably my lips, too. All this just from her simply being *near* me blows how I've felt about other women out of the freaking water. I could probably forget about all of them with one more good kiss.

She's been inside for several minutes, but when I put my mug down and cup her face in my hands, her cheeks are still wintry cold. Maybe it's the difference in temperature from my mug. Whatever it is, I know I don't imagine the way she presses the side of her face deeper into my palm and lets her eyes flutter closed. Her eyelashes are dark and practically cast shadows on her cheeks. I expect her to open her eyes again, look at me and pin me with one of those gazes of hers that undoes me. But she doesn't. I guess she must be waiting. And in truth, so have I.

I lean towards her and slant my lips over hers. Her mouth doesn't taste like tea or questionable Chinese food—it tastes like her. And I can hardly be expected to not go back for seconds (and thirds and…) once I realize how intoxicating that taste is.

**

"Mmm… You may think it looks like a mess, but I approve of all these pillows and stuff piled on here," Jules says. "It makes it sort of like a little fort."

I chuckle. "You don't suppose we're a little old for pillow forts?"

"Pssssh. You can never be too old for pillow forts."

I'm inclined to agree with her. But at the moment, the term 'kissed me stupid' applies all too well to me. At this point, I'd be inclined to rob a bank with her if she asked me to.

Besides, we really have created a little fort. Given the late hour, I could easily fall asleep like this. She's settled herself against my chest, her hips nestled in between my legs. Our fingers are a complicated knot I don't want to unravel. In this deliriously happy post-make-out state, being with her clothed is better than most of the time I've spent naked with anyone else. I marvel again at the natural way our bodies seem to fit together. Sure, it makes me think of other things. But one step at a time. Or at least, that's what we'd told each other a few minutes ago, when our kisses had gone from feverish to full-on desperate. Too fast is still too fast. Damn it.

I know this is only temporary. She'll come to her senses soon, and I'll be left with a nice little memory. Not that I want her to get up and go, of course, but I'm too much of a pessimist these days to believe this is anything but too good to be true.

The cat is perched on the corner of my coffee table, flicking her tail back and forth while she stares at us. Juliana rubs her fingers together again to beckon her, but the cat is frozen in place like a fuzzy, hissing gargoyle.

"What's its name?"

"Uh...."

"You don't remember your cat's name?"

"She's not really *my* cat," I say. "She belonged to my father. He named her Birdie."

She snorts. I'd laughed when Mac told me the cat's name, too.

"Mac had a weird sense of humor," I explain. "He found her behind his garage when she was a kitten. I guess she'd been kicked out of her litter or something. It was amazing she was even alive. He fed her rice milk out of an eyedropper and fattened her up with tuna after she could hold it down. She was totally attached to him after that. Except first thing in the morning—she'd sit on his windowsill in his breakfast nook and watch the birds in his crabapple trees. I guess that's how he got the name."

"You guess? Why don't you just—oh."

I swallow hard, not wanting to have to confirm what she'll ask next.

But she doesn't say a word, or ask the obvious question about what happened to Mac, or mention the cat again. She curls against my chest and squeezes my fingers between hers.

"So, is it all right if I stay a little bit longer?"

"Is it all right if I kiss you again?"

She turns her face up to grin at me. I don't need any other validation than that before I surge up and claim her mouth.

***

"You weren't going to leave without saying goodbye, right?"

Jules startles and clutches her heart through the puffy winter coat she's shrugging on. "I was trying not to wake you."

"What time is it?" I grind the heels of my hands into my eyes, realizing I'd fallen asleep with my contacts in.

"Almost six. I need to try to sneak in before Mama realizes I didn't come home."

My heart sinks in my chest. I wonder if she doesn't want to acknowledge anything that happened last night—the kissing, the talking, the falling asleep curled up together—like it was some sort of mistake.

"Mama is prone to asking a lot of questions I'm not sure we're ready to answer," she says. "At least, not until we can talk a little more."

"We talked a lot last night."

"You know what I mean, Ezra."

I actually don't have the first clue what she means. Maybe it's because I'm still groggy. Maybe it's because I don't want her to leave. I know it's because I don't think we did anything to be embarrassed about. And I'm a guy who knows a lot about embarrassing evenings. But I nod at her through a stifled yawn and get up to at least walk her to the door.

"Wednesdays are still laundry day, right?"

"Isn't it obvious?" I kick one of my laundry baskets for good measure.

"Fair warning, as soon as you walk in the door, Mama will conscript you into helping dust or vacuum or whatever else she can think of for the big shindig. You don't mind?"

"Not at all."

We linger in the doorway for a moment. Then she puts her hand on my chest and stands up straighter to kiss me. She's only a couple of inches shorter than me, so it's not far for me to duck down to return it.

"Good. I'll see you later today, then," she says.

"You will. And we'll talk if you want to."

"I do want to."

There's a definite nip in the air when I open the door for her, like it might start snowing any minute. I watch her get into her car and drive away. I feel lost without her next to me as I settle back on the couch and crumple into a heap.

She was just here. She stayed all night without me begging

her to, and without any ulterior motive than to just be with me. She was here. She *wanted* to be here.

And if I press my nose into just the right place in one of my pillows, I can smell the faintest trace of her perfume lingering there.

I fall asleep like that, not caring in the slightest how moogly-eyed and love-struck that might make me. I'm a total idiot, and I know it.

CHAPTER SEVEN

Mama A is a whirling dervish, scrubbing and dusting every surface of her home. According to her, Juliana is supposed to be helping, but got a phone call ten minutes previously and has been holed up in her bedroom ever since. Truth be told, I'm a little relieved. How would we have been expected to greet one another? A hug? A kiss? A casual wave, like we didn't spend last night in each other's arms? I've never been good at knowing what level of affection is appropriate in mixed company, even when the parameters of a relationship are well-defined.

After I start a load of my wash, Mama A puts me to work, just as Juliana had predicted. Being a good head taller than Mama, I'm tasked with dusting the tops of bookshelves and ceiling fans. It's mindless work, so I can't help that my eyes wander to the stairs. I wonder if I'll see Juliana at all. I wonder if she's avoiding me.

She comes down around the time Mama A insists on making me lunch. I'm elated to see her, at first. When she barely acknowledges me and takes a glass of water and a sandwich to her room instead of sitting down and eating with us, my stomach clenches in the most uncomfortable possible way. I'd made myself available to talk, like she wanted. I hadn't made any untoward moves when she'd been at my place last night—and that had been hard in more ways than one. I felt like things were going well. Maybe even better than well. So what's with the cold shoulder now?

I know I should text Anja and explain what's going on. The more I think and overthink about this, the more it's bound to stress me out, and the more I stress—it's not a difficult leap from confused to disheartened to drinking. But last night still feels like such a special secret between Juliana and me that I'd feel bad mentioning anything to Anja without telling Juliana first.

I'm beginning to feel like I should have known better. I should have thought with my head and not my heart and lips and hands. I guess it could have been worse—I could have thought with something farther south of my hands. I've done that exactly enough times to know how bad it can be.

I'm loading my clean clothes into the back hatch of my car when Juliana finally seeks me out. I stand still and stupid, waiting for her to make some sort of move and let me in on what's appropriate. When she doesn't do anything, I shut the hatch and lean casually against my car.

"I'm sorry we didn't get a chance to talk. I had a call from work to deal with, and then when I came down... Well, I didn't think we should talk in front of my mother."

"Right, yeah. I understand." It's dawning on me that maybe I'm Juliana's dirty little secret. I'm a holiday fling, hidden and not thought of again once she's home and amongst men who actually deserve her. The way she keeps looking towards the house, through the windows like she's worried Mama A might be watching—well, that says a lot.

"I *do* want to talk to you. I just—I got sort of blindsided by something, that's all."

"Look, it's all right," I tell her, shoving my hands in my pockets. "We can just let it be what it was. It was a lot of fun. It doesn't have to be anything more. It doesn't have to mean anything."

She rears back. "Is that *really* what you think I was going to talk to you about?"

"I think you might be too nice to just say it, in case I... Look, I get that I'm not really a desirable guy. And you live in another country. It's all right if you're looking for casual. But casual really doesn't work for me."

She looks like she wants to slap me. "That's *not* what I meant. At *all*. We'll talk later, once I've figured out what to say. If you're interested in listening, that is." She strides up the walk and slams the front door behind her.

It sinks in that I was kind of an asshole to her. I want to kick myself in the ass, but I settle for pulling my hair and groaning before sliding behind the wheel of my car to chain-smoke my way home.

Anja's and my mother's voices both ring in my head again that alcoholics in recovery and burgeoning relationships don't mix. I really should have listened in the first place.

***

Other times in my life, a small setback like this would trigger a binge of the highest order. I'd get a handle of Wild Turkey, a couple of two-liters of club soda, and maybe a growler from Comrade if I was feeling particularly thirsty, and lock myself in my apartment. I'd call in sick to work and watch the bottles disappear. I'd savor the burn, the blurry edges, the way time speeds up and slows down all at once. Six months ago, I'd have been drunk for five days after realizing how badly I'd screwed up my chances with the girl of my dreams in less than five minutes.

Let it never be said that I don't possess a modicum of self-control. As I'm stacking my folded clothes into my dresser and begin to feel that sort of intense yearning coming on, I unlock my phone. Anja programmed nearly every AA meeting in the greater Denver Metro area into my calendar so I always know where one is. There's one starting in twenty minutes at a church not too far from my apartment. I opt to jog there instead of drive—it's the one habit I've carried over from my drinking days. Running would help sober me up and sweat out enough alcohol from a bender so I could go into work and not reek of booze. Now it just helps me clear my head.

I sit in the back of the meeting, my chips clutched in the palm of my hand. I remind myself that things could be worse… they could *always* be worse, and I'm a testament to that.

Then I remember the way Juliana fit perfectly against me, and my spirits sink all over again. I don't *want* that to be it. I don't want to pretend like nothing happened. I don't want to pretend that I wouldn't take a night like that one with her again if she offered. It doesn't matter that whatever I forge with her is fleeting, and I'll be left totally crushed when she gets on her plane back to Brazil. I *want* to be crushed by her. Then at least I could say that I had her, if only for a moment. Wanting her like I do is such a huge mistake.. And the problem is that if I could take back everything I've felt since the first moment I saw her, I wouldn't. I'd live these days over and over and over again, because God—she seems so disastrously worth it.

***

It snows overnight and most of the day before the Christmas party. When I arrive at the Almeidas' around dusk, the Christmas lights on their house are especially lovely, and the always-warm little house seems especially cheerful and inviting. I juggle the gifts in my arms before going up the shoveled, salted walkway, and let myself in. The house smells of cinnamon and pine. I try not to dwell on the unanswered email I'd sent Juliana after my AA meeting yesterday, apologizing for being brusque with her, and greet everyone with smiles and

"Merry Christmas" on my lips.

Anja has a special sense for when things are bothering me. She links arms with me after I set the gifts down, grabs a plate of appetizers, and forces me out onto the back porch. She noshes on a bruschetta while I light us cigarettes. All it takes to get me to open up about the whole sordid situation is one of her significant looks.

"I wondered why Jules was so quiet today," she says after I pause long enough to take several drags before my cigarette burns down to ash. "You need to talk to her, Ezra. For real."

"I know I do. I just don't know what to say. I think I might have really hurt her."

"I think you might have, too. Which makes it all the more important."

"I'm just so bad at all this. The last time I showed interest in a woman I... Well. You know what happened."

She nods, and I know she's thinking about how she'd found me in the ER, gauze shoved up my nose and my eyes blackened.

"You're a different person now, though," she says.

"I'm still a fuck-up, Anja. Eight lousy months doesn't change that. And I don't want to fuck *her* up. Everything I've touched has turned to shit lately. How the hell do I live with myself if I do that to her?"

She purses her lips for a second and studies my face. "*Everything?* You sure about that?"

"I've got the deviated septum to prove it," I say, pointing to my nose.

"Look, I stand by what I said last time this came up: I'm not sure you're ready for a new relationship. But Jules is tough. If anyone's tough enough to figure out how to be with an alcoholic and make things work, it's probably her. She and Mattias have that in common."

She steals another cigarette from my pack. "And she went

to you. That's pretty indicative. I don't know, maybe giving things a go wouldn't be the worst thing in the world."

"I figured you'd lecture me on keeping all this from you," I admit.

"Your business is still your business. You need to tell me when you're going to drink, but who you talk to, who you flirt with, who you... whatever. That's still up to you."

"She lives thousands of miles away. I don't know how to cope with that."

She nods. "I'll bet that she's not sure how to cope with it, either. This is pretty new territory. You need to have this conversation with *her*, not with me."

I know she's right. We stub out our cigarettes and go back inside as a cold wind picks up. The amount of people in the house has doubled since we slipped out, and more and more are people I don't recognize. We go for some hot mulled cider while I pretend not to notice that Juliana is acting as though she hasn't seen me.

The house is practically full to bursting when the toasts begin. I've switched to straight club soda (which lacks a certain something, but I gulp it down anyway). Mattias has been hanging with Anja and me, introducing us to people he actually knows and recognizes, but when Lukas stands up on the coffee table, much to Mama A's chagrin, he gets up to join his brother. It's tradition, Anja explains: every member of the family says something, thanks everyone for coming. Lukas, ever the comedian, always starts and gets everyone's attention.

He's written his speech in limerick, and within seconds, he has even my sad-sack ass rolling. It's breezy and light and funny, exactly what you expect out of a character like Lukas, but his crescendo is what really gets my attention.

"...and middle sister, how we've missed her—we'll be so pleased next month when we forever get to keep her!"

He's slipped it in, maybe thinking no one will notice. But

enough people gasp and rush Juliana to ask what he meant by it that I know Lukas meant to spill the beans. She confirms aloud to the entire ensemble that she has, in fact, accepted a position within her company here in town. She isn't going back to Brazil, at least not forever. She's flying back to pack up, then moving back home for good. It was official as of yesterday. She doesn't get the chance to give whatever speech she might have had lined up before she's mauled with hugs and kisses from the ravenous crowd of people who adore her.

I look at Anja agape. She shakes her head in silent insistence that she knew nothing about this. Across the room, I catch Juliana's gaze with my own.

I told you we needed to talk, she mouths to me.

I nod, like I'm actually brave and noble enough for this talk. But right now, with an ocean of possibility stretching out in front of me and inexplicably scaring me shitless, I am neither brave nor noble. I kiss Anja on the cheek and tell her I'll call her later. She tries to follow me out to my car, but I brush her off and promise her I'm not on my way to doing anything stupid. I just need to think, and I need to do it alone.

I barricade myself in my apartment and turn my phone off. I marathon cheesy 80s movies to distract myself from my incredible yearning for a drink. When that doesn't work, I exhaust myself with push-ups. I smoke three packs of cigarettes with the windows thrown wide open. I stay put, safe and locked away inside my own head, and try to process what this means. Why I'm scared when I should be thrilled. And finally, why I took off instead of taking that charming, gorgeous woman in my arms and kissing her senseless in front of the entire party.

CHAPTER EIGHT

I feel like a coward when I wake up in the morning. My head aches and my heart is torn up with longing. I feel miserable. Which 'is the exact opposite of what you should feel when the woman of your dreams announces she's staying in the country when you'd been so sure things were over. When I turn on my phone again I have half a dozen texts from Anja telling me Juliana is looking for me. I run a shower as hot as I can stand it and stay under the spray until my skin feels raw. Why the hell am I such a coward?

I put it aside while I'm at work—I have to, or I'll drive myself crazy. At least it's a busy day. I only have one free appointment spot on my schedule at the very end of my day. I check and recheck it between sessions, torn between wanting the money and wanting to leave early. It's open right up until I go into my second-to-last session.

That's when Juliana calls in.

I try to weasel out of it, like the louse I am. Ethically it's questionable whether I should see someone I know—particularly someone I know like I know Juliana. I'm prepared to make my case to the manager-on-duty, but a glance over the schedule for the rest of the day reminds me that I'm the only one available. This must be my shitty, bailing karma coming back to bite me.

I wait for her intake paperwork, then go out and introduce myself like she's never seen me before. She plays along with a scowl on her face — I'd be a moron to not notice it. My heart races as I lead her back. When I usher her into my room and close the door behind us, she crosses her arms and glares at me.

"I wanted to talk to you, Ezra. I really *needed* to talk to you," she says.

"And you couldn't think of any other way than to blindside me at work?"

"Well I tried going to your apartment, but you weren't home."

"Yeah, well. I've been here."

We stare at each other for a minute. "Did you just come to yell at me?"

"I—no."

"Okay. So what do you want done?" I gesture to the table. "They're going to charge you even if you storm out right now."

Her demeanor changes. "I mean… A massage, I guess? I told you, I've never had one."

"Right. So what's hurting? Anything?"

She mutters something I can't understand, then shrugs her shoulders. "Nothing, really. I just want to see what all the fuss is about, I guess."

"Okay. So I'll step out and let you get ready, and knock when I'm coming back in."

"Ezra?" she calls as I'm opening the door. "What, ah… What do I do?"

I can't believe I'm about to tell her to take her clothes off. And yet, what else can you say? You can't really give a massage through a thick sweater and jeans.

When I close the door behind her, I hightail it to the

bathroom and splash water on my face. I'm a consummate professional. I've never once even been tempted to cross a line with a client. I've got ten grand worth of student loan debt— one moderately pretty client would so not ever be worth risking my reputation for. I have to pretend she's just any other client on my table, and not the girl I'm a lovesick moron over.

I rub a paper towel over my cheeks roughly and stalk back to my room. I wait an extra second before knocking and letting myself into the room. She's lying on her stomach under the blankets, propped up on her elbows and looking over her shoulder. This is exactly why I don't work on people I know— with any other client, I'd put on my soothing, therapist voice and tell them to lay down and relax. With her, I have to keep my voice in check when I say, "You can lie down. Relax."

"Face in this horseshoe thing?" she asks.

"Yeah. That."

Why am I being such an asshole to her? I ought to be jumping for joy that this is just one of a million moments I can now spend with her since she's staying here. I have a shot with her, and that should thrill me more than it should upset me. I should be making jokes, not snapping at her. Maybe this is just another reason why this is all a very bad idea.

"So, erm, I'm going to get started," I tell her. I place my hands on her back through the blankets and rub up and down her spine. "You can tell me if I'm working too deep or too light anytime, all right? If something hurts or tickles, let me know."

"I'm not ticklish."

I file that in the therapist part of my brain. At least, I think it's the therapist part. "Still. Just let me know what to adjust and we'll go from there. You won't... hurt my feelings or anything." I'd say the same thing to any client to make them comfortable with the idea of telling me what I need to do differently to accommodate them. With her, the statement is fully loaded, and we both know it.

I give the same basic massage to most people who walk through my door the first time. Get them used to my hands through the blanket and sheet, undrape their backs, work top-down on the back of their bodies, toes-to-head on their fronts. But because this isn't most people, I have to steel myself to undrape her. I pull the blankets back to the base of her spine and keep my gaze straight ahead. I stare at the clock, which I swear is mocking me, and register only what I'd register with any other client—a trigger point here, tight muscle tissue there, a deep scar on her hip that might be sensitive to too much pressure. As I work in a little deeper, I feel her skin pebble underneath my hands.

"Are you cold?"

"A little."

"We've got a heating pad on the table. I'll turn it up for you."

"Thanks. I guess my blood will need to thicken back up to cope with winters here." She shivers again when I go back to my work. I train my eyes straight upwards.

"So…pressure all right?" I ask, mostly because that's always what I'd ask of anyone on my table, and it's *almost* working to pretend she's anyone and not someone I'm so crazy for.

"I don't really know the difference between all right and not all right," she says. "But it feels good."

"If it doesn't, just—"

"Let you know?"

"Yeah."

For a few minutes I can pretend that she really is any other client. We're silent and I get into my groove. She tilts her head in the face cradle and stares at me until I look back.

"It's a coincidence, you know," she says. "Me staying. It's been a possibility in the works for a while. When you were over on Wednesday and I was in my room on the phone the whole time—that's what I was doing. My boss made her decision and we were figuring out all the logistics. When I'm starting, where I'll be living, all that. It's sort of a major deal—I'll be running the entire office here. I've worked my ass off for this. It's a coincidence, meeting you and liking you and also staying. That was what I wanted to talk to you about at the party last night."

Was I actually vain enough that I thought maybe she was staying *for* me? Her brothers and mother hadn't been enough to keep her in the country when a work opportunity came up, so the notion that I could be a deciding factor was probably ridiculous. I don't think I did think that, not really—but maybe I hoped that she liked me enough that I played a tiny part in it.

I guess that sort of is what she's saying, though.

"You should be really proud of yourself, then. Congratulations."

"Thank you. I am proud of myself. And I'm really happy I'm staying."

I realize I'm going to knead her back into sore mush if I don't move on. I switch to her leg and chance a look down for the first time and admire the copper glow of her skin. My pale skin seems even paler in comparison. I wonder if she's naturally this dark, or if she's perpetually sun-kissed. I have to stop myself, though, because thinking about her sunbathing in Brazil, of all places, is right up there with picturing her naked. I can't think like that while I'm working. Right now she has to be any other client, any other body, nothing more.

I've got my knuckles buried in between the bones of her feet when she speaks again and unhinges my defense. "I hoped that maybe you'd be excited," she says. "That maybe you'd make some time to spend with me. Like the other night."

"I liked the other night," I say quietly.

"I did too. I hoped we could do it again."

"I'd like that. But if it's all right, can we not talk about it right now?"

"Oh. Yeah, sure." A little disappointment there.

"It's just that I'm trying really hard to stay professional here," I say, my voice strained. "I can't think about how much I want to kiss someone when I'm trying to do my job."

"Oh, right. Boundaries."

"Exactly."

I see the blankets bob up and down as she laughs.

"What?" I ask when she offers no explanation.

"It's not exactly easy for me on this end either," she says. "Knowing just how well my massage therapist kisses."

Shit. Shit, shit, *shit*. This is why you don't work on people you know, Mackenzie, you ass.

"This is why I don't work on people I know," I go ahead and tell her.

"I should have gotten my first massage from a stranger, huh?"

"You never know… There could be another therapist on staff that kisses even better than I do."

"I don't really want to find out. I'm pretty happy with how you kiss, if that wasn't obvious."

My heart leaps. I have to start thinking about things other than kissing her, and fast.

After that, time ticks away almost too fast. I sneak a few more downward glances, enough to notice her pedicure when I've got her turned onto her back, a little birthmark on her left wrist, and the way she smiles tightly and bites the corner of her lip when I hit a particularly tender spot on her neck. I can stay focused enough to not think of how pretty the color of her nail polish looks, how the birthmark resembles a pair of lips, and how I'd felt her teeth scrape against my mouth the other night. *Almost.*

I run my fingers along the side of her face in closing. She opens her eyes, looks straight at me, and smiles.

"Not too bad?" I ask.

"Amazing."

"I'll step out and let you get dressed. Ah, do me a favor and don't mention knowing me when the girls at the front desk check you out? I actually could get into a little bit of trouble for working on someone I know without saying anything."

"I'll tell them you were the very picture of professionalism."

"I tried. It's not so easy where you're concerned."

That seems to trigger something in her, and she smiles at me coyly.

"I'll see you later, all right?" I tell her with finality, and leave the room. I have to splash another handful of water on my face after I scrub my hands to keep my composure. I grab one of the mini-bottles of water we keep on hand for clients post-massage, and return to my room....

...but Juliana is already gone.

***

I take my time heading home. I make a couple of needed stops for gas, cigarettes, and cat litter, and it gives me time to process everything that happened during Juliana's session. I don't feel like I've crossed any lines, but I also know something significant happened. The way she was talking—it was like she was *claiming* me. Or trying to. I feel like I know her enough now to be able to tell for sure now what she means when she speaks. Perhaps she was never that difficult to figure out in the first place. Maybe it was just a matter of sifting through all my own bullshit in order to put two and two together. I suppose I don't necessarily have to understand her feelings to understand why she feels them.

I could wax poetic about how I'm not worthy of her. How I'm certain she's setting her sights way too low when it comes to me, and that it's only a matter of time before she figures it out. Why would she want me when she could have literally anyone else in two different countries?

With my bags in hand, I take the steps two at a time to my

apartment. I am, but shouldn't be, surprised I find her squatting outside my door, her arms hugging her knees to her chest. No one has ever waited outside my place for me. But then, when has this girl done things other girls have done for me?

Never, in the best possible way of the word.

She gets to her feet, and we stand and stare at each other for a minute. Then I unceremoniously drop the bags at my feet and open my arms to let her fall into them. My eyes haven't even shut all the way when her lips seal over mine. I pivot her until she's backed up to my front door and crush myself against her. I need to kiss her lips, her face, her neck, every inch of skin I can find that I couldn't wait to touch like that an hour ago. I had my hands on her professionally before—now I need them on her because I want her. And it's finally registering that she wants me, too. My chilled hands roam her torso and loop around her bare wrists. I pin them in place on the door behind her and kiss her until my head spins. She pants for a second when she rips her lips away from mine and attaches them to my neck instead. It ought to give me the freedom to see well enough to jam the key into the lock, but instead my eyes roll back in my head when her mouth finds my pulse point. I fumble blindly for another few seconds, catch her in my arms when a shove of the door nearly sends her tumbling backwards, and I kick the bags at our feet over the threshold before we stumble behind them. I can't let her go. Not now.

"This is okay, right?" she says between gasps when I nudge the door closed behind us.

I grasp the back of her neck and force our mouths flush. I kiss her deeply, trying to rid her of any doubt that I might not want this as much as she does. I groan as her tongue writhes against mine, and I feel my hips buck against hers.

"Oh, thank *God*," she mutters against my lips.

We're through the doorway to my bedroom within seconds, and she drags me down on top of her when her knees hit the edge of my bed. I hover over her, one arm keeping me from crushing her while the other smooths over her torso. The buttons of her coat come away easily under my fingers, and the pair of us wiggle and roll around until both of our jackets and shoes are tossed on the floor by my bed.

She throws her weight against me so I'm on my back while she straddles my hips.

I can't do anything but stare in lust and wonder as she inches her sweater up her torso and tosses it aside. The streetlights peek in through the slats of my window shades and set her dark skin glowing. What I hadn't looked down at before I'm seeing now in spades. Like so much else in my life, all I want is *more*. More skin, more touching, more her.

Her arm twists behind her, clearly working at the clasp of her bra when a rational thought finally crashes around me. I gurgle out a request for her to stop, to wait, and see her arms fly to cover her chest protectively. I sit up on my elbows, lean her face towards mine, and kiss her soundly. "I don't want to stop. It's just that I keep certain things in the bathroom and—"

"Right," she says, relieved. "I'll wait here."

I can't help but kiss her long and slow before I leave the room. My head spins as I flip the light on in the bathroom. My face in the mirror is flushed, thoroughly kissed, and piqued to everything around me. I'm so hyper-aware, in fact, that I know before I open the medicine cabinet what I'll find there. Or rather, what I *won't* find there.

Funny how replenishing your supply of condoms becomes less of a priority when you aren't bringing girls from a bar back to your place on a regular drunken basis.

My heart sinks, but it's nothing in comparison to the aching protestation from my groin. The girl of my goddamn dreams is here, in my apartment, half-naked for fuck's sake, and all I can find is lube. There are convenience stores literally seconds away from my place, but Juliana is here *now*. The spontaneity, the impulsivity of this incredible moment is gonna fly out the damn window the second I go back to my room and go for my shoes. Who the hell even knows if she'll still be here when I get back? It'll probably be just enough time for her to come to her senses.

My erection mocks me all the way back to the bedroom. When I see Jules spread out on my bed, having taken the liberty of shirking the rest of her clothes and wrapping herself up in only my comforter, I physically ache for her.

"So those things I keep in the bathroom," I say with a wince, "turns out I didn't have the stock of them I thought I did."

"Oh." She sounds as disappointed as I feel.

I start searching around for my shoes, my coat, everything else we managed to get off me before I came to my better senses, then say, "I know it kills the moment, but there's a gas station like, two minutes away…."

"Ezra…."

"I know, it sucks, but I had a lot of sex without protection when I was messed up." I shove my left shoe on, frustrated when it gets stuck on my heel. "I know I'm clean, but probably only by the grace of God, really. And you mean more to me than that. Just, please wait?"

"Ezra," she says in that sing-songy way she convinced me to dance with her at the wedding. "Take that shoe off and come here."

I toe off my sneaker and approach the bed. She sits up, yanks at my wrists, and I crumple in a heap next to her. She laces her fingers in my hair and our lips meet, tentatively at first, then with all the primal fervor of before.

"I'm not getting up and leaving. And neither are you. Not right now. We don't need a condom for what I have planned."

My spine tenses and releases with every wicked word she says.

Her mouth trails back to my ear lobe, which she suckles

luridly before she lies back, her dark hair a curtain against my
pillow under her head, and grins up at me.

She's right: there is plenty to do, no condom required.

***

Hours and both of us falling asleep later, I run my fingers
through her hair. She wakes, stretches like a cat, and yawns
loudly into the crook of my elbow before smiling up at me.
"Time?" she asks sleepily.

"Almost midnight. I didn't know if you needed to get home
or not."

"Do you want me to go?"

"Not at all."

She smiles and pulls the covers around our waists up to her
chin. "Then I won't."

I kiss her forehead and untangle my fingers from her
tresses. She whines at me when I move to get out of bed. "I'm
happy you're staying, but I still really need to get up for a
minute. I'm not going far, promise."

She pouts at me, but I know it's in jest when she does that
wink/bat thing with her eyes. I want a better name for that.
Especially now that I'm going to get more time with her.

"Want me to get you some water or anything?" I ask as I
pull my underwear back on.

"I'm all right." As I leave the room, I spy her making a nest
out of my pillows. It's maybe the most heart-bursting thing I've
seen her do tonight, and *that* is saying something. I take a look
at myself in the mirror as I'm washing my hands. There are a
few errant red marks from Juliana's long nails and nipping
teeth, particularly around the patches of my skin in between the
whirling black and grey ink on my chest. She seems to be
entranced by the tattoos that nearly cover my left chest, back,
and arm—as entranced as I am frankly embarrassed by a few of
the images, permanent remnants of drinking nights that got
way out of control. Her tongue outlining them had felt too

good to ask her to stop, so I decide to wear the marks proudly, like the tangy sweetness of her that lingers on my lips and tongue. Because against all the fucking odds stacked against me, I fell asleep naked with her. I touched her everywhere someone can want to be touched. I've tasted nearly every inch of her skin. I'm going back to bed with her. She's here, and, inexplicably, she wants me.

She'd never have looked at me twice nine months ago, and I wouldn't have wanted her to. Any girl who settled for Drunk Ezra would be settling for a real loser. And the jury is still partially out on whether or not I'm *that* much better sober.

Regardless, she's in my bed tonight. She may be in my bed a lot more nights in the near future. I grin to myself, still in a bit of disbelief about my incredible luck, and stride back to my room.

Her face is illuminated by the light of her cell phone. She tosses it onto my bedside table when she sees me come in.

"Just letting Mama know I'll see her in the morning." She slides over to let me back between the blankets, warm and inviting from her body heat.

My throat goes a little dry. "Did you, ah, tell her that you're with me?"

"I told her I'm crashing at a friend's place. I figure I'll tell her which friend in the morning and let her decide what she wants to decide."

She slides over towards me and looks as though she's mulling something over in her head. After a pause, she says, "If you want me to, anyway. I don't have to tell her anything. Or I can tell her everything. Well... everything that's PG, of course."

"I'm okay with telling her everything PG." I try to sound nonchalant about it, but it thrills me to my very core.

She shivers and kicks at my shins playfully when I wrap my arms back around her. "Your feet are *freezing*."

"My bathroom tiles are always subarctic," I say, trying to sound contrite. "Why wouldn't you think I'd want you to tell her?"

"Technically we still haven't really talked about it. We've talked around it, sure, but about what you and me *are*? Not yet, anyway."

"We agreed we want to spend time together. Especially with you coming back here for good."

"I do. But I know you're in sort of a weird place. I don't want to mess that up, you know?"

I nod. I appreciate how respectful and careful she wants to be, but I'm also already wondering how she can't see how much better I am around her. I saw her drinking at the wedding and it barely fazed me. She was standing next to me when I had a glass of champagne in my hand, and I didn't drink it. Maybe it's my own willpower I've never given much credit to, but it can't be only coincidence that I don't crave around her.

"I don't think you're going to mess me up, Jules. I can't make the same promise about me to you, though."

"I'm a big girl. I can take care of myself. And I know what I want." She kisses me tenderly and beams at me. "You're coming to Christmas, right?"

I groan. "Actually, I'm spending it with my mother."

"Oh," she says, her tone a little crestfallen. "Anja said she'd invited you to be with us."

"She did. I'm coming to dinner Christmas Eve. I'm heading to Constance's house straight from there for the next day. It's the first time I've spent Christmas with her since I was really little—I can't bail on her." There's Gemma, of course, too, but I don't know if I'm ready to unload all of the sordid elements of my biological family on her just yet.

She sighs. "I'm going back to Sao Paolo the day after. Only for about two weeks, just long enough to pack up my stuff and get it shipped up here."

Disappointment crests over me. Two weeks sounds like an eternity when I didn't think she'd be slipping through my grasp again at all. A part of me really does want to bail on Constance and Gemma, but that seems too much like something I'd have done nine months ago. I'm not that guy anymore. I *can't* be that guy anymore.

"I don't work tomorrow," I say. "So there's that."

"There's that." Her hands begin to roam across my still-bare skin and tug at the waistband of my shorts. "Why'd you put these back on?"

"I didn't miraculously find condoms in there," I say. As soon as the words come out of my mouth, I realize how thick I sound.

"Have I not made myself clear enough yet?" she asks. Her hand slips fully under the waistband and her lithe, talented fingers circle me. "We don't need condoms quite yet. Why would we when there's…."

Even in the dark, I can see she's grinning like the Cheshire Cat. That is, until my eyes roll straight back into my head.

CHAPTER NINE

Juliana comes back to Denver three days before my nine-month sobriety anniversary. It's not a moment too soon, too, because as soon as she mentioned to her family where she'd been the night she spent at my place, Mama A began hounding me like I was already her new son-in-law.

"I knew she'd find someone to ground her one day," she'd said to me. "I think you're it. You're perfect for one another."

It took an impassioned phone call from Jules to convince Mama to cool her jets and remind her we aren't anything official *yet*, but she still grins at me like she knows something I don't every time I see her.

We have dinner plans a few nights after Jules gets in. It's torturous to know she's in town and not be able to see her, but she's getting settled into her little cottage-sublet and I'm making up for a few sick days I had to take after the new year with extra hours at work. It takes the edge off how much I've missed her.

Her new place is in the newly gentrified and posh LoHi, just a short walk from some of the trendiest bistros in town. She's got her sights set on one in particular for what I've only now realized is our first, real, proper date. Desperate not to look as exhausted as I've felt the last few days, I thumb through the dress shirts I own, and can't seem to decide which one looks the least ratty. There's a cigarette burn on the sleeve of the white one. The navy one has a dark stain on it I set in by drying it. In the heyday of my drinking, I didn't have a steady enough hand to own and operate an iron without scorching my clothes, so the grey one would never work. I'm aware I need new clothes. But, honestly, broke, recovering-alcoholic massage therapists don't have a lot of occasions to wear a collared shirt—and when we do, like for a wedding, we typically rent them.

It strikes me that I have one more. It's not mine, per se, but I do have it. It's buried in a flat plastic storage box under my futon where I never have to look at it. It's tucked in with an obnoxious, stained tie with dancing turkeys in Pilgrim hats, a couple of old books and photo albums, and a blanket that'd been on my bed in Mac's house since I was old enough to remember. The shirt probably wouldn't fit me anyway (Mac had about fifty pounds on me, after all), but it's there, and I entertain the thought of cracking open the lid and trying it on.

But it might still smell like Mac. And if it does, I can't let that scent out. Once it's gone, it's gone forever. So I shrug on the navy one, hoping the stain isn't too noticeable in a dark restaurant.

There's an abysmal amount of traffic driving north. My phone rings a couple of times, but as I keep getting cut off by semis and idiots smoking pot behind the wheel, I don't answer. By the time I finally pull off at her exit, navigate the twisty old neighborhood to find her place, and find parking on the crowded street, I've got two voicemails and three text messages from her. I quell my nerves and knock on the door of the bright green bungalow, the small bouquet of flowers I brought with me behind my back.

"This really great woman I'm nuts about thinks I'm standing her up for our date tonight," I say when she opens the door. "Would you mind telling her that Denverites have no fucking clue how to drive and let her know I brought contrition flowers?"

Jules grins a mile wide. If it weren't for my holding the flowers off to the side when I pull them out from behind my back, she'd crush them between us when she leaps into my arms. Kissing her makes me delirious.

"Can you blame me for being anxious to see you?" she murmurs between kisses.

"Not at all."

We stumble through the front door, lips reminding us each how the other tastes, hands roaming to recall how well we fit together. I pull away to get a good look at her face — flushed as it is, it looks a lot like it did the last time I saw her on the porch of Mama A's house when we said goodbye on Christmas Eve. It strikes me as even more lovely because I know this is the first of hundreds of times I'll get to see it. My head swims at the thought, and I have to kiss her again.

We collapse together, our lips still tangled, on an overstuffed, over-wide chaise in the corner of her very put-together living room. She sinks into the brown and white velour pillows, pulling me by the collar to spread out on top of her. Her legs loop with mine, holding me there so all I can do is kiss her, fill my senses entirely with her, her, her. It flits through my brain that making it to the restaurant for our seven o'clock reservation is never going to happen if we don't straighten up and get going. But why would I want to go anywhere other than here, with her, losing my mind with how miraculous she feels underneath me?

She has the same idea, apparently, because her fingers begin working at the buttons of my shirt. The skin of my chest burns when her fingertips graze over it, mapping the lines of my tattoos again as if she's memorized them. My own fingers creep under the cashmere sweater she's wearing. Her skin is as wickedly soft as I remembered, begging for every inch to be touched and kissed. Her lips find my earlobe when I graze my thumb under her navel, and the little gasp she utters echoes in my ear. I rear up on my knees enough that there is space between us to fumble at buttons, tug on hems, and work the front-clasp of her bra and the fly of my slacks. More fumbling and writhing, a few well-placed kicks and pivots of hips, and there's nothing between us. I look down on her in awe, as if I hadn't seen her naked just a few short weeks ago. She smiles up at me, her eyes hooded and lips plump. Once our gazes are locked, her eyes flit over to the small coffee table between our chair and her couch, where her purse lies partially open. I already know what she's implying I'd find in there, but I have a staunch rule against going through a woman's purse. And besides, *I'm* not going to be ill-prepared twice.

I press a kiss to her lips, her jaw, a trail of them down the smooth column of her throat, in between her breasts, pausing for a moment against her stomach before turning away from her to fumble through the pockets of my discarded pants. She must recognize the tearing sound the foil makes, because anticipatory whimpers bubble up and spill over her lips. I turn back, hover over her, and kiss her breathless as her knees fall open under me.

She pulls me down on top of her and pivots her hips up to meet mine until we're both gasping with relief. *Finally.*

It's slow at first. She's writhing and bucking her hips to meet every thrust of mine, but I take my time because she feels so good. I close my eyes and let myself sink into her deeper, let the sounds she makes engulf my senses as we build our rhythm. It's steady and perfect. The perfect part must be her.

For the briefest second I let my mind wander. I remember other girls, other beds, other times I've been inside a woman, and only then do I acknowledge my own clarity. Other moans laced with lust and desperation, other hips snapping against mine, begging to be filled and pleased as quickly as possible—I can remember them, but their memories are hazy and muddled. I remember obliging their whims and demands, my head never really clear, never quite cognizant enough to realize that girl wasn't what I actually needed—just what I momentarily wanted.

But not now. Not with Juliana. When she presses her lips the patch of skin under my ear and groans my name, I feel every centimeter of her mouth, every puff of her breath. It's only her. The sounds she makes. The way her body writhes under mine. Her smell, her taste, her smooth skin and soft hair. She's every ounce of my awareness. I could be with her like this forever and it would never get old, dulled, or muted. My heightened senses, so blissful, so intense, threaten to betray me far too fast.

I hang on as long as I can, because every sound she makes is perfect. When the pressure at the base of my spine is too much to hold back, I grunt her name and snap my hips with an overwhelming finality.

A little whimper of release echoes from her throat into my ears, and she cups the back of my neck to hold me still on top of her.

Panting, exhausted as I am, it's several long minutes before I can actually breathe enough to speak. When I look down at her, she smiles blissfully up at me. I kiss her again and again, until my arms are too shaky to hold myself suspended above her. I fall into a heap on the throw pillows next to her, and snake my arm around her shoulders as she wiggles and presses herself into my side, her head lolling on my chest.

We lay there in satisfied silence while I rationally piece together the thoughts that churn about in my brain. It renders me speechless, to the point where I only snap out of it when she tickles my sides and tilts my face down to look at her.

"What is it?" she asks.

I smile at her, the sort of irrepressible smile that comes so easily for me when I'm around her. "That was...." I sigh in wonderment.

She giggles, and begins traces the outline of one of my tattoos with her fingertip. "That *was*. I know."

I sigh. How do I explain this to her without sounding completely insane? "That was... I don't remember the last time I did that sober."

Her fingertips fall away. She leans up on an elbow and cups the side of my face with her hand. I press my lips against her palm, not ready to look at her after this confession until she forces me to.

"How did it... um, compare?" she asks.

"It doesn't. Not at all."

Her eyes go wide with worry, and I realize she's misunderstood my meaning. I click my tongue in my mouth, shake my head, and nudge her nose with mine until our lips brush together. I stroke my knuckles down her cheeks and along her jaw until our gazes lock again. "What we just did? That was incomparable. I can't even explain to you how much better that felt than... well, than *any* time before."

She looks relieved and nuzzles her face, pressing tiny kisses to the side of my neck and jaw.

After a second, I continue. "I'm not sure if it's because I'm sober, or because I'm with you."

"Can't it be both?" she says.

"Must be," I agree.

"Good."

"Excellent."

The smile we share is dippy and lust-filled. Our kisses after become lazy and sated as we stay, curled up in that chaise long after the restaurant has probably given up on our reservation.

But really, who needs a fancy dinner out when you're lucky enough to have a girl like this in your arms?

***

Juliana is the type of person you'd want to get snowed in with. Her feet are never cold, she seems to have a steady supply of blankets and coffee beans and condoms, and she owns a copy of every Monty Python property known to man and can quote *Holy Grail, Life of Brian,* and most episodes of *Flying Circus* word for word.

She's the sort of person you want to make love to over and over again, even if you're exhausted and your back is aching, because when she falls apart, she makes some of the strangest, most gorgeous sounds known to creation. This is my own opinion, of course—although I don't think I'd like verification of this fact from other men she's been with. I'm happy to just blanket-statement this.

Even lazy, first-thing-in-the-morning sex makes her make noises that I swear to God I've never heard a woman utter. I really don't think she's faking, I think she's just *that* vocal. She really, really likes what she likes—and I can't get enough of figuring out what those things are.

She's the sort of person you can spend every night of the first three weeks she lives back in her hometown with and still not feel like you've gotten enough of her. You can spend quiet moments with her, each absorbed in different books or marathoning *Friends* on Netflix, and that's just as exciting and interesting as fighting skiing traffic and wandering around a little mountain town, coffee in one hand and her hand in the other. She has fantastic, interesting opinions on art and politics and American versus Brazilian culture without being an utter snob. She's funny without trying to be. She's a gracious loser at cards and board games, but she loves to rub it in when she wins. She hums in the shower. She murmurs to herself when she's sorting out something in her head when it's keeping her awake at night.

And if I thought for a second, for even the slightest of seconds, that I had any chance of not falling madly in love with her, I know for sure after three weeks that she's everything I've been looking for. I know I'd be insane to let her go, because she's the sort of woman I didn't dare to hope I'd even get a chance to meet, let alone go to bed with. And she scares the living shit out of me.

I know subconsciously that she's not actually as perfect as she seems. But these days, I regard anyone who doesn't have years and years of being a slobbering drunk as having their lives totally on track. It's a low bar, but then again, I *am* that low bar. I'd ask, again and again, what the hell Jules is doing with someone like me if it weren't for her asking me not to do so. I've done it so many times it's begun to irritate her. And hey, that's fair. It's probably irritating having her—boyfriend? This is way more than just sex—whatever the hell I am to her and we are together be so goddamn insecure. But how can I not be when there's still so much potential for me to fuck up so exponentially? I suppose in a situation like this, you either let the goddess-like qualities of the woman you're with freak you out into a downward spiral, or you rise to the occasion.

The problem is, I've never been particularly good at rising to the occasion.

***

"Your mother is staring at me," Jules says after she follows Anja and me out onto Mama A's snowy porch. Anja laughs a puff of smoke out of her lungs and I wrap my arms around Jules to keep her warm.

"I noticed. Sorry about that," I say.

It would have been any other dinner at Mama A's if I hadn't brought Constance with me. I'm not entirely sure what possessed me to do it, but I can't really take it back now. She's here, and since the moment she stepped through the door, there's been a weird air of forced pleasantry and awkwardness between her and Mama A, her and Anja, her and Jules. Constance is not an intimidating woman to look at; she's tiny, barely five feet tall and maybe 110 pounds dripping wet. She's as fair as Mac was ruddy, hence where I got my pasty complexion, even though I did end up with Mac's flaming red hair and dark eyes. But everyone, save for the unflappable Mattias and Lukas, who've been acting like they always do, seems to have no clue what to make of her.

"It's fine. It's just not how I thought my first meeting with your mother would be. Hurry up and come back in, will you?"

"We'll be in in a second," Anja says. She smirks at me when the porch door slides closed.

"What?" I ask.

"You two," she says, a smile tugging at her mouth, "are pretty cute together."

"Shaddup." I shove her hip with my own.

"I mean it as a compliment, not to harass you. All the wedding pictures with the two of you showed it, too. You look good together. Complement one another. And she seems to be doing good for you. It's been, what, three weeks since she's been back? You haven't texted me once in all that time saying you're craving."

"I think she is. I really, really... really like her."

"Just... promise me you'll be careful, okay?"

"Are you trying to lecture me on condom use?" I snort. "We were in the same sex-ed class in high school, remember?"

"I know *that*. I'm saying I'm still your sponsor first and foremost, so I have to do the sponsorly thing and remind you to be cautious, for the good of your recovery. I just want to be sure this be a good thing that keeps you on track, and not an intense thing that burns you out and derails you. Okay?"

"Look, for whatever it's worth, I think we're both on the same page about... well, a lot. She keeps telling me we can slow down if I need it, but I feel like everything is going exactly at the pace it should be, you know?"

"That's good to hear," she says with a smile. She stubs her cigarette out in a pile of snow on the porch railing and tosses it into the ashtray. "Do you suppose it would ever have occurred to us in high school that we'd end up with siblings who are basically clones of one another?"

"It probably should have, since *we're* sort of clones of one another. Although I'm not, you know, exactly *with* her. Yet, anyway."

She grins at me and chucks me playfully on the jaw. "You're right about the clones thing. But you're *obviously* together, Ez. Come on; let's go inside. It's fucking freezing."

I want to ask her how she knows, how she can tell so implicitly what Jules and I have become in the weeks she's been back while I'm still over here, trying desperately to figure it out.

It doesn't take Mama A but the first helping of our meal to finally crack through my mother's rough exterior. Mothers, it seems, love telling embarrassing stories about their children to other mothers right in front of said children. After an especially funny story about ten- and thirteen-year-old Lukas and Mattias ruining an entire row of planted vegetables in the back garden with their bikes and rollerblades, Constance laughs with everyone else and looks at me with a soft smile.

"Well, Ezra was never wild. He was the quiet one of the twins," Constance says.

There's a familiar dull thudding in my chest at the mention of Dylan. If it weren't for not wanting to be rude at Mama A's table, I'd tell Constance to cram it, and fast. Coincidentally, that was a phrase she drunkenly shouted at me a lot while I was growing up, polite company or no.

"Twins?" Jules asks, her eyebrows raised. "You didn't tell me your brother is your twin brother."

"Uh, yeah. He is. Can I get another couple of *bolinho*,

please?"

Lukas passes me the platter of the little fried rice balls, but nothing seems to be able to deter Constance's story.

"Ezra was almost an hour behind. He was more than happy to ignore my contractions and stay right where he was—the doctor almost had to go in and get him by force," Constance says. "But he was the most mellow baby. Didn't cry a lot, didn't fuss… So long as you didn't take his spit pillow away from him, he barely made a sound."

My fork clatters to my plate. Oh *God*….

"Spit pillow?" Lukas asks, looking at me like he just won the lottery of most embarrassing childhood story. "What on God's green Earth is a *spit pillow*?"

"Oh, it was this manky little crib pillow he wouldn't part with. He hauled it around after he started teething, and we figured it wouldn't hurt him since he couldn't bite anything off it and swallow it. But even after he cut all his teeth, he took it everywhere—except preschool, thank God. We tried to break him of it for years, but he'd go bananas when we took it away from him. Every time I looked at him, there he was—one of the corners in his mouth, the rest of it tucked under his head. It was sort of precious if you could get over how gross it was."

"Oh, Jesus," I say, rubbing my eyes with the palms of my hands. Jules squeezes my thigh under the table, but she and Anja are still giggling.

"He finally gave up on it when he was about six. But we couldn't throw it away, just for posterity's sake. Whatever happened to it, Ezra?" Constance asks.

My palms sweat a little. "I, um, don't know. We left it. *Behind*."

I give her a significant look, and she drops her gaze to her lap. I don't mean to sound cruel—it's true; it wasn't one of the things we took in the move when Mac packed us up and left—but I emphasized the word 'behind' on purpose. And she falls quiet because she knows why.

The table falls back into an awkward sort of quiet, and I feel like an asshole. I shouldn't have said that, I realize. But words aren't something you can snatch out of thin air.

"I'm going to put the kettle on," Anja says, getting up from the table. Mama A tries to object, and they end up squabbling all the way into the kitchen about it. Mattias and Lukas start to clear the dishes, and I watch my mother drum her fingernails on the table for a minute before she scoots back and gets to her feet.

"It's a long drive for me. I think I need to get going," she says, prompting Mama A to come back in and try and talk her out of it. Constance manages to beg off and thank her profusely before heading to the front door.

I whisper to Jules that I'm going to walk Constance out, and leave the lingering tension behind as we step out into the cold, February air. It's begun snowing again since dinner started, and a light dusting covers everything. I help her brush off her windows, and we each light cigarettes as her engine warms up.

Constance sighs. "I didn't mean to bring up your brother to upset you," she says between drags.

I shake my head. "It probably wouldn't kill us to actually talk about it. Him, everything before. But not in front of my friends." I'm careful to use the word 'friends,' even though the Almeidas are more than my friends. They're my family, my real family these days, and I'm pretty sure Constance realized it the minute she walked through the door. It's the best reason I have for why she was so spiky with them at first, even after saying for months how much she wanted to meet them.

"I know. I'm sorry, sweetheart." Terms of endearment are strange coming from her mouth. "I'm… The whole mother thing has never been something I've been good at. Not like her in there." Constance gestures back to the house and clearly

Mama A.

I opt not to try to deny it, because to do so would be needlessly condescending. And I've already been kind of a jerk to her once tonight.

"We can talk this weekend, maybe? If you aren't working?" she asks.

"I work Saturday. And Jules and I have plans on Sunday."

"The weekend after, maybe?"

"Maybe. Soon, I promise."

As she tosses her cigarette butt, she grins at me, a trace of a smile returning to her lips. "Jules seems like a sweet girl. I don't know if I showed it, but I like her, Ezra. And she seems to love you a lot."

"I wouldn't go quite that far," I say, my eyebrows practically raised to my hairline at the pointed way she uses the word 'love.'

"Give me this little thing as Mother's Intuition. She does. I can see it on her face when she looks at you, even if she hasn't said so yet."

"I'll take your word on that."

"I'm going for real now. Thank them again for me. And next time I'll do better. I promise."

I give her a hug, something I'm still not used to doing. Even when I was a kid and she wasn't messed up, she still didn't show a lot of physical affection. "You did okay. And, for what it's worth, bringing up my spit pillow? That did feel pretty motherly to me."

She smiles like she's proud of herself. I suppose she should be.

I wave her off, telling her to hug Gemma from me, and watch as she pulls away. As I turn to go back inside, my hip bumps the corner of Juliana's car-share vehicle. I purse my lips and look towards the house to see if anyone is peering out at me. I poke my index finger into the snow settled on the windshield.

Can't you see that I love you? I write.

She might see it later, or she might not. She usually stays at Mama A's overnight Wednesdays and drives into the city in the morning. The falling snow is light, but will probably cover it up by the time I leave a little later to go home. Maybe I ought to brush it off when I leave. I like looking at it, even though I'm pretty sure that telling her I love her—even if it's already starting to feel true—before we've even declared our relationship status is one of those things that scares people off. But then, it's always felt true. It felt true the moment she made me dance with her at the wedding.

Hours later, in my own bed in my own apartment, I realize I never checked the windshield when I left. Then I realize that I don't regret it at all.

CHAPTER TEN

Few things can tear me away from Juliana's mouth when we're kissing and half our clothes are off, particularly when we're on what we now think of as "our" chaise. But I figure that her stomach growling audibly is something we need to address since it keeps happening.

"Why don't we go get some food?" I say mid-kiss, eliciting a snarl from her in reply.

"We're busy," she whines, and latches onto my earlobe. My eyes roll back into my head, but still I push her back.

"We can get back to this when your stomach isn't about to digest your other organs. C'mon, where do you want to go?"

She pouts, but she doesn't complain when I grab my car keys and lead her out the door. She's no closer to a decision, though, even after I drive idly for several minutes while she debates with herself under her breath on whether or not Indian food will sully the mood later.

"Jeez, Jules, I'm about to override you and just swing into the next grocery store we pass and we'll cook a couple of plates of pasta."

"Pasta? Pasta sounds safe. And quick."

I decide not to say that we'd have already ordered and likely gotten appetizers at a restaurant if she'd been more decisive. I've learned over the last six weeks that when she's hungry, Jules is about as petulant as an eight-year-old whose favorite toy has been taken away.

It's a quick right turn into the next market we pass. We start filling a small cart with everything we'll need for a basic Bolognese, which is about the only thing I can cook with guaranteed success. I smile while she plucks other non-necessities off the shelves, because truly, I brought this on myself taking her into a grocery store hungry. We're nearly done when we remember our need for tomato paste, and have to go back down the canned goods aisle.

And that's where I see him.

He looks exactly the same as the last time I saw him, except his knuckles aren't swollen and my nose isn't broken and bloodied. He's still a fair amount of roiling rage festering under a very cool, put-together facade—and I can likely only tell because he's my twin brother. Estranged or not, I still can see that much about him. He's dressed like he just got off work, with his dress shirt sleeves rolled up to his elbows, and his cell phone cradled between his shoulder and his ear. He's wearing his glasses—we both have piss-poor vision, although I've always preferred contacts to frames—and at first, he doesn't see me. When he does, I know he wishes he hadn't.

A sea of rotten memories crash over me in waves. Mac's funeral, packing up his house, the explosive fight weeks later. It's all muddled the way most of my memories from my drinking days are. Half the time I can't tell which was worse— the shitty things I did, or the shittier excuses I had for doing them. Before I have time to dwell, I feel my hand raising in greeting of its own volition. I shouldn't be surprised when he abandons his cart mid-aisle, throws his coat over his shoulders, and storms away.

It's like he's clobbered me in the nose all over again. And I deserve it, of course—but it's been almost a year. I'm kind of surprised. The Dylan Mackenzie I knew would have at least told me to fuck off and maybe given me a single finger wave as he did. It rattles me that I don't even earn that much from him.

"Was… was that your brother, babe?" Jules asks, her voice dulcet.

I'd forgotten she was even there. I wish she wasn't. That wasn't something I wanted her—or anyone else for that matter—to have seen.

"Yeah. That was Dylan," I say. I hope she won't ask what happened, why he stormed off. I don't want her to know this story.

I'm not that lucky, though. "What happened?" she asks.

"It's a long story, Jules." Now I'm desperate to not have this conversation. And desperate for a cigarette. I really, really need a cigarette.

She plucks a can of tomato paste off the shelf and tosses it in our cart. "Okay," is all she says, but I know that isn't going to be the end of it. She's humming, but it's not casual, easy humming. It's determined-to-figure-something-out humming.

She waits until we're back at her place, the groceries strewn over the counter and a pot of water coming to a boil on the stove. She's sweating onions and garlic in a pan and I'm chopping vegetables and opening cans before she turns to me and pins me with her eyes. Damn her eyes. I can't hide from them.

"Are you going to tell me why you and your brother aren't on speaking terms, or do I have to play Twenty Questions to get it out of you?"

I swear under my breath. "I really, really don't want to talk about it, Jules."

"Why not?"

"Because it was a long time ago." That's a lie, but I'm not

eager for her to know it. "It's not a story I'm proud of." That is putting it fucking mildly. "And there's a very real chance that if I tell you, you'll wind up hating my guts."

"Well, now I have to know."

"Christ, Juliana," I say, and storm over to the door that leads into the tiny backyard off her kitchen. There's no snow today, but the wind is cold and unforgiving. It takes me six flicks to get anything more than a spark out of my lighter and light my cigarette. She doesn't follow me outside. In fact, she's still stirring the contents of the saucepan when I come back inside, two cigarettes and wind-burned cheeks later.

"You both have the storming-off thing down pretty good. Even if you didn't look exactly like one another, I'd be able to tell you're brothers just from that." Her tone is different. It matches the strange cock of her hip and her tense shoulders. She hasn't looked at me like this since that day before the Christmas party when I was, admittedly, being kind of a dick to her. I hate her looking at me like she is, but instead of making me feel like an asshole, it riles something in me that's equally indignant and frustrated.

"Look, not every set of siblings are crazy-close best friends like you and your brothers," I snap at her without even thinking. "Most siblings *don't* get along. Some even outright hate one another, even if they're civil to each other when they're together. And then there are some of us who can't be in the same place as one another without fists flying."

She slams the spoon she'd been using down on the counter. "First of all, that's not fair. I don't know who you've been watching, but Mat and Luk and I bicker and fight just like anyone else. They drive me crazy, especially when they're trying to be protective, but they've been that way ever since our dad died, so I deal with it. I don't hate them when they drive me nuts, I love them because they're my *family*. And second of all, I have plenty of friends who get along just fine with their brothers and sisters. Older, younger, step, twin, whatever. So don't give me shit about something that clearly chaps your ass when all I did was ask a simple question. I'm your girlfriend. Don't I get to ask questions like that?"

"You can ask, but it doesn't mean I have to answer."

"Nice, Ezra. That is super-mature."

My blood begins to boil. Why can't she just let this go? Her persistence matches my inner embarrassment, and I'm desperate to end the conversation anyway I can. I think that's the only reason why the words come out of my mouth. "You want to know what happened, Jules? Do you really?"

"Jesus Christ, *yes*, or I wouldn't have asked!"

"Fine. The last time Dylan saw me, he punched me in the nose. The snoring you tease me about? He deviated my septum. Your mother shoved gauze up my nostrils the first night I met her to keep my fucking brains from leaking out. There, are you happy?"

She stands stock still and blinks rapidly. "Why would he do that?"

"Because that's what some guys do when their drunken, screwed-up asshole of a brother fucks their girlfriend."

I could knock her over with a feather. I wish I'd lied instead, although no more than I wish I didn't need to lie about this. I want to be honest with her, but this is the worst thing I've ever done. This is the thing that was the final straw before I figured out what a massive, drunken fuck-head I was and realized I had to do something about it. This was rock bottom.

"Oh, *Ezra*," she says. It's the disappointment in her voice that kills me. But now that I've told her, I have to say more or else she'll think I'm still that guy. And more than anything in the world, I'm desperate to not be that guy anymore.

"She wasn't... She wasn't exactly his girlfriend. They were dating but... I was at a strange bar I didn't really know because I'd been invited there for some old co-worker's birthday. I was there later than the party went, and I saw this girl across the bar I thought was good-looking, so I went over and talked to her. I didn't recognize her, even though I'd just met her at our dad's funeral the month before, but I didn't recognize her because, surprise surprise, I was drunk then, too. I had no idea it was her until way later. I guess she had some guilty conscience when she realized later I was too much of a dipshit to wear a condom, and told him what happened. I got home a couple of days later and Dylan and his fists were there waiting for me. He socked me, told me to go to hell, and that was the last time I saw him until tonight. There's more bad blood between me and my family than you could possibly imagine, Jules, and I didn't want to tell you this sort of shit because that's the guy I *used* to be—he was a real loser and I hate the shit out of him. Can you blame me for wanting that guy to be no part of your life?"

"You didn't use a condom. So, does that mean…?"

"I didn't knock her up or anything, fuck, but is that really the point? Does he need any other reason than me fucking her to hate my guts?"

She snaps the burners off with a couple of flicks of her wrist and leans against the counter with her arms folded. Finally, she says, "I don't get it. I don't understand the draw of drinking like that."

My mind reels. "Of course you don't. You're not an alcoholic."

"I know I'm not. But I'm trying to put myself into a frame of mind where drinking like that, drinking that much and getting that blitzed seems like a good idea, and I'm sorry, I just can't do it. My father died when I was fifteen. Did you know that?"

"Mattias mentioned it once."

"I acted out after he died. I was Daddy's Little Princess so I took it hard. I took it harder than both Mat and Luk combined. Maybe if I'd been older, I'd have gone a little crazier but… I don't know, I still just don't get it. And I'm trying, Ezra, I really am, but I can't wrap my brain around it. Why did you do it? Why did you drink like that? Did you even feel bad about it?"

"I didn't know who the hell she was! She was gone the next fucking morning. I barely remembered what happened. *Because I'm an alcoholic.*" I must sound like a broken record, and a frustrated one at that, but it's all I can come up with. "My brain doesn't work the way yours does. You have a couple of drinks, get a good buzz on, and then stop because you don't want to feel like shit the next morning or you need to drive yourself home safely. It's rationality, but my brain doesn't have that trigger. I stop drinking when I lose consciousness and not a second before. I don't just stop when the bottle is empty; I open another one. I puke, then I rally. That's what being an alcoholic is for me, Jules. You can't understand it because you aren't one."

"But you did stop, eventually. You're sober now. You have been, what, ten months now, right?"

"And do you not realize these ten months have been the hardest months of my life? Don't you get that I've wanted a drink every single day since my first day of detox, and every day I have to talk myself out of it? Christ, that's why I'm with Anja half the damn time, because I usually don't trust myself to not buckle and go to the liquor store when she's not around to keep me in check. Mattias and Lukas? They watch my ass like hawks in case I might have snuck a drink past Anja without her noticing. My brain *doesn't work right,* Jules. What more is there to get than that?"

She curls in on herself. I wonder if I've been purposely wheeling on her, getting into her face and yelling at her, or if it's a defense mechanism. I take a step back because a tiny, rational part of my brain knows I'm getting out of control. It's not the sort of lack of control from when I drank—it's the sort of lack of control I imagine Dylan felt when he balled up his fist the day he confronted me. And no matter how much of a fuck-up I am, I refuse to be the sort of fuck-up who'd ever get violent, especially with his girlfriend.

"I'm gonna go." I grab my cigarettes, wallet, and phone. I've got my coat half on when she smacks her hand against the door and blocks my path.

"If you leave right now, are you going to drink?" The way she says it really isn't a question. She's accusing me, not asking.

"No, I'm going to think about why I'm being such an asshole to my girlfriend. I'm going to get away from you before I say something I regret. Let me by."

"No. Please, Ezra, don't leave."

"Jules, I need to." She grabs my wrist when I reach for the handle, and it's everything I can do to not pry her fingers off me and throw her aside like a ragdoll. I'm scaring myself. This isn't me now... This is me a year ago. I'm not supposed to be like this, not anymore. Especially not around her.

"No," she says again as I yank my hand away from her. She makes to grab it again but I'm afraid if she touches me, I might burn us both to the ground.

"I don't trust myself around you right now, all right? Let me go before I do something stupid."

"If you leave, you'll drink, won't you? Ezra, please, I can't let you do that," she says, her voice wavering like she's close to tears.

"Let me go, Juliana."

She staggers backwards and I slam the door behind me as I retreat down the sidewalk to my car. Tears are burning behind my eyes—I can't let her see this part of me. I hate it too much.

It takes all the willpower I have left to call Anja. I whimper something half-human into the phone, and she tells me which meeting I should head to so she can meet me there. Our cars pull in one after the other, and I fall into her arms. Like a mother with a fretful newborn, she holds me and tells me that

I'm all right, that I'm going to be okay, and I try like hell to believe her.

***

I smell about as good as I look after spending a night on Mattias and Anja's couch. I leave their place with only a note saying I'm going home and thanking them for what they did for me last night before either of them wakes up. Not only did they have the dubious honor of pulling my ass back together last night, they'd also been the ones to calm Juliana when she'd called Mattias in hysterics, claiming she'd pushed me into a relapse. I'm sure I'm going to get a call from Anja soon enough when she gets up and finds me gone, but I'm also sure she'll understand that I need some time to decompress before Juliana comes over.

It was Anja who suggested I have Juliana come to me, and show her I didn't self-destruct last night. She'll be over in the afternoon, and in the meantime I call out of work and go ape on my apartment. I scrub anything and everything, I vacuum up all of the cat hair that's settled on every surface, and air out the smoky, stale air with wide-open windows. Early March weather is always unpredictable, but today is thankfully mild so I don't freeze to death. I take a scalding-hot shower and make coffee as the sun starts to set, then curl up on the futon with a pack of cigarettes, deciding that the open windows will carry away most of the smoke before it can sink into the furniture. I've nearly finished the pack when I hear a gentle tap at the door. My heart gallops, and I will myself to not screw this up.

Jules' eyes are dark-rimmed and sleepy, and a ratty ponytail at the top of her head and rumpled clothes clearly state that she's had about as pleasant a day as I've had. I stand aside and let her in. The cat dive-bombs her ankles and laces between them, purring like a motorboat. The damn thing still barely comes near me, but she loves Jules. Maybe if she dumps me today, I'll give the cat to her—she'd probably take better care of it, like Mac did.

"You clean on bad days too, huh?" Jules says before settling down on my futon. The place smells heavily of bleach and white vinegar, laced with tobacco.

"Yeah." I ought to, but don't, apologize about the cigarette smoke.

I sit down on the coffee table so I can face her straight on. She shrinks her legs back against the couch so I'm not touching her. So much for hoping she might fall into my arms. I stew for a second before I launch into the speech I'd been rehearsing as I'd scrubbed the tiles of my shower.

"Look, I'm sorry about last night. I can tell you that until I'm blue in the face, but what I can't do is take back any of the bullshit things I did when I was fucked up. All I can tell you is that I'm trying to be better than who I was back then. I don't want to be that person anymore—that's why I got sober. I realize that I don't really have a lot of credibility with you right now, and I don't know what to do about that. I'm hoping you'll tell me so I can try and do it. And if you can't, if that's not an option… Then I'm sorry. I'm sorry I wasted your time and hurt you."

She unfolds her arms and rubs at her face. "You don't waste my time, Ez. What I said about not understanding… That was true, but I shouldn't have said it. I shouldn't have gone at you like that. You probably thought I was judging you even after telling you all the time how much I admire you and Anja for straightening up. That was terrible. I'm sorry I did that."

"I'm not that guy anymore. I *promise*," I say, trying not to sound meek or unsure. I need her to know that I mean that.

"I know you aren't. I wouldn't be with you if I thought you were." She uncurls a little, and our knees almost touch.

"Makes sense why my brother hates my guts now, doesn't it?"

"Would you still have done what you did if you had realized who she was?"

It's a fair question, and one she deserves an answer to. "I don't know. I'd like to think I wouldn't."

She's worrying the Cupid's bow of her lip, turning it bright red and blotchy. It looks like that after I kiss her sometimes.

"But it's not ever something you'd do now," she says. It's not a question.

"I wouldn't put myself in that position at all. I told you, I don't—"

"Want to be that guy anymore, I know," she interrupts. "That girl isn't entirely blameless in all this, either."

I tried telling Dylan that. I don't know why he wasn't with her that night, or remember why she flirted back and came home with me. For all I know, Dylan might have been with someone else that night, too, and that's why she was out by herself. Until he speaks to me again, sometime between now and the eventual heat death of the universe, I won't know for sure whether or not that punch landed solely because I had sex with that girl, or if that was merely the last straw for Dylan concerning me and my drinking.

"All right," Jules says, snapping me out of my thoughts. "But don't storm out on me like that again. You scared the shit out of me."

This is the part I've really been dreading.

"I can't promise that. There are gonna be times I need to duck out and pull myself together. I... I don't want you to see me when I'm shitty and craving and mean. It's the worst part of me. I don't even want to see myself when I'm like that."

"That's what a relationship *is*, Ezra," she says. "It's seeing each other at their worst. It's not negotiable stuff."

"I don't want to scare you off."

She bumps my knee with hers. It's the first time she's touched me since she came in, and it sends a jolt of electricity through me.

"You won't. I'm tough enough to take a fight or two."

"I'm probably more of a fight than I'm worth, honestly."

This time she doesn't bump my knee—she swats it with her hand. "Don't say that."

"I figured you noticed that last night."

"Stop. Don't try giving me an out. I don't want one. I'm in this if you're in this," she says. Her eyes challenge me to question her on it. I don't, and I don't want to.

I lean towards her and seize her hands. The connection is electric. She does that gorgeous wink/bat thing. Then something else hits me.

"You, uh… You've never called this a relationship before. And last night we… we used words we've never used before. Like girlfriend."

Her cheeks flush, which makes her tired-looking face that much more lovely. "Oh, I… I guess I thought that was obvious by now."

"I hoped it was. I've hoped that's what we are for a long time. I didn't want to…."

"*Stop* thinking you're going to scare me off."

I nod. "I loved hearing that word, though. Say it again?"

She leans forward and nudges my nose with hers. Our mouths hover near enough that it'd take just a little pivot to push them together, but she pins me with her eyes and holds me steady. "This is what a *relationship* is, Ez. I think ours is strong enough to get through some of this crap, don't you?"

"Yes. Yes, I do." I don't think I'm lying. I'm not just saying it so she'll close that gap and let me kiss her like I so desperately want to. I want her, and I want this relationship to work more than I want anything, other than to never drink again.

When she finally does kiss me, her lips are all the sweeter knowing what we just made it through.

CHAPTER ELEVEN

Sundays are the one day a week Juliana and I always have off together. Unless we have some plan involving brunch or a drive that requires an early alarm, we stay in bed late and refuse to acknowledge the sun's come up until we're satisfied with one another. This morning, however, when I roll over to tuck my arm around her and kiss her until she wakes up, the bed is cool and my arm falls flat, empty. I rub my eyes and see it's only about nine, but that still feels a little early for her to be awake before me. My girl loves her sleep.

I haul myself out of bed and peek in the kitchen, thinking maybe she's putting the coffee on. There is coffee percolating already, but I don't see her until I hear her a minute later. Her voice rings out over a newly started shower, and I'm not sure why I didn't think bathroom immediately. I shrug it off as still being too sleepy, and pad back to bed. Then her voice changes.

I've never heard Jules sing before.

I press my ear to the closed door and listen to the words rise from her throat. She's singing in Portuguese, not English, but her voice is sharp and clear and, like everything else about her, beautiful. It's even lovely when she cuts herself off mid-sentence to swear, still in Portuguese, maybe about shampoo in her eye or nicking her leg with a razor. Then she starts up again. I press the door open quietly and slip in without letting too much of the steam from her too-hot shower escape, and silently slip out of my pajamas. When I poke my face around the shower curtain, she turns to me with a smile, like she was expecting me to join her all along. She pulls me under the spray with her and wraps her arms around my neck.

"You sing?"

"Now and then," she says with a shrug. She leans her head back to rinse the conditioner out of her hair, and I admire the length of her neck and the light stretch of her muscles under her bronze skin. I pull her a little closer, and when she looks up at me, she winks at me in that half-way and then drops her gaze down between us. She gives me a look that's equal parts amused and a little baffled that I'm, well, totally aroused.

"I liked hearing you sing," I say in my own defense.

"My singing made you horny?"

"A little. It is also the morning. But I liked listening. Sing again?"

"I can think of way more fun things we can do naked in a shower together."

"Who says we can't do both?"

She laughs. She flicks a few strands of her hair plastered to her chest back over her shoulder and wraps her arms tighter around my neck. "Close your eyes, then. I feel weird when people watch me sing."

I oblige, and the bathroom fills with her voice all over again. I'd go weak at the knees or something if slipping in the shower weren't so dangerous. But God, the things this girl can do to me. The things I love finding out about her. Her voice overtakes my mind, and I bask in the lyrics I can't understand.

The only thing about the moment that isn't perfect is the water turning icy a second later. But then, since it only ends the singing and not the rest of our morning together, what's the harm?

***

Being with Jules curbs my desire to drink. I haven't lied about that. But I'm still an alcoholic, still not even a year into recovery, and for all the magic she is in my life, Jules isn't going to change that all on her own.. The few-and-far-between nights I spend in my bed alone are the worst, but as the weeks wear on, my yearning for a drink (or twelve) comes on a little stronger every day. Every hour, really. If I thought the desire would weaken the closer I got to one full year of sobriety, I was apparently dead wrong.

I suppose I could connect it with what falls next month—the one-year anniversary of Mac dying—but that's just grief talking. My drinking was bad well before Mac died. More likely it has to do with that crap day I ran into Dylan, who for better or for worse, I'm really beginning to miss. We haven't been close in a few years. Not coincidentally around the time my drinking started to get really, really bad. But it doesn't seem all that long ago. We even went and got tattoos together—a Scottish thistle on my left shoulder blade, his inner arm—on our eighteenth birthday.

When it comes to missing my brother, I'm not sure if it helps or hurts that Mattias and Lukas treat me so much like one. We tussle when our conversations get heated, never enough to actually hurt one another, of course, but enough to burn off the testosterone in our bloodstream. Mattias and I tease Lukas about the people he dates. Lukas and I razz Mattias for not getting Anja pregnant yet, when we all know that a baby is something Anja wants above all else, and soon. It's all in good fun, this sort of guy stuff. It's good to have them. But I find myself thinking sometimes about how Mattias's dry humor is similar to Dylan's. That Dylan and Lukas both wear their hair a little long and shaggy, and are left-handed. It's comforting and weird at the same time, because eventually I remember that while they've taken to calling me "brother" when we're hanging out, we aren't *actually* blood. My bridges with my blood are basically ash on the wind these days.

It's in support of Lukas that I'm settling in a booth with Jules, Mattias, and Anja at a late-night cafe so far across town, I'm not even sure it's Denver anymore. The place hosts an open mic night once a month, and we'd all been floored when Lukas announced he was signed up to play. I'd seen a couple of guitars in his apartment on occasion, but I'd figured they were showpieces, not things he actually used. For all I knew, they were left behind by some ex of his, like an old hoodie or pair of underwear. No. *Really.* You could sell all the items Lukas's exes have left behind in the past few years and probably pay rent for a month with the proceeds.

What surprises us all when he takes the stage is that, not only can he play, he's actually *good.* His ten-minute session blows away most of the other people who'd come before. He's playing Brazilian songs their father loved and played to them when they were kids, Mattias explains, and as we watch, Juliana hums softly next to me. My mind flits back to the other morning, and I tuck my arm around her hip and rest my head against hers.

Lukas has budgeted his time for three songs, and at the end of his second, he gets easily the most thunderous applause the audience has given any performer. He takes a little mini-bow and smirks in our direction as he plays a few chords. Juliana stiffens next to me and scowls.

"He wouldn't dare…," she mutters under her breath.

Mattias bangs the table next to her elbows and laughs. Lukas says into the microphone, "I know she's not on the signup sheet with me, but I can't play this song without my sister's help. She's a little shy. Can I get a little encouragement for her?"

The crowd applauds again, and I poke her in the side. She swears and shoots both her brothers a death glare. Still, she saunters up and stands next to Lukas at the microphone. When he begins to play, she begins to sing.

It's a folk song, Mattias explains, one that their father and Juliana used to sing together. But I don't need the explanation—it's the same one Jules sung the other morning. She'd asked me to close my eyes, because people watching her made her nervous—but there she is, up on the little makeshift stage, and everyone in the place is staring at her. I'm pretty sure my heart should swell with pride during a moment like this, but instead, a pang of jealousy rips through my gut. Because *everyone* is watching her. Complete strangers, Anja and Mattias, even Lukas looks up from his guitar and looks at her like she's the real star of the show. And I wish they wouldn't. Something baser and far more jealous than I'm proud of kicks in and I wish they'd just disappear, so this could be *my* moment with her again. It's not so wrong to want another moment like this with my girlfriend, right?

I'm jealous—every fiber of my being is teeming with jealousy. And I don't exactly know why.

They're sent off when the song finishes to a cannonade of applause. Stewing in envy as I am, I excuse myself outside for a cigarette with just a quick nod.

Anja joins me. I wish she hadn't, because I prefer stewing by myself.

"You okay?" she asks, using the end of my cigarette to light her own because I haven't lit her one. I'm too irritated to think about it.

"Fine."

"That's convincing."

I groan. "It's nothing."

I can tell by the look on her face she doesn't buy my lie. "Did one of the guys say something to upset you while I went to the bathroom or something?"

"I'm not upset," I snap.

Her expression turns dour. "Seriously. What's wrong? You weren't like this five minutes ago."

I want to deny things again, but that would be ridiculous. I let my shoulders slump and shake my head. "I just had this thought that that would be something she'd only share with me. She said she was shy about it."

"What, singing?"

"Yeah. I only heard her do it for the first time the other day."

"That's what's bothering you? You've only been dating her a couple of months, Ez. What sort of relationships have everything all out in the open so quickly?"

"I didn't think she'd be so open to singing in front of a room full of people she doesn't know, all right?"

"That's a little possessive, don't you think?"

"I'm not possessive," I say. "Forget it. You obviously don't get it."

I shouldn't say things like that to Anja. She's the one person who nearly *always* gets the shit going on in my head.

"Is everything all right with you since that fight? You haven't said anything else about it." Anja says.

"We're fine," I insist. "Never better."

She blows smoke through her nose. "You're still being careful, right? You're not... Never mind."

I roll my eyes. "Of course we're being careful."

"I don't mean condoms. I mean—is it possible you're replacing booze with sex? With *her*?"

My left eye twitches. I really wish Anja had stayed inside. "What the fuck?"

"It happens sometimes. It's something to be cautious of. I don't want the nitty-gritty about what you two do, but it's a new relationship. Is it possible?"

It's a new relationship! I think. Of course we're fucking like rabbits. That's what people do when they first get together. "Our sex life is fine, Anja, and none of your damn business."

"Why are you getting so pissy with me?" She actually sounds hurt—it's pretty hard to hurt her feelings. She's not easily riled.

"I'm fine. I just don't appreciate your nagging."

She stubs her cigarette out on the wall and shakes her head. "It was a question, you know. I ask you questions sometimes. I'm your sponsor, Ezra. That's my job."

"I'll let you know when I want a drink, Anja. Leave what goes on between me and my girlfriend behind closed doors to me, all right?"

She throws her hands up in the air. "Why don't you cool off out here and come inside when you feel like being less of an asshole?"

I roll my eyes and puff away at my cigarette as she storms away. The fucking nerve on her.

When I do finally go back inside, I bypass my seat and head towards the bathroom to wash the smoke off my hands. There are two unisex bathrooms, but one has an out-of-order sign on it and the other is locked, so I shove my hands in my pockets and lean back against the wall to wait.

It's Juliana who breezes out a minute later. She's shaking her hands in the air to dry them off, and grins when she sees me.

"Is that violinist still playing?" she says in lieu of a greeting, then shudders when a shrill shriek of strings reverberates through the cafe.

"What, you couldn't hear it in there?" I ask, nodding towards the bathroom.

A devilish grin crosses her face. "Oh, it's super-quiet in there. Very, very soundproofed."

Without another word, she's pulling me through the door

and securing it behind us. This isn't something we do, have ever done, and if my head were on a little straighter, I'd probably tell her no and make our excuses to head out early. But right now? Right now I'm desperate to feel her as mine. As soon as the door closes behind us, I have her pinned to the door with my hips flush against hers.

Her lips are pliant and lush under mine. I slip my fingers into the belt loops of her jeans and press into her further, melting us into each other as our tongues glide together. Her fingertips graze my belt buckle, mine move to lift the bottom hem of her shirt up to wiggle my hands under the cotton garment and find her breasts, pull down the lacy cup, and tweak her nipple until it's turgid and sensitive. This is the sort of thing teenagers do in a coat closet at a party after a couple of hits from a bong and bad keg beer, not twenty-somethings in a cafe bathroom. But the thought of peeling my hands off her, of pushing her away? Never going to happen now. I want her too badly, and she clearly wants me, too.

I spin her around and back her up until she's flush with the sink, then lift her by the hips until she's perched on the edge. Our lips separate with a loud pop to hoist our shirts over our head. I greedily slide the straps of her bra down and nip at the exposed skin. She throws her head back, the most lovely little half-gurgle, half-moan getting caught in her throat before it can slip past her lips. I love that noise. I'd die a happier man than most if that was the only sound I heard for the rest of my life.

I use my teeth as much as my lips, tongue, and fingers as I work her breasts, claiming them with tugs and twists maybe a little harsher than normal. She writhes from where I have her pinned with her shoulders pressed against the mirror, and tugs on the hair at the nape of my neck. An uncomfortable little squeak escapes her throat, so I haul her off the sink and kiss her hard while I work in earnest at the fastenings of her jeans. I wiggle my hand between layers of fabric and her smooth, supple skin to burrow my fingers between her thighs. Another kiss or two, and she'll be ready. I *need* her to be ready.

A higher part of my brain says to kiss her the way she likes being kissed after a long day when she wants to forget how shitty the world can be and lose herself in a few minutes of ecstasy. I love kissing her like that, making her feel loved and desired and gorgeous, but that's not how I kiss her right now. I kiss her like she's oxygen and I'm drowning, gulping her down like she's the only thing that can save me. She's water for a parched throat. She's sustenance for the starving. I kiss her like she's everything and if I don't possess her, I won't know how to carry on. Her fingers are laced in my hair and her hips are undulating against mine. If my pants were down around my ankles like hers are, we'd be connected by now.

So I can't wait, and I don't. It's painful to stop kissing her, but try as we might, it doesn't work to stand and do this, and that sink probably can't be trusted for how this is going to go. I spin her in place, her hips turning willingly under my palms, and whip my pants down to my knees. I half-kiss, half-bite her shoulder and force her forward until her forearms press against the mirror. I can see her mouth fall open when I trail my fingers between her thighs again, nudging them open and tilting her ass upwards. She's soft and warm and perfect when I sink inside her.

I grasp her hips like she'll disappear if I let them go, and start a punishing pace—slow is not in my lexicon right now. She feels too good, and the noises coming from her mouth and our skin as it slaps together with each thrust roars in my ears. I attach my mouth to the crook of her neck and force myself to feel everything. This is the one time it's okay—even *better*—to feel everything. The flesh of her hips is pliant under my grip. When I look down, I see her face contort in a hundred ways at once, and God, she's breathtaking when she's like this. She can't keep her eyes open and she's so flushed I wonder if she remembers how to breathe. She mutters my name like it's the only word she remembers.

As I study her face in the mirror, I get a glimpse at my own… and what I see is terrifying. I'm feral. My eyes are crazed, my eyebrows knitted together like I'm possessed. My skin is red and feverish. I almost don't recognize myself. I look insane.

Maybe I *am* insane.

"Ezra, God!" Juliana cries, and I feel her clench around me. It snaps me away from looking at myself in the mirror, and I remember I'm the reason she's making those delicious noises. I clutch her hips tighter and guide us until she's quivering beneath me and I can barely hold it together. I mutter something obscene in her ear and she nods rapidly. Then, with one final roll and grunt, I'm spilling inside her.

Inside her.

Inside… oh, mother*fucker*.

I rear back, and the sight of myself uncovered and slick with her jars me. We're always *so* good about using condoms. I haven't been this stupid since….

"Shit. Shit, Jules, I didn't…."

She must feel the stickiness between her thighs before she whirls around and sees me holding myself in my hands. She holds her hands over her mouth to muffle anything she might say.

A pounding on the bathroom door snaps us into action. After a quick search, we pull our clothes back on. She splashes a handful of cool water on her face while I make sure we haven't left any actual trace of what we've done anywhere, other than the hint of rumpled clothing and swollen lips. She uses a hot, damp paper towel to wipe off the counter where she'd been pinned and I slowly open the door. To either our endless relief or undying horror, it's Lukas on the other side of the door. He laughs at us at first, but I cut him off by storming

past him. If I hear him laughing like that anymore, I might sock
him in the jaw.

Anja's stare when I return to the table is like a sucker punch
to the gut.

You're wrong, Anja, I want to tell her. I'm not using her
like that. It just... happened. Unprotected.

I can't find the words to say anything at all.

We all part ways without Lukas being a pain about what he
saw. Anja ignores me to the point of not even hugging me
goodbye. I was planning on going back to Jules's house with
her for the night. Instead, we find the closest 24-hour
pharmacy and head straight for the family planning aisle. She
swallows the Morning-After Pill with a bottle of water as soon
as we get back in the car. "Crisis averted," Jules says, although
her voice is still shaky.

I mutter something under my breath about the crisis
actually being far from averted, but she doesn't press me on it.
I drive her back to her house and instead of finding a parking
space, I idle in front of her house.

"What are you doing? I can walk back from where you park
with you."

"I'm just gonna go home, I think," I say.

"What? Why? Because of that?"

"I don't know if I should be around you when I'm not
acting like myself."

I'd been avoiding looking at her. I snap my eyes up when
she bellows, "Fuck that. Fuck you going home alone. You're
sleeping here, all right? You're not skulking off to pout on your
own because we both got too impulsive to remember to put a
condom on. You're my boyfriend and I want you with me
tonight. Get your head out of your ass, Mackenzie." Her body
vibrates in the sort of anger she's only ever shown me those
couple of times we've fought. My shoulders slump and I lean
over the console between the two seats to take her in my arms.

"I'm sorry," I tell her again and again.

"Stop apologizing like everything is your fault all the time," she murmurs back.

I have to bite back an apology for apologizing so much. Then I find a parking space and, exhausted, we both head inside.

She's changing into her pajamas—the very ones I met her in—when I glance over and see the marks. Four deep, purpling bruises mar her hips and at the curve of her neck and shoulder, I see what can only be a blossoming hickey.

"Holy fuck, Jules."

She gasps when she looks in the mirror and sees them, too. "I didn't realize…."

"Jules, I'm such an asshole. I'm so sorry."

She scowls and crosses the room. I don't want her touching me, but she forces her arms around my neck and kisses me soundly.

"You didn't hurt me," she says. "If you had, I'd have told you."

"You're bruised."

"I bruise easily. It's fine. If it had hurt, I'd have told you to stop, and you would have stopped."

Would I? I want to think I would have. I desperately want to think I would have.

Anja's voice sounds in my head again. I beg her to shut the hell up.

It's several more kisses and tugs of her arms before I stop vibrating and lay down in bed with her. She snaps the light out and nestles into my arms. I comb my fingers through her hair, finding its glossy waves calming as I rake through them.

"I should go on the Pill, just in case that ever happens again," she murmurs sleepily a minute later.

"I'll be more careful, I promise. I don't mind using condoms. I… I don't know what came over me." My voice cracks around the edges.

"It's okay. I mean, we'll still use them if you want, but I should have been on the Pill forever ago." She arches her neck back so she can look at me. Her eyes are full of forgiveness I'm still not sure I deserve.

So I tell her, "I don't know if I deserve you, Juliana."

"Don't ever say that again. I *want you*, Ezra. Get that through your head," she whispers, her tone rough enough to drive her point home.

She falls asleep a little while later, but my mind is racing so fast I can barely pull air into my lungs. What the hell came over me? And how do I make it stop?

CHAPTER TWELVE

The window across from the chaise in Jules's living room faces east. I'm watching the sun rise as I chew on the filter end of a cigarette. I want to light it, but it feels like too much effort right now to put shoes and a jacket on to go outside. It's been several days since I slept more than a couple of hours at a time without long periods of restlessness in between. My eyes burn from it. Nothing I've tried—not sex, not jogging, not any sort of herbal remedy Jules keeps on hand for just such an occasion—has helped. Nothing probably will, not when it comes to Mac's anniversary.

The sun's warming the soles of my feet through the window when Jules steps out of the bedroom, looking tousled and gorgeous. She nudges my thigh until I scoot over enough for her to curl up on the chaise next to me. I think she's fallen asleep on my chest until I hear her speak.

"You never talk about him. Will you tell me about him?"

I want to say no, but I imagine that the day someone died, you *should* talk about them, even when it's painful.

"What do you want to know about him?"

"What'd he look like?"

I pull up a picture of Mac in my mind and it brings a stinging smile to my face. "Big, broad. Hair like mine, eyes like mine. He could have been a linebacker for how wide his shoulders were. He had to turn to the side to go through most doors."

Once I start, it's difficult to stop.

"He never drank coffee, only tea. He'd make it so bitter and stout, though, it smelled and looked like coffee. He had this sort of laugh that just echoed—like, seriously, it bounced off the walls, it was so strong.

"He couldn't sing—which didn't stop him from trying. And he had this hideous tie with turkeys on it, in these ridiculous little Pilgrim hats he wore on Thanksgiving. It didn't matter if it was just me and him and Dylan for Thanksgiving, he insisted we all wear a collared shirt and tie and slacks, and I'm pretty sure it was just so that he could get away with wearing that ugly tie. He loved it because Dylan and I hated it." I'm smiling, but really, it's taking everything in my power not to sob.

"And you really called him 'Mac?' Not 'Dad?'"

"Always Mac. Everyone called him Mac. He'd yell at our friends if they ever tried to call him 'Mr. Mackenzie.'"

"He sounds like a wonderful guy."

"He was. I... I really miss him, Jules."

She holds me as I start to full-on blubber. I miss him so much it hurts. It sinks in all over again that I'll never get him back. I'll never get the goodbye we didn't have. All I'll have are twenty-five years of memories of him, and the ones that ought to be the sharpest are the most muddled because of my drinking.

It's a long while before I'm put together again, although I still feel hollow. Juliana kisses my forehead, smooths my hair, and slips off the chaise to make us coffee and breakfast. She's taken the day off work, although I didn't ask her to. I'm appreciative, even if I do think that grieving is probably something I should be doing alone.

"Can I ask how he died, Ez?" She comes back over to me, two steaming mugs in her hands.

"Stroke. He was home alone. The cat made enough noise to irritate his neighbor, who came over and found him. But he was already gone."

She swipes her fingertips across her lips, lost in whatever words she's trying to come up with to comfort me. "It must be terrible to die alone," she says, although I can see immediately that she regrets it.

I try not to think about how Mac died alone. It makes me hate Dylan for not stopping by that day and checking in on him, makes me really hate myself for spending the day, one of my days off, drunk out of my mind and ignoring the ringing of my phone until later. I was so drunk I missed the call telling me my father was dead. I'll never forgive myself for that.

"Does he have a grave we can go visit? Or you can go, and I'll wait in the car… We can get flowers, or candles…."

"Can we talk about something else? Can we try spending today like it isn't… today?"

"We can do whatever you'd like, baby."

We end up settling on her couch, *Doctor Who* streaming on Netflix. An actor with a Scottish brogue is a guest star, and it hurts all over again. *I wish I had one of them*, Mac used to say. *Be a real proper Scotsman if I did.*

I'm thankful when her phone rings and she pauses the show to answer it. I try not to listen in on the conversation, but it's next to impossible with how emphatic she becomes the longer it carries on.

"Ez…," she says. "That was work."

"Go on, honey," I say.

"I figured they could handle one stupid day without me, but apparently I'm the only one who knows what the hell we're doing on this project."

"It's fine. Seriously."

I watch her get dressed through the open bedroom door, then follow her in.

"I won't be long," she says when she sees me grabbing my jeans and shoes. "I'll steal your car so I'm there and back as fast as I can be."

"No, I'll walk with you. It seems like a nice day. I think I'll take the light rail down to my place for a little bit—the cat will tear up all my shit if she doesn't get fed today."

Her eyes flash with concern. "Are you sure you're up to being alone?"

"It's just for a couple of hours," I say, trying not to puff when I speak, despite how fast my heart is beating. "Text me when you're wrapping up and I'll catch the train back. Maybe we can go to Cafe Brazil for dinner."

She thinks it's charming how much of a liking I've taken to Brazilian food since we started dating.

We walk down the steep embankment of LoHi's main drag and cross over the pedestrian bridge over I-25. She clutches my hand like she's trying to root me to the ground, and I'm grateful because it feels for a second like maybe I'm not going to lose my mind today.

We walk as far as the central train station together, where she can catch one of the downtown shuttles to her office and I can catch a train. We stumble over one another, each insisting the other catch their transport first.

"You'll be late. I still have fifteen minutes to wait," I warn her.

"But…."

I kiss her hard on the mouth. "Thanks for being worried over me today," I say. "But I'm fine." I'm lying. But I don't want her to know that.

"I'll meet you back here in a few hours, all right?" she says, looking over her shoulder at me like she's afraid to let me out of her sight.

"Sure thing." I blow her a kiss and try my best to smile. I know without seeing it it's a seriously fake-ass smile. Does *she* know just how fake it is? If she did, would she have let me out of her sight?

She disappears in the crowd a moment later, and I can't help but feel that my sanity went with her.

***

When I get back to the apartment, the cat is pacing back and forth, growling and hissing. I check her food dish and litterbox—it's been a couple of days since I've been home, so she's probably a bit irritated by how empty one is over the other. She's clawed the shit out of the corner of my TV stand and the half-wall that separates the kitchen from the living area. I'll bet she's pissed in my bed, too. I debate the merits of trying to take her back to Jules's place so she isn't so destructive here by herself, but there's no way I can get her in a carrier and on the train.

Then I stop and wonder—maybe, just maybe, she remembers what happened last year. It seems ridiculous, though—cats can't possibly have that sort of recollection, can they?

After a few minutes by myself, I realize that I'm at a total loss for what to do with my day. I can't focus on TV or a book. Spending so little time here lately means there isn't anything to clean save for a thin layer of dust, and I've been doing all my laundry at Jules's instead of Mama A's. I keep picking up my cell phone and putting it down again, locking and unlocking the screen to see if anyone—one person in particular—has sent me anything.

It's something else that's been weighing on my mind. On the day our father died, Dylan and I should be able to call a truce. He told me he never wanted to see me again, stormed away from me at the store all those weeks ago, but today is different. Or at least, it *should* be different.

I take the chance and text him. I tell him I know he might not want to speak to me, but if he does, I know what he's feeling. I miss Mac, too. I don't elaborate on how my heart is aching, how I can't stop picturing him lying on his living room rug, all alone and dying. I have to force myself to stop, or I'll drive myself crazy.

Dylan doesn't text me back. Maybe I shouldn't expect him to. And yet, I keep checking my phone every couple of minutes, hoping he'll put aside his ego and be my brother again. Just for a second, I want us to be like those two guys who got a Scottish tattoo together, who had each other's backs no matter what, even though we couldn't be more different despite looking exactly the same.

It's probably impossible, considering what I did. But I still want it.

I can't keep sitting here doing nothing, though. I'm starting to get antsy, and antsy is a bad thing for me. I haul myself up and put on sweats and running shoes. I blast music in my ears and take off out my door, the winter wind stinging my cheeks and eyes as I try jogging off the anxiety that won't stop growing in my gut, no matter how much I try to ignore it.

I don't want to wait at stop lights, so I end up turning corners in a big circuit. The neighborhood is mostly residential, with a little office park set off the high street and a strip mall across the way. I've done well ignoring the strip mall in the last year, though that hasn't stopped me from remembering that's where my brew-pub was—is. Just because I don't go anymore hasn't made it disappear. When I break through the office park, the light is green, the little walk signal popping up as I get to the corner. I could turn back, take a different route through the neighborhood behind me, or press onward and jog along the same side of the street as Comrade. I know I should go backwards, but my feet sprint me forward. It doesn't matter, though, right? Seeing the place doesn't mean I have to go in.

I'm dead in my tracks when I spot the neon sign, already illuminated and glowing against the brick and the early afternoon drear. My brain is fighting two contrasting images: Mac's eyes, his smile, the actual look on his face when his mustache-covered lip curled up in preparation for one of those booming laughs of his, flickering out and disappearing forever, and then there's the look of a bitter, hoppy microbrew, perfectly poured in a well-chilled glass. One might make the other go away, but only one is available to me. *No, Mackenzie, you can't have either. Not anymore.*

It's a painfully long minute before my feet are pumping beneath me. I full-out run back to my apartment and throw myself on the futon, panting and shaking. A thin layer of sweat coats my skin, but it's not the sort that should come from exercise. This sort of sweat only makes me shake harder as I pick up my phone again. My fingers skirt across the touchscreen of my phone, typing in another message to Dylan.

Me: I miss Mac. I know you hate me, but just don't hate me today.

The cat is yowling. I try to pick her up to quiet her down, lest one of my neighbors overhear her and think I'm torturing her, but she skitters under my futon and hisses. I hiss back, run a shower, and stand under it until the water actually runs cold.

I text Jules, who tells me she's got at least two more hours at work. Anja has conferences after school, and besides, I'm pretty sure she's still pissed at me. I can wait out Jules's two more hours at work. I can handle my shit for that much longer.

The cat's crying is getting louder. More irritating. The longer she carries on, the more I think she *must* know what today is. She's never this loud, never carries on like this. I think, though, about what it must have been like to see Mac that last day like she did. I'm not sure how capable of empathy, love, and attachment to their humans cats are, but what must it have been like? Maybe it was enough to imprint a memory. Cats are probably smarter than I give them credit for being.

My phone trills. I can barely hear it over her yowling, but it's just a text. My blood sluices like ice through my veins. It's Dylan.

Dylan: You don't get it, do you, Ezra? Leave me the fuck alone. I don't know where the hell my brother went, but whoever you are is exactly like our mother, and I don't want anything to do with her, either. *I* don't have any family left.

I read the message over and over again. My knuckles turn white from how hard I'm gripping the device.

Another comes in.

Dylan: And for the record - Mac would hate what you turned out like, too.

There's nothing preparing me for how much that hurts. Because I've been thinking it myself, but getting the confirmation... Holy shit, that fucking *hurts*.

I should probably cry. It's a natural sort of thing to do when your brother tells you you're basically dead to him. I should ball myself up and wallow and feel like the piece of shit I am.

I scroll through my contacts for my mother's number. Anja isn't available, and Jules won't be for a while yet. It's okay. They can't be at my beck and call all the time. That isn't their job. But Constance... She can help. She has to be able to help.

I keep pressing send, over and over, and each time, the call rings and rings and then goes to voicemail. Her outgoing message is chipper and optimistic, so unlike the woman I knew growing up who called her sons terrible names and told them they were good for little and worth even less. Why do I want her to help me? Why do I want her in my life? She's awful. I don't want my mother.

I want Mac.

I want my dad.

I lied to Juliana earlier—Mac wasn't always Mac. When I was really young, Mac was Daddy. I grew out of the word when I was a teenager, but if he were here now and could see me, losing my mind and craving and shaking, a cigarette dangling out of my mouth as I listen to the fucking cat carry on like I'm sacrificing her to some pagan god, I'm pretty sure he'd be Daddy again. Mac, Daddy, whoever he was, could fix things if only I'd let him. I didn't want him to fix me when he was alive, because there wasn't anything wrong. Now everything is wrong. I realize that now, the way I couldn't until the ENT on call at Mama A's hospital told me how bad my nose break was. If Mac were here, I'd tell him how fucked up I am. I'd tell him I'm sorry for everything. I'll never get that chance, and I'm furious. I'm furious with myself. I am such a piece of shit.

I try calling Constance one more time, even though I hate her and don't want her, because I know there's no way Dylan will take my call. The call goes to voicemail, as I should expect it to, but instead of barking out a panicked message, demanding she call me and come and help me before I do something really, really stupid, I ball up my fist, arch my arm backwards, and aim for the dead center of the window. I don't even realize I've whipped my arm forward and flung the phone out of my grip until the window shatters and my cell disappears through the hole in the middle.

The cat shrieks. I might be shrieking, too.

I hate my mother. I hate my father, for leaving me. I don't have a brother. Whatever is left of me isn't fit for human consumption. Why is Juliana wasting her time with me? What am I to Anja but a pathetic project? Mattias and Lukas can't possibly think of me as anything but a pain in their asses. Mama A, sweet Mama A... She deserves better than an interloper like me invading her family's life.

"Oh my fucking God, cat, shut the fuck up! He's not coming back for you! You're stuck with me!"

I rip open the freezer to pull out a fresh pack of cigarettes. Of course I'd be out now. How the fuck did I manage that?

I stuff my feet into shoes and yank the front door open. I shouldn't have left my car at Jules's... The closest gas station that sells American Spirits is four blocks away and scary-close to Comrade. Maybe I can make do with some Camels, or Marlboros....

A blur of tan fur whizzes past my feet and down the cement stairs. All the air leaves my lungs

"Birdie!" I scream, finally using the cat's real name, "Birdie, come back!"

I fling myself out the door and race down the stairs. This was the one thing I could do for Mac—I couldn't stay sober at his funeral, couldn't be with him the day he died, couldn't even say goodbye the right way, but I could take care of his cat. His declawed beast of a cat who's already disappeared from my view. I can't fuck this up too.

It's better on foot. I can check the park and in people's backyards. Up trees. She can't have gone far, I tell myself, and I can't fuck this up. I just can't. I owe Mac more than that.

My legs are leaden and it's nearly impossible to keep them steady underneath me. I keep moving forward through sheer force of will. There's no trace of her in the office park, no sign in the neighborhood behind my apartment. Dusk is coming on, but without my phone, I have no way of knowing what time it is. There's more traffic on the streets. I should go back home and see if my cell phone is salvageable, because surely Juliana will have called me by now.

She shouldn't, though. She shouldn't be bothering with me. Why is she bothering with me?

There's a park and a bike trail on the far side of the strip mall Comrade is in. There's signage warning about the presence of coyotes. I have to check there—I have to make good to Mac, even if I'm useless in every other way.

My legs are rapidly numbing and my throat feels like it's on fire. I've been calling the cat's name over and over, long enough to go hoarse and craggy. The park is empty, the streets are getting more crowded, and tears are burning at my eyes.

There was one day I never told Anja about. It was after she'd given me my one-month chip, and in spite of how proud she was, I hadn't been able to control myself. I'd gone into Comrade while my laundry was running, and ordered my favorite of their drafts. The bartender was different, must have come on new after the incident with Dylan and my subsequent sobriety. She'd poured me a drink, given me change for the ten I'd slid across to her, and puttered on about her business. I'd stared at the glass, at the frothy head and the bubbles floating up from the bottom. My hands were clammy and absolutely itching to take hold of the glass. Instead, I'd grabbed the red chip out of my wallet and rubbed it hard between my finger and thumb—maybe that was when the engraving began to smooth away.

I'd taken off, the beer untouched, collected my still-damp laundry, and gone home. I left the drink on the bar, and deciding that must be the epitome of self-restraint, I'd never mentioned it to Anja, because it didn't count because I didn't drink it.

Rationally, I know there's no way that beer from ten months back is still on the bar.

But something I can't deny, can't stop, makes me go in and check.

CHAPTER THIRTEEN

Here's what I know: I'm Ezra Mackenzie. I was twenty-six on my last birthday in November. And I was twenty-three days (three and a half weeks, 553 hours, however you want to measure it out) from being sober for exactly one year when I fucked everything up by going into a bar, ordering a drink, and forgetting everything else that happened during the past three days. I had myself a nice little three-day bender to make up for the eleven whole months I was sober.

At least when I do something, I do it big, right?

I shouldn't have a sense of humor about this, but it's a defense mechanism that feels almost not terrible right now when everything else feels so hopeless. I'm lying in a hospital bed, tubes coming out the crook of my arm full of stuff that's supposed to keep my brain from swelling up and dying, my leg slung up above me and hurting like hell. I feel like every bit the complete piece of shit that I know I am, so I need *something* to keep me going. So gallows humor it is.

I remember the first couple of drinks at Comrade—the calm that washed over me with the first few sips, the lightheadedness that came with finishing the second, the hazy feeling that this really wasn't so bad, I could handle this, I'm totally in control, and if I'm not, who cares, by the time I ordered the fourth. And then there's all these weird fragments, these pieces I'm sure made sense in my stupor but now mean absolutely nothing. I couldn't tell you how I ended up where I did when the cops found my sorry ass this morning. Maybe it's locked in the recesses of my brain or something. Maybe it'll come back to me in a day or a week or a month as I berate myself for being such a spectacular moron.

This hospital I woke up in is on the complete opposite side of town, closer to where Constance lives than where my apartment is. In addition to fluids, they're giving me just enough prescription-grade ibuprofen to offset the pain of my broken fibula—another mystery of my relapse is how I made it across town, probably on a broken leg. They think I might actually have walked on it after I broke it. *That* I feel like I'd remember by sheer virtue of how much it hurts now when I so much as look at it.

I wonder if they've called an In Case of Emergency out of my phone, but then I remember that my phone is back at my apartment, probably shattered to shit with a seriously dead battery. It snowed sometime last night—it's probably double-dead, done in if not by my excellent throw through the window, then by water damage. They haven't asked me for a contact name or number, at least, not that I can remember or would have been cogent enough to give. I think I still have Juliana's card in my wallet, but her old Brazilian phone number would be useless. I hope they couldn't contact anyone, and that I can sign myself out of here without having them ask me about my family, my friends, my girlfriend. I want more than anything to pretend this didn't happen, but after three days of not answering my phone, I'm betting that's a pipe dream.

Even if she hasn't already guessed this is what happened, I know I'll have to 'fess up to Anja and give my chips back. I'll have to start all over again.

The weight of what I've done is all-consuming—I'm a failure. I'm a loser and an idiot. I've let Anja and Constance down when both of them have found ways to stay sober. I've let Mama A and Mattias and Lukas down, who only wanted to see me get better and stay that way.

And then there's Juliana, who had been expecting me home. She'd been expecting me for dinner, for the night, for everything. I wonder how many times she might have called me, trying to figure out what I was up to all day. I wonder if she got worried when I didn't reply and never came back. She *had* to be worried—of *course* she was worried. I wonder when worried became angry. When angry might have become panicked. She didn't sign up for a three-days-missing boyfriend. When I think of putting her through that, my leg thrums in pain and I have to sink down lower in the uncomfortable, lumpy hospital bed with my face in my hands. I'm so far past humiliated and ashamed, it's pathetic. *I'm* pathetic.

I try to shift around in bed, and it sends a jolt of pain up through my leg and into my gut. I grasp for the call button on the outdated, corded phone attached to the bed frame. The last thing an idiot like me needs is to add Narcotics Anonymous meetings to my repertoire for a new prescription drug addiction, but ibuprofen isn't anywhere near enough for me right now.

A nurse comes in. She's got a halo of dark hair, big pretty eyes, and full lips ever-pursed in a smile. I can tell she's doing her best not to look at me like I'm completely pathetic. For a minute she looks familiar, but I'm sure it's just because she's probably been on duty for hours and has checked on me before I was ready to realize what's going on.

"How's the leg, Ezra? Scale of one to ten, ten being the worst?" The pain I'm feeling must be plastered all over my face.

"E-eight," I gulp out between deep, sucking breaths.

"Maybe nine." It's worse than I can ever remember feeling anything hurt before, even my fucked-up nose the last time my shit-for-brains ass ended up in a hospital bed.

She pulls out a key from a long retractable chain at her waist, unlocks a door above the sink in the corner, and pulls out a tiny bottle. She sticks a syringe in the vial, then presses the contents of the syringe into my IV tube. Whatever it is is powerful—it's only a couple of minutes before I can breathe again.

She checks my vitals, makes a couple of notes on the computer plugged into my IV pump, and then, instead of leaving, pulls up a chair by my messed-up leg. "You know, you're lucky the police found you when they did. There's another freeze warning tonight. And if you'd been on that leg any longer, you'd probably have severe nerve damage."

There's something biting and nasty on the tip of my tongue, but I can't find it in me to be mean to the woman with the drugs. I nod and shove the back of my head deep into the limp pillow and stare at the ceiling. Whatever she's given me hasn't made me sleepy—yet—but I hope if it looks like I'm about to drop off, she'll leave.

"One of the other nurses told me you were asking for your personal effects a little earlier; do you remember that? We figured you wanted your shoes to try to take off, although I really don't think you'll be going anywhere on that leg without crutches for a while. And we won't give you those until you're being discharged and someone from OT can come in to help you on them."

"I don't want to take off," I say, and I vaguely remember why I must have asked for it to begin with. Subconsciously, I think I was looking for it when I wiggled around and jarred my leg. "I just want my wallet. There's something in there that I—"

She holds out her hand. In her palm are several colored, nearly-rubbed-smooth anodized aluminum chips. *My* chips. I look at this woman with her kind face, and try to figure out how she knew it was my chips I wanted. She tips them into my palm and I clutch my fist to my chest. Not that these things mean anything now, but for a second, having them makes me think maybe this wasn't all as bad as it seems.

"You're missing your one-year medallion." Her tone has taken a different tone. I've heard that tone in meetings time and time again.

"Won't be getting it now."

"It's a hard one. Don't beat yourself up—lots of people have to try and try again. This isn't failure—it's a reset button."

She's an addict, too, I realize without her having to say it.

"You've had visitors in the lobby for hours now, but we wanted to wait until you were lucid enough to consent to see them."

"W-what? Who?"

"A very bossy woman with a thick accent who keeps telling us she's a nurse, too, to get us to do what she wants. Two guys your age. Two pretty girls, a blonde and a brunette, who're spending about as much time fighting with one another as they are hugging and crying. And your mother. If you'd like to see any of them, I'll bring them in. If not, I'll tell them you're not ready for visitors and have them come back tomorrow."

How the hell did they find me? I wonder. "Did I tell someone who to call?" I ask, searching my hazy memories for one where I'd have done something like that.

The nurse looks sort of hurt. "*I* recognized you, Ezra. I called your mother. I thought it was the best thing to do, considering. You don't remember me, do you?"

I stare at her long and hard until I piece together why she looked familiar. Then I remember Thanksgiving—she'd been there. She'd had to leave before pie, but she'd been one of Constance's friends from her AA meetings. We talked for a few minutes about our jobs, and I remember now thinking she had the same sort of energy as Mama A and wondered if that was just a nurse-thing. I feel like a total asshole as it comes rushing back at me now.

"I'm sorry…," I say.

She waves me off.

"Don't worry about it. I'm excellent at forging almost no impression whatsoever—that's how I got away with my own bad habits for so long. Constance was going out of her mind by the time I called. They all showed up just a little bit after that."

"I want to see her," I say. "Constance. I want to see her," I clarify, surprising myself. I didn't want anyone ten minutes ago. Surely I should say, "I want to see my girlfriend," or "I want to see my sponsor." But no—for not the first time since I was old enough to know better, I want my mother.

The nurse nods and pats my good leg through the blanket. "I'll bring her in. It'll be all right, you know. I know that sounds like something everyone just says, but I promise you it's true. Believe me—I've been there."

"Thank you." I lean back and will my heart not to pound out of my chest. I wish it was Mac about to walk in the room, not Constance. It stings too much to think about Mac right now, though. I push him out of my thoughts because the last time I thought too much about him….

"Ezra!" I look up to see Constance rushing towards me. "Oh, honey, oh, I'm so, so glad to see your eyes." Her eyes are glistening and her hands are shaking.

"Mom?" I haven't called her that in decades, but it slips out and doesn't feel terrible. It makes things a little less hopeless for a second. I try the name again. "Mom… I'm sorry." It's all I manage before I begin to sob.

"Oh, honey." She perches on the side of my bed and throws her arms around me. For so many years, there was nothing comforting about my mother's arms. Her embraces were scarce, and never soothing when they were offered. Now they provide all the comfort I crave. She pulls me up and folds me against her chest. Her fingers comb through my hair and I hear her shushing me, her voice low from the back of her throat. "You have nothing to be sorry for, nothing at all. We're just so relieved you're all right."

I shake my head back and forth in disbelief. She pulls away and holds my face in her hands, forcing my eyes to lock on hers.

"Honey, listen to me. This is a setback. This is just a setback. This doesn't define you. This doesn't make us any less proud of you. Do you understand me?"

"But... I f-fucked up...."

"We *all* fuck up, Ezra. That's the constant in our lives, especially for people like us. You'll put this behind you, and next time you'll do better. This doesn't ruin everything. It just starts something else." She strokes my cheeks with the pads of her thumbs to blot away my tears. This tiny gesture means absolutely everything. Every moment growing up when I craved a mother who didn't stink of red wine, who never said my name at a normal pitch that wasn't jarring and abrasive, comes back to me in an instant. I feel every one of those feelings begin to pour out of me like water. I shake like a leaf, but she's there. She holds me tight and tells me she loves me and how sorry she is. My body convulses as sobs rip out of my chest and throat. And she's there.

When the shaking, the sobbing, the intense self-loathing finally comes to a head and mixes with whatever the nurse shot into my IV, Constance (Mom) lays me back and smooths my hair against my forehead. "You need to rest, honey," she says. "You need to rest and relax."

"I can't fail again, Mom. Please tell me what to do so I don't fail again."

"Tomorrow," she says. "We'll figure it out tomorrow. Right now you just need to rest."

I do. After all, there's plenty more time for self-loathing tomorrow.

***

In the year since my last hospital stint, I forgot how often nurses come in to check on you. Some try to be quiet and even apologize when they see they've woken you up. Others bang the door open and closed, snap on lights, and talk to you with no regard as to whether or not you've been sleeping. Because of this, I sleep fitfully when I manage to sleep at all. Mostly my head races to every possible conclusion it can in the state I'm in. I don't see the nurse who's friends with Constance again that evening; she must have left for the night. I feel bad that I don't remember her name, that I can't even pick it out of the list of nurses' names scribbled on the white board across from my bed.

I drift off around dawn, and at last get some quality sleep. When I wake up, Anja is sitting in the chair next to me. My skin turns icy—I wasn't ready to see her yet. I wonder if I was ever going to be ready to see her.

"Ez," she says, her voice somewhere between a gasp and a sigh. "I'm so glad you're okay."

I should apologize, right? That's the logical thing to do. My vocal chords don't seem to be working, though. I try to smile, but it's a grimace at best.

"This is a ridiculous question, I know, but… how do you feel?"

"Like hell." My voice is craggy and whatever smile I might have donned fades fast. "I feel like hell. The only things I can remember are pops and flashes of stupidity, and when I woke up, I'd ended up in here with a fucked-up leg. Were you expecting I'd feel just fine and dandy?" I shouldn't snap at her and I know it, but it doesn't stop me from doing it.

She bristles, but she takes it. It's a year ago all over again. She'll smile at me when she wants to cry for me. She's my best friend, my sponsor, the person who knows me best.

"I'm just so glad you're... alive. That someone found you," she repeats.

I scarcely feel alive even though my heart is beating, even though my brain is racing. Maybe it was just the bad night's sleep and the deep, unyielding sense of shame, but I feel like I'm going out of my gourd. What did I do the last three days? Why did I go into that stupid bar? Why did I chuck my phone out my window? What was I thinking? Why am I such a fucking moron? When can I have another drink?

"I'm really not up to company right now, Anja. Can you...?"

"There's some things I need to say first. I got a substitute for my class for the morning only, so I'll be quick. But Ezra, I'm sorry I wasn't there."

"Don't act like this is anyone's fault but mine."

"No, that's not what I'm saying. I'm just—Juliana texted me that she had to go in, and I should have tried to get a sub and...."

This grates on me, the thought of the two of them talking about me like I needed to be coddled, needed to be watched like a teenager left alone in a house full of flammable things—even though I did end up burning the proverbial house down, didn't I?

"I didn't call you," I say, my voice still too sharp. "I didn't ask you to be there. I wanted to be on my own."

"I *should* have been there. That's my job. I was supposed to be there for you to turn to when you started craving."

I rub my eyes. "You're not my babysitter. I didn't pick up the phone. I didn't reach out to you. That was my mistake, not yours."

"We saw what happened. Mat and Jules and Luk and I... We went to your apartment and saw the window. Your cat is gone... I'm guessing you know that?"

I nod. It hurts my head to think about it and my heart to know I lost that part of Mac because I was so careless. "I was chasing after her. She took off and I went after her. She ran in the direction of the bar." Did she? Did she really? Or did I just want an excuse?

"Oh, Ezra...." She was trying to be supportive and loving, but she's finally let the disappointment edge her tone. She *should* be disappointed in me.

"Look, I know it's your job as my sponsor to make me feel like shit because I fucked up, but can you please just wait until later? Is one day of self-pity too much to ask for? If you want my chips back, they're there." I point towards the bedside table where I'd dropped the little tokens last night when Constance came in.

She sighs and runs her fingers along her temples. "We need to talk about that, too. I... I don't think I can be your sponsor anymore." She says it like she wants to shield me from it. But this sort of rejection can't be shielded. "I know some people who can be your new one, but I need your permission to tell them what happened first."

I stare at her in disbelief. I knew she'd be angry at me, knew she'd be disappointed. I never pegged her to just up and waltz out on me, especially now, when it feels like I need her the most.

Maybe she's sensing my thoughts, because she moves so she's sitting on the side of my bed and grasps my hand in both of hers. "You need a sponsor you can trust, one you can call anytime, day or night, whenever you feel the urge come on. How long did you feel the need for a drink coming on without calling me?"

I gape at her. Apparently that's all she needed to know.

"I'm not giving up on you. I'll never, ever give up on you. You're my best friend and I love you more than you probably understand right now. But I need to be just your best friend for

whatever comes next. I can't be your sponsor and watch you…
I can't be your sponsor. I'm sorry, I really am…."

"There isn't anyone in the world I trust more than you.
You have to know that." It's true. I trust Juliana and Mattias
and Lukas, but Anja is the only one who knows what's going
on in my head. So why doesn't she know that right now it
sounds an awful lot like she's breaking up with me? *It's not you;
it's me. We can still be friends. I love you, but….*

"If you trust me so much, why didn't you call? Why didn't
you come over after you broke your phone, go to Mama A's,
something?"

"I didn't have my car! I left it up at Juliana's, and I was
going to take the train, but… Anja, you can't do this. *Please.* I
can't do this without you."

"I feel like shit about this, Ez, I really do, but you have to
understand I'm trying to do what's best for you. If something
like this happens again—"

"Then it will happen because it will be *my* mistake to make!
All of this was *my* mistake to make! I thought I was doing the
right thing at first, I really did, but everything just fucking
snowballed on me all at once. The fucking cat was crying and I
know it was because of Mac and I started to miss him so much
I couldn't breathe or think straight, and then Dylan texted me
something nasty—"

"Oh, Ezra." Will it ever again be possible for her to say my
name without sounding so sad? "I'm sorry. I know it must have
been bad, because I know you wouldn't fall back without
something pushing you. But I think we're too close, and maybe
that's why you didn't call me. Is it possible you didn't want me
to see you at your worst? I think that might be why friends
aren't supposed to be sponsors."

"This is so fucked up, Anja. This is so, so fucked up that
you're telling me this now." I can't sift through the betrayal, the
abandonment in my brain to know that maybe this really is for

the best, and that maybe we just need to be friends and not sponsor/sponsored. Maybe that's how it always should have been. But I can't appeal to that higher sense right now. Right now, she's the enemy. She's the one giving up on me. Right now, I get to hate her fucking guts.

"I know it is. And you can hate me all you want. But I'm doing this so you get better, so you don't end up like this again. You're so much stronger than you believe you are, and I don't know how to get that through your head. I'm hoping someone else can."

"That's just a pretty way of saying, 'I'm giving up on you, you loser.'" I'm unable to keep the spite in my voice in check and maybe not even trying.

"No! No, that's not it at all! I'm sorry. I'm so, so sorry." Tears roll down her cheeks.

"I'm sorry, too," I snarl. "I'm sorry I'm such a fuck-up that you can't be bothered with me anymore."

"Ezra, stop, you know I don't—"

"Get out, Anja. Just... go away. Leave me alone."

"Ezra, please...."

"Get. Out."

She drops my hand and is out the door so fast, I hear something like an echo of the sob she makes as the door closes behind her. I'm not proud of making her cry. But it's either her or me. And if it's going to be her *and* me, I want her gone before I start.

***

My mother isn't back for hours after I chase Anja off—I'm guessing she doesn't want to expose Gemma to me with as volatile as I am right now. I decide to let whoever in, because I can't possibly be any worse to Jules or Mama A than I was to Anja. But just because I am slowly coming around to understanding why Anja is giving up on me, it doesn't mean I have to like it. It doesn't feel like any less of a kick in the ass while I was already down for the count.

No one comes, not for a while. I'm about to press the call button and ask for something to knock me out so I can sleep the rest of the day when yet another nurse comes bustling in. What the hell is it with this hospital? Why are there so many nurses constantly coming in here? Isn't there supposed to be some great nursing shortage?

It becomes clear she isn't here to take my temperature or change out my IV, which I probably don't even need anymore. I'm ready for someone to show me how to navigate some crutches so I can limp out of here with my tail between my legs, but this woman isn't here to do that, either. I don't think the first thing an occupational therapy nurse, or really, any nurse, should offer me is to wheel me outside so I can smoke. I sort of want to kiss her.

I was on my way to get cigarettes, I remember as she wheels me to the elevator. *Did I ever end up getting any?* The nurse pulls a pack of Marlboros out of her scrubs pocket and hands me one. I'm so desperate for nicotine I won't dare complain they aren't my brand. I study her name badge as she holds her lighter up for me to lean the tip my cigarette into the flame. Before I puff out the first acrid drag, I resister her name, Lydia, and her department, Outpatient Rehabilitation Services.

Rehab. I let the word swirl around in my brain, and I think she's letting me before she says anything.

"You're ready to be discharged any time now, Ezra," she says like we've talked about things like this before as old friends. "Technically, the hospital doesn't really care if you go out and drink again, so long as you don't mess up the wrapping job on that leg of yours." She lights a cigarette of her own, and something tinkles around her wrist—a bracelet with what looks suspiciously like an AA medallion strung on it. Is that a six I see emblazoned on it, or an upside-down nine? It's not a months chip; it's one of the lacquered ones that denote years. What must it be like to be sober for that long? Will I ever be sober that long, or am I doomed to repeat my failure every year on Mac's anniversary, or birthday, or....

"It has to be your choice what you do next," she says between drags. "We can't and won't make you do anything other than ask you to come back in a few weeks to have your cast taken off. I can answer questions about our rehabilitation programs if you have any, or I can sign off that I spoke with you, and your doctor will release you as soon as you learn how to work a pair of crutches. It's up to you."

In a way, it feels like she's giving me permission to go out drinking again. And God, is that tempting. I want to skip the hangover, of course, avoid the hospital stay and bills, but to drink *just* enough until I'm happy and carefree and not hating everything the way I am right now... I ended up missing out on three days of work, so my ass has probably been fired, so that wouldn't interfere....

I can't believe what the hell I'm thinking. I stare at the woman and her half-ash cigarette and realize what clever reverse-psychology she just employed. She wasn't being lazy or unkind or uncaring... She must get a hundred people to sign up for rehab like this.

"Pretty sure this fuck-up of mine cost me my job," I say. "I'm pretty much broke."

"We work with everyone from white-collar workers to homeless individuals. Don't worry about the money, at least, not for a minute or two. Do you want to get clean again?"

"I don't want to end up like this again." It's true. Sitting in a wheelchair, a sharp breeze drifting up the back of my hospital gown chilling my ass and spine, smoking a cigarette like it's oxygen—I think this is even worse than being socked in the nose by my twin brother, as far as rock-bottom moments go. "I let everyone I love down. I can't do that again. I'll do whatever it takes to make sure I don't."

"All right then." She flicks her cigarette into a nearby sand ashtray. "Let's go back inside so we can talk in private and see if one of our programs might be a good fit."

I greedily puff down the end of my own and let her wheel me back in. Something feels lighter, feels less awful. Maybe it's the nicotine. Or maybe I know that I can be better, if I want to be.

***

It's only about an hour later when everyone arrives all at once: Constance and all the Almeidas. I'm not sure who I'm more surprised about seeing—Anja or Juliana. I wouldn't have blamed Anja for never wanting to see me again after how I treated her. The nurse, Lydia, is clearing away the intake paperwork she's been going over with me, and holds out her hand to shake mine. She says she'll see me soon and hurries out, letting my whole sordid, strange, wonderful family get a good look at the loser I am right now.

Mama A rushes to me and kisses my cheeks. She asks again and again if I'm all right, even though it feels like nothing will ever be all right again, I keep telling her that I am because I know that's what she needs to hear. Mattias and Lukas find chairs near me and drop down into them, their shoulders hunched, their faces tense and nervous. Anja stands by the door, her arms crossed tight over her chest. I can tell she's still hurt from this morning, but it means a lot to me that she's there, and that she's not looking at me like she completely despises me. And that she's not glaring at me, like Juliana is. It makes me feel about three inches small, but I want to cling to the fact that Jules is here. She's here when she probably shouldn't be, not after what I have put her through the last few days.

"Thanks for coming." My throat is so dry it's difficult to talk.

"We all wanted to see you yesterday, but we get that you

weren't ready," Lukas says, his own voice surprisingly emotional.

"You okay, brother?" Mattias asks. Maybe Anja didn't tell him about the nasty way I spoke to her. He wouldn't be so concerned if he knew what a dick I was to his wife.

"I'm fine. I mean, I'm not right now. But I will be. And I'm really sorry." I look from face to face to face. Mattias and Lukas are still concerned. Anja is still angry, but willing to forgive me. Mama A looks like she's trying not to cry. Constance is steady, and it soothes me to look at her. I have no idea what Juliana is thinking. It kills me that I don't know what she's thinking. But for the next few moments, I can't let her be the center of my awareness, because she's far from the only one I've hurt. She's far from the only one I'm *about* to hurt.

"I feel like I must have put you through hell this week, disappearing like I did. I wasn't thinking straight. I'm sorry if I had you all worried."

"Don't apologize," Mattias says. "Not to us."

"I need to. I need to explain myself," I say.

"It's okay, brother, really. We're all just... so happy you're okay," Lukas says.

Constance circles around the bed and sits next to me, her arm snug around my shoulder. "Was that paperwork for...?"

"Rehab," I affirm, then look at the other baffled faces staring at me. "The hospital runs an outpatient rehab program. I'm starting it immediately, so this doesn't happen again.

"I... I want—no, need to let you all know that I have no hard feelings if this isn't something you can handle," I say without a quaver in my voice. I've practiced these words over and over in my head as I signed every piece of paper Lydia put in front of me so I could get through them without breaking down. "I love each and every one of you, but I can't expect you all to stick around, not when it's gonna be hell. I don't want to put you through it. I just—if you guys choose to walk away, to not let me be a part of your family anymore, I need you to do it now. That'd be the best way, I think. For me, anyway."

Mattias and Lukas and Mama A look between one another, the looks on their faces so confused that they actually startle when Juliana says, "He's trying to give you all an out."

I startle, too. But Juliana knows my 'out' speeches. No wonder her voice sounds so bitter.

"No, I'm letting you *all* have one," I say to her.

The look she shoots back pains me. But I've thought about what Anja said this morning good and hard—if this isn't something Anja can handle, who's been through it before and knows exactly how hard this will be this time around, I won't—can't—expect any of them to sign up for this.

Lukas looks at his sister, then at everyone else before he stares me down, groans, and rubs his face. "Bullshit. Fucking bullshit."

"Lukas!" Mama A starts, but Lukas cuts her off.

"I'm sorry for my language, Mama, but no, *fuck* that. Fuck that. You're my friend, Ezra, all right? You're practically my second brother and I'm not gonna bail just because you're sick. I get it, all right? This is a disease, and you're about to start your own different version of chemo or something, so you're gonna be tough to swallow for a bit. But family doesn't bail because shit gets rough. I'm not letting you take off anywhere, no matter what you say," he says, his face defiantly set.

"You don't ever get to ask us to walk away, Ezra. That's not how this works," Anja says.

I feel sobs threaten to overtake my chest. "You didn't tell them what I did to you this morning, did you?" I say to Anja. "I made her cry, guys. I was angry at myself for fucking up and I took it out on her. Chances are good I'll do that to all of you, and hell, I might not even have the decency to apologize after. That isn't okay with me, but I know I'm gonna do it. It's only gonna get worse. I can't take it back, but the least I can do for you all is to keep it from happening again. And if I can't control the terrible things I say and do, I can at least control whether or not I see you."

"I did tell them," Anja says, and there's her significant look. "But I know why you did it. I can handle it. And it's not like you're going to be that way because you want to be. I know how this works, remember? *They* know how it works because of me. That isn't what I meant when I told you I can't be your sponsor, Ezra. It meant I want to be your friend more. We all do."

Mattias says, "Look, man, you're family. You're in my blood. I'm in. We're all in."

"We can handle you being an asshole. We can't handle you not being in our lives. Thanks for the offer, but no thanks. We're staying put. You're not gonna shake us that easy," Lukas says. He gets up out of his chair and leans down to embrace me. It's not an awkward guy-hug—it's a proper embrace. Before I know it, they're all doing the same thing, until we're a mass of limbs and IV lines and fresh tears on all of our faces. They've forgiven me, even though I probably don't deserve to be forgiven. It's extraordinary.

But when they all pull away, we realize that Juliana hasn't come any closer to us. And they can all tell that she and I clearly need a minute.

Mama A and Constance both kiss my temples and lead the way out the door. Everyone follows, and Lukas and Mattias joke that they'll kick my ass into gear later for giving them such a scare. It's as lighthearted as it can be when their sister is glaring daggers at me.

The silence between us is thick for a long, long time after we're alone. Then, "God *damn* you, Ezra Mackenzie. God fucking damn you."

"Jules...."

"No. You got to talk; now it's my turn. I was worried *sick* about you. We all were. I figured you just needed some space at first, so I wanted to give it to you. Then you went and broke your phone so no one, not even your boss, could get hold of you. You disappeared. You could have died on us, wandering around for three days while it snowed without a roof over your head. You could have gotten behind the wheel of a car and died on us, and I swear to God, I would have figured out a way to bring you back from the dead to kill you again myself if you had."

She's so angry that she's vibrating. I sit and take it. It gives me a minute's respite from being angry at myself for a change.

"You were going to break up with my family, so I guess you were gonna break up with me, too, huh? Just like that? Because you decided for me I can't handle it? That I can't handle you?"

"I don't want to hurt you," I say quickly when she pauses for breath. "I'd rather never see you again than hurt you over and over and over."

"I can handle a little hurt when it comes to you. That's what happens when you love someone. Can't you see that I love you?"

The tip of my index finger turns cold with the memory of dipping it into the snow collected on her car-share's windshield and writing that same sentence. It must be a coincidence—she never mentioned seeing it, so I assumed she never did. And yet....

"I want forever with you, Ezra," Jules says, her voice cracking around the edges. "I love you. I want you to wake up with you in the mornings, and fight with you when you're being stubborn and when I'm being irrational, and kiss you to sleep at night. I want bad Chinese food and pillow forts and cats you can't remember the name of. I want *you*. I love *you*. And if all of that means I have to put up with a nasty version of you for a little while then I'll take it. I'll suck it up. Because you're it for me. Do you understand that now? Just, please… don't scare me like that again. I thought you were gonna die before we got a chance to do all of that. Don't you dare scare me like that again, all right?"

"Can I talk now?" I ask, still trying to process her words.

"Yes," she snaps, though I can tell she doesn't mean to.

"You've never said 'I love you' to me before."

She chews the side of her mouth. "Of course I love you, you idiot."

"I love you, too."

If I could get out of bed and swoop her into my arms, I would. All I can do is reach out for her and pull her against my chest when she falls onto the bed with me. She curls into my lap and shakes with anger until anger becomes emotion and she starts to cry. I stroke her hair and tell her I'm sorry, and she in turn tells me to shut up and kiss her already. I tilt her face up and cup her jaw, then kiss her long and hard. Something begins to unfurl within my chest, making it easier to breathe. But then, it's always easier to breathe when I'm kissing Juliana.

We break apart only when we realize we've somehow tangled up my IV, and a little alarm blasts to signal a nurse. We untangle it, laughing from frustration and fervor, and then when the alarm stops, my lips are on hers again. Her arms are wrapped around my neck. She's here. *She's here.*

I could think of all the ways I don't deserve her, her forgiveness, her affection, her promise of forever. Her love. Especially her love. But I kiss her, again and again, and tell her in so many words (how many do you really need, though?) that I love her, too. That I have since I met her. That, lovesick fool that I am, I always will. That she is everything I don't deserve but have always wanted.

I've been sober again for about 24 hours. It's all just beginning, of course, but at least, oh at least, I have her.

CHAPTER FOURTEEN

You want to know something that sucks? Rehab. Rehab fucking *sucks*. I held out the vain hope that maybe it might not suck too bad by virtue of being an outpatient, and not being hounded all the time by overzealous nurses and orderlies. I was mistaken.

I detox first. I'm promised it won't be as intense, because I don't have many months' worth of stored booze in my bloodstream, but I feel misled almost immediately. I thought the days I spent detoxing the first go-round were the worst days of my life. I was, again, mistaken, because now I've been teased. My body had enough alcohol in it to remember how much it liked it, so the withdrawal is fucking brutal. My entire body shakes. My body temperature can't regulate itself. And I hate everyone, from the doctors and nurses who tell me I just need to keep going and it'll get better, to Mac who I (wrongly) blame for feeling like this. It's something like the worst hangover you've ever had in your life, combined with a stomach flu and vertigo. It's the sort of thing that would make any sane person never want to pick up a bottle again. Picking up a bottle again is all I want, though. If I could only have a drink or two, this feeling would go away. It'd be better—for a little bit, anyway. After what might be two days or maybe two weeks, I'm done and can go home. Which is another problem entirely. My apartment isn't anywhere near this hospital. Not only that, the first of the month is looming and I'm officially out of a job. I don't know how long it will take me to find another, all things considered. I have a little money in savings, but I have no idea how I'm going to pay my rent. I make an uncomfortable call to the leasing office and arrange to break my lease. They'll give me time to get back (literally) on my feet in order to pack up and move out. Constance has a spare bedroom she offers up to me without my even having to ask. We agree it's a temporary solution, because the only thing I want less than to be an unemployed loser going through rehab is to be an unemployed loser going through rehab *who lives with his mother.*

Once everything else is dealt with, I get to deal with something I find even shittier: living day-to-day, sober, and not being able to do anything but suck it up and deal. My rehab is your fairly run-of-the-mill Twelve Step variety, with lots and lots of therapy to boot. Sometimes I'm at the hospital for what seems like an entire day, for a morning group session and an afternoon one. Sometimes it's hours upon hours of one-on-one time with my randomly assigned shrink. I hate it, but wherever they tell me to be, I'm there. It all feels like a very long, very intense AA meeting that just won't fucking end. I'm angry and sad, and I hate myself for ending up here again. Being around Gemma, I have to hold in a lot of what makes me feel angry and sad, lest I terrify her. Perhaps that's why I'm so insular when I'm at my group meetings.

One of the treating therapists gives me a choice: be angry and sad quietly and live with the threat of another relapse because I haven't coped—or talk. And yell. And cry. Get it the hell out. Stop wallowing. Stop feeling sorry for myself. Talk, yell, cry, over and over, as much as I want to and need to.

I resist at first. The people in my group sessions are nice enough, but I don't trust them. I don't want to talk to them. It took me forever to find my footing when I started going to meetings with Anja… how do they expect me to open up and let all my ugly out for a room full of strangers to see? But the therapists reiterate their point again and again—I need to make the choice. Talk or don't talk. I still don't want to talk, but I have to concede that when it came to *that day*, not talking did a lot more harm than good.

I try. I offer a couple of reserved statements here and there, feelings that aren't really feelings but reflections of what everyone else is putting out there. It's enough to get my shrink off my back, but mostly I still keep my eyes trained on the ground when someone begins to yell or sob during group therapy until a counselor applauds them for their bravery and tenacity and encourages the rest of the group to do the same. I do notice that whoever it was that had that breakdown (break*through*? Damned if I know) seems… lighter the next time we meet. Less edgy. Smiles a little easier. I envy them that, because I'm tired of being sad, and I hate that I'm so angry.

I couldn't even tell you who it was in group that made me snap, but it finally happened. I yelled. Screamed, really. I told whoever it was that if they honestly thought they're the only one who felt like shit all the time they could go fuck themselves. That every single one of us is having a long series of the worst days of our lives.

The counselor and everyone else blinked at me for a long, awkward moment.

"Sorry," I said, suddenly much, much calmer. "That's just… how I feel."

It's really weird to have people applaud you after you've called them all assholes. But apparently, that's some sort of progress.

The next time I talk, I have a little more control over my words. The time after that, I have even more. I find I like talking to some of the people in group more than others. I decide I like people in group a lot more the more I open up and allow myself to know them. We're all different, but we get along surprisingly well. We understand one another in ways most of my friends and I just quite can't. As the days go by, things *do* start to get easier. Not all the time, of course. There's plenty of crap moments, moments I wish were hazy and muddled with booze-goggles so they wouldn't upset me so much.

But I've made my choice. I talk. I scribble in a sketch book and find I'm not too terrible at drawing. I take the medicine they give me. I reach out to Anja after weeks of near-total silence and accept what she can do for me, and what she can't. And for now, that's to continue to keep her distance from me while she forgives *me* for the rotten things I said to her. I get a new sponsor. I remember I'm not only doing this for me—this is for Juliana and the rest of my family, too.

Slowly but surely, it starts to make sense.

***

After a few weeks, my leg comes out of its cast, and on the very next weekend, Jules, Mattias, and Lukas agree to help me pack up and move out of my apartment. I'm honestly afraid of what I'll find when I step back into my apartment. Jules and I get there before the rest do, and she holds my hand while I approach the front door. My key fits smoothly in the lock and turns.

"Did I leave this open when I…?" I hate to ask her such a painful question, but I know she and Anja and Mattias came over at some point the day I took off and found the place a wreck.

"Mattias got to the door first. I'm not sure."

I look around. "I'm surprised my TV is still here."

"Looks like maintenance came in to take care of your window."

It's true; they have. There's not a shard of broken glass anywhere to be seen. That seems strange, since I've never known the maintenance department to not half-ass anything they've ever been in my apartment to take care of. This is the same bunch of guys who left moldy drywall in my mop bucket when they came to fix a leak in my bathroom ceiling.

My eyes flit around the unusually tidy unit (Jules doesn't have to tell me that she and Anja cleaned up while I was in the hospital—I know it instinctively), and my heart lurches when I see the cat's bowls. I look at Jules' feet. If Birdie were here, she'd be twining around her ankles, mewling pathetically.

"Still no sign of her," Jules says, reading my mind.

I shake my head. "There was one cat who looked a little like her when I called the animal shelter, but it was a boy. They told me they'd call if she turned up, but...."

"I'm sorry, sweetheart," Jules says.

"She wasn't mine. She never felt like mine. But the least I could have done was take care of her for Mac," I say, pressing down the thick lump in my throat the best I can.

"You did, though. Sometimes cats run off and you can't find them. Try not to beat yourself up over it, okay?"

She was the one piece of Mac I had left, I think. And she was probably torn to shreds by a coyote.

"You could still find her. You've got the Craigslist ad up still," Jules says, but I can tell by her inflection she doesn't really believe it. She wraps her arms around my neck and holds me there for a long time, and I give myself permission to cry into her hair.

When she pulls away a few minutes later, she wipes my cheeks with her thumbs and kisses me. She has a soft, tentative smile on her face. Juliana always has a smile on her face for me, even when I don't deserve it. I wish I'd noticed that more, before.

"I love you," she says. "It's going to be okay."

She holds me again, and, honestly, I can't and shouldn't ask for anything more than that—those three words are so much more than I probably deserve from her.

In the minutes we have before the guys arrive, we put on a pot of coffee and pack some of my clothes, a few books, my computer—the basics I'll need for the interim at Constance's house. A portable storage unit will be dropped off in a couple of hours for everything else so I have it out of the way while I figure out where I'm going next. As we're stripping the bed and folding up my towels, Jules starts to mutter to herself. It's clear there's something else on her mind, and I have to pester her to figure out what it is.

"I was just thinking about how you were hardly ever here, except to feed the cat."

"Well, it's kind of a dump, isn't it? Your place is nicer. Plus, it's easier for you to get to work from there than from here."

"Constance's is so far…."

"It's not that bad from your place. Now that I can drive again, I can come by more often."

"Is it weird for Constance, you staying nights away with me?"

"Um… I'm pretty sure she realizes I'm an adult with a girlfriend and a sex life," I say, although the last bit stings. I haven't spent too many nights with Jules since I was released from the hospital. I'm on a slew of meds for my recovery, and they're kinda killing my sex drive. She hasn't said anything to imply that it's been tough on her the nights I stay over and just drop off to sleep as soon as we climb into bed, but I feel like a rotten boyfriend for it. Once I'm a little farther along in the program, they'll ween me off and I'll be back to normal. For whatever normal means for someone like me, anyway.

"Are you really not getting what I'm suggesting here? I feel like I'm being kind of obvious," she says, her eyebrow quirked at me.

I open my mouth to reply, and that's when I get it. "*Oh*. I... Um. Are we ready for that?"

"Are *you* ready for that? 'Cause I would have asked you weeks ago, but I wasn't sure you'd go for it. I want to help, Ez. I want to see you be successful. And it sucks not sharing a bed with you."

She does the thing where she scrapes her bottom teeth along the Cupid's bow of her mouth and turns it red. I go to her and wrap my arms around her waist. "I love that you want to help. But I don't want to be a burden or something you have to take care of all the time. I have to learn to take care of myself."

"So learn to take care of yourself at my place. I'm not asking because of what happened, I'm asking because I want you there. You were practically living there before—what'd be so different, really? I want forever. Maybe this is how our forever starts."

What is it about the word 'forever' when it comes across her lips that is so thrilling? A warmth settles in my chest and she tucks in closer to me and presses her lips to the patch of skin under my ear.

"Please?" she asks.

I reply with a feverish kiss that I hope tells her everything.

***

Later that evening, as I look over the apartment now empty of all but the one thing I'm leaving behind, Mac's voice echoes in my head. Not in the bad sort of way something haunts you. The sort of way that's comforting, soothing even.

You never take your broom when you move, Ezra, he told me when I was ten. Dylan and I had managed to pack up all of our things from our bedroom, and Mac was claiming only what he felt was his out of the kitchen cupboards. He'd wrangled my help in packing some cleaners and detergents as our very last act in the house. On impulse, my hand had wrapped around the broom handle. Mac had shaken his head at me until I put it back where I had found it. I'd asked him why.

You leave your broom behind for the people who come next who have to sweep out your memories, Mac had told me. I was confused, but I obeyed all the same, because why question Mac? We left it for Constance, double- and triple-checked the security of the trailer hitch, piled into the car, and left.

Jules creeps up behind me and slips her arms around my waist. She presses her lips in between my shoulder blades through my shirt, and I tuck my arm around her shoulders when she moves to snuggle into my side. She smiles at me in that lovely, soothing way only she can.

"The guys are on their way to Goodwill with the stuff you didn't want, and then they're going to meet us at my place. We'd better get going."

I nod, but my legs aren't ready to move. Even though I'm leaving it on shaky terms, leaving this place feels right. I'm ready to leave this apartment and all its drunken, terrible memories behind and forge a new, clean life with Jules. But this place was still home for a long, long time.

"You're not having second thoughts, are you?"

"I'm not, I promise," I say. "I'm just caught up in my head."

"You want another minute?" She nods towards the door.

"Just one."

"I'll go get the car started then." She kisses me on the tip of my nose, but I pull her in for a proper kiss before she leaves. When she's gone, I rub my palms along my arms where I feel goosebumps pebble up and down my flesh.

Mac helped me move into this place. He sat with me while I signed my lease, he made trips up and down the stairs, lifting boxes I shouldn't have packed so heavy with a smile on his face like nothing could have made him happier than to move me into my own place. This was the first—the only—place of my own. Dylan had moved out years earlier, so maybe it was just that Mac was happy I was finally growing up. Maybe he was just proud of me. I'd like to think it was the latter, even when I think back on how he kept catching me taking nips of my flask throughout the day. He hadn't said anything—thinking back, he never did when he caught me drinking—and averted his gaze. I wonder if he'd looked away to pretend he didn't see, or to keep me from seeing that, in those moments, he wasn't so proud of me after all.

"I'm really sorry," I whisper to the empty room, like Mac is there, Birdie purring on his lap in between hissing at me. "I'm trying to do better. I'm *going* to do better, I promise."

I must stay wrapped in my thoughts longer than I realize, because Jules taps on the doorframe and nods over her shoulder.

"They've already dropped off the Goodwill stuff and they don't have a key to my house," she says. "I don't want to rush you, but…."

"Sorry. I'm good now."

I turn towards the door, still trying to banish the image of Mac from my head when Jules strides across me towards the kitchen.

"You forgot your broom," she says as she picks it up and makes to bring it out with her.

I grasp her by her forearm and shake my head. "You never take your broom when you move," I tell her.

"What? Says who?"

It's been ages since Mac, Dylan, and I moved out of my mother's house. But still, why question Mac?

"Said Mac." It's all I need to say. She nods and twines her fingers in mine, then we leave my apartment—and all its memories—behind.

CHAPTER FIFTEEN

The same sort of thing happens the first few nights I live with Juliana. We'll be settling in for bed, me working through some of the reading and journaling exercises that my group counselors want me to do, Juliana rubbing what seems like mounds of cocoa butter into her skin, and I'll start to want her. I'll want her so badly it aches. Or, at least my head does. My heart does. Anything south of that is a no-go. This seems both unfair and messed up, because I'm only twenty-six. Other than being a hopeless drunk, I'm healthy. So why the hell can't I get it up to make love to my amazingly gorgeous girlfriend?

She'll smile at me, slip between the sheets, and read until I'm ready to turn out the light on my side of the bed and hunker down. She'll roll around a little in bed, trying to get comfortable around my weight next to her, I suppose, and then end up touching me somehow. Usually she wedges her fingers under my arm or torso. Sometimes she rolls all the way over and nestles her head in the crook of my arm. Eventually, I'll gather her in my arms and we'll fall asleep that way, absorbed in each other in all ways except the way I'm craving most and can't get myself fully geared up for. I could chalk it up to being tired—it really is amazing how tired you can be when you literally do nothing all day but think about not drinking—which is actually thinking quite hard about drinking. But there's a niggling sort of feeling I can't quell that there's something else going on, something in my brain chemistry that's affecting me physically.

But she's unendingly patient, this girl of mine—she seems content with these little touches, with this sort of innocent bed-sharing. It helps me feel a little less useless, and a little less bothered by my uselessness.

A very little bit, anyway.

***

It doesn't take more than a couple of days to unpack my things. On the day I finish once and for all, I'm finding a place for my kitchen stuff when she gets home from work, a scowl set deep in her face and her shoulders hunched up to her ears.

"Rough day?" I ask.

She mutters something that sounds vicious, even though I don't understand Portuguese. This is where most boyfriends would pour her a glass of wine, but she's thrown away anything in her house that has any alcohol content whatsoever—even her NyQuil and rubbing alcohol. Instead I make her a cup of tea as she launches into a tirade about a new solar panel sales rep her company is working with who seems like a good guy, but has a bad habit of taking credit for ideas that aren't his. I slip off the precariously high heels strapped to her feet as I sit on the ottoman and listen. She falls silent and her jaw hangs open when one of my knuckles finds a tender spot in the arch of her foot.

"I'm not venting so you'll do th—oh!" she yelps when I move a fraction of an inch.

"What, it's not like I do anything else all day, other than search job ads and roll on my foam roller. You might as well get something out of me being your man of leisure."

"You're not a man of leisure. You're recovering and that's important," she says, a little too seriously.

"I'm trying to add a little levity to your day, Jules. Let me rub your damn feet before I forget how to do what I was trained to do."And maybe I don't want the reminder of my recovery, but I won't say it out loud. I already know I've got to get moving in an hour or so if I want to make my AA meeting at the church across the street.

She's a little less enthusiastic with her complaints as I work up into her always-tight calves, and her words fall away entirely once I knead her muscles into mush. I scoot her legs off my lap and curl into the chaise next to her. She lolls her head on my shoulder and grins up at me, like she hadn't been tempted to kill the sales rep in question twenty minutes ago.

"How do you do that?" she asks, her voice dreamy.

I shrug. "How do you calculate carbon emissions acceptable for minimum environmental detriment?" Not a bad phrase to have memorized for a guy who barely made it out of high school.

"No, I mean… The massage felt good and all, and my feet feel better, but I'm not feeling so nasty now. That was you."

"Oh. Well. I don't know what to tell you on that," I say, because it's true. "I'm glad, though. It's good to know I'm good around here for something."

Her scowl returns. Clearly I'm not as good as calming her down as she says I am.

"I hate it when you say that sort of stuff about yourself, you know. I know you think you sound self-deprecating, but it worries me."

"Jules, I haven't worked in almost two months. Literally all I do with my time is read the classic novels I lied about reading in high school English and go to my rehab sessions. I *am* sort of a loser right now. That's not exactly up to interpretation. It's just true. I can't even—"

I stop. I wonder if she knows what I'm about to say, since she's more than aware of how useless I've been in bed in the weeks since my relapse.

"You're not a loser. You're brave. I see how brave you are, even if you don't. It frustrates me that you don't see it. It really does."

I hang my head. "I don't know what to tell you, honey. I'm sorry you're frustrated with me."

"No, it's not... You're just... I don't...." She's cute when she stammers, but it's unnerving when she's stammering because she doesn't know what to make of me.

"I'm gonna head to my meeting. I can pick us up food on the way home, if you'd like," I say, because yeah, I want to get out of this weird mess I've managed to make since she got home.

"No, it's all right. I'll cook. Have a good meeting."

She doesn't send me off with a kiss, which sort of hurts. I palm my cigarettes and stalk down the street, smoking two in rapid succession before I let myself into the church basement meeting room and find a usual spot near the back. I'm prepared to sit there and stew, which is usually all I do at these meetings despite my new sponsor, Ryan, pushing me to open up.

After the opening salvo, when everyone begins to look around shifty-eyed to see who's going to be the first to speak up about their day, their week, their year or whatever, I feel this strange wiggling in my feet. It's not just that I'm antsy to leave so that I might be able to set things right with Jules again, although that's a part of it. I can't seem to stay still in my seat. I want... I need to get up. The problem is, if I get up, everyone is going to assume I'm going to be the first one to talk. So I'll have to get up and talk, and let out all the crap in my head about how useless I feel, how I keep sliding backwards instead of pummeling forwards, how I can't seem to do anything right. And we've heard that story over and over again, day after day after week after week. It's not *the* prevailing theme of an AA meeting, but it's certainly one of them.

I think that's when it clicks. I'm not the odd-man-out here, just like I'm not the odd-man-out at rehab. I can talk about what's going on in my head here, and these people aren't going to judge me like I judge myself, like I'm worried everyone is always judging me, because it's the same sort of stuff that's going on in their heads.

My feet wiggle again, and I stand. There's that sort of hush that comes over a group of people when someone is about to be the center of attention, and I clear my throat.

This particular group doesn't employ the standard, "I'm Whoever and I'm an alcoholic," you see on TV, which is one of the reasons I prefer it over other meetings. You can say your name or not. At the moment, introducing myself doesn't really feel necessary. Instead, what feels necessary is this:

"I just… I feel like I have no idea what I'm doing. I fucked up two months ago and I've had to start all over again. And no matter how many people tell me I'm doing everything right, I still feel like I have no idea what I'm doing."

My brain turns on autopilot, and my words just… flow. I don't remember half of what I say as soon as I say it. I don't realize I've even stopped talking until people start clapping for me and a few people I've always thought of as strangers get up and ask if they can give me a hug.

I'm not special. I'm just like everyone else here. And that, in fact, might be the best thing to be.

***

Me: Look, I know we aren't talking right now, and I get why… I just wanted you to be the first to know I spoke in my meeting tonight. About the relapse. About everything going on right now.

There's a long pause in which I can actually smoke two

whole cigarettes before Anja texts me back. Then:

Anja: So how do you feel now?

Me: About a billion times lighter. I wish you'd been there. I feel like you would have been really proud of me. I'm pretty proud of me, too.

She doesn't text back. Instead, she calls, and she's sobbing. We're on the phone for a long time, apologizing to each other about how much of a mess we've been lately and telling each other we love one another. It still stings not having her as my sponsor, but I have my best friend back.

That means more than I can possibly say.

***

Juliana is still in her work clothes, her feet stuffed into a pair of fluffy bunny slippers while she stirs a pot of something hardcore spicy—some sort of red bean mixture, I figure, given the pot of rice on the burner next to her.

"Go okay?" she asks, not looking up from her rapid stirring.

"I talked about the relapse."

This gets her to stop stirring and look up and me. Like Anja, she understands the significance of this. That this is one of the biggest things my counselors and Ryan have been harping on me to talk about since it happened, to deal with it fully and put it behind me. I don't think I can be blamed for not wanting to talk about the day I flushed all my progress from the last year down the drain in one fell swoop, but I kept saying I wasn't ready, I didn't know when I would be ready.

It had poured out of me like water at the meeting. I could barely believe I was the one talking.

"That's a good thing, right? That's what they've been wanting you to do."

I nod.

"That's awesome, Ez. I'm really glad to hear it." Her face is a full-on smile, but her lips twitch, like she wants to say something else and doesn't quite know how or what. Instead she goes back to stirring the pot.

"Jules, put the spoon down a second."

"It'll burn. What's so import—"

I cut her off with my mouth on hers. My fingers find my way into her hair to guide her face towards mine, and I back her up against the counter nearest the stove. My body presses hungrily into hers, and I can feel her hesitate a moment before she sinks into me.

There's freedom in talking, a lightness that only comes when you get your bullshit off your own chest and out into the ether. It weighs your heart down less and gets you out of your own head. When I stepped through the door, all I could think about was Juliana and how much I want to be worthy of someone like her. I have so far to go in that respect, so much work still to do before I'm anywhere near good enough, but finally feeling like I'm trying and succeeding—it stirred something deep in my gut and set my body ablaze. And I think she's the only way to truly quench it.

I pivot her into the bedroom, not even bothering to turn off the burners on the stove before I sweep her into my arms. She doesn't hesitate helping me out of my clothes as I tug on hers, and only when we're both naked do I feel the full weight of everything that I said, every admission of my mistakes and fuck-ups, truly melt away.

"I love you, Jules," I say, and lay her down. My body melts into hers as soon as I lower myself on top of her, finding any and every inch of skin to kiss and worship as she hums my name in return with sweet, melodic grace.

It's the first time since that aggressive, stupid moment in the cafe bathroom we don't use a condom—she's gone on the Pill since I moved in, and feeling her, every inch of her, is heaven. Everything about us in this moment is perfect and infinite. There's something different about the way we make love. We don't hold anything back. She knows she can finish me when she gasps into my ears how much she loves me, and she holds me when I'm shaking with aftershocks of pleasure and struggling to catch my breath. For a second, I think about how much I love her and it scares me. You shouldn't be scared of how much you love someone, but I am with her, a little bit. She didn't ask me to love her—she only asked me not to give up on us. To give us the future we deserve together.

That, I tell myself over and over again, is what I'm doing. We're giving ourselves a chance, and I'm giving myself one. We're aiming for forever at the same time I'm aiming for 'better.'

CHAPTER SIXTEEN

It isn't even all that long after that revelation at the meeting that I feel things begin to slide. I go on a few job interviews, but I am apparently too honest in my interviews, because people don't seem to want to take a chance on an addict who hasn't even earned back his three-month chip. I hear a lot of "You do great work; call us when you're a little more stable," and "Shouldn't you be focusing on your recovery?"

I think my luck is turning around when a chiropractor decides to bring me on full time, and seems utterly unfazed by my admission, my meetings and group schedule, and my lack of personal clients. I'm literally putting together a website and business cards with her office's information when she calls at the last damn minute and changes her mind. This sucks even more than the people who'd told me thanks-but-no-thanks from the beginning. And I think I'm understandably bitter about it, all told.

Jules says the same thing, but far more delicately. It's no secret that an engineer is going to make more money than a massage therapist, but I'm not used to the idea of not contributing financially at *all*. We strike a bargain that I'll keep the house clean and cook—well, more like learn how to cook anything besides pasta and rice. At least that keeps me busy while she's at work.

Still, I'm not sure how Jules can stand me being around all the time. When she gets home from work, I practically pounce on her—not even in a sexual way, but in the sort of way one craves human contact after being alone with one's thoughts. And with her projects at work ramping up, I get the impression that some nights she just wants a little peace and quiet. So, with the weather on its way to balmy, I get back into running and become uniquely acquainted with the library nearby, so she can have some time to decompress,. Only half the books I check out are on addiction, if that's interesting to note.

There isn't anything wrong with our relationship—at least, I don't think there is. We don't bicker, we make love as often as Jules has energy. And she always seems to have energy. We go on day trips into the mountains with Mattias and Anja or play soccer in City Park with Lukas and whomever he's dating at that particular moment. Lukas and I have become closer, too, since I'm free during the weekdays and he tends to work mainly nights and evenings. When Anja and Mattias buy their house, it's the five of us who paint the place from floor to ceiling and decorate for their housewarming. The three of them come up to our place for dinners as I figure out how to mill about the kitchen and not start fires. We dine with Mama A every Wednesday, even if I take care of our laundry during the week as needed. And the longer I'm sober, the more I realize other sober allies are important—Constance is slowly becoming my mom, not just my mother, and Gemma has gotten so attached to Jules as to call her 'her big sister.' I'm still not sure the kid really realizes that I'm her big brother, but that's neither here nor there.

We seem like any other couple, with friends and family we love, and a little rental house that is slowly becoming less hers and more ours. We're playing house and playing it well. And I'm only an asshole, like, forty percent of the time.

... maybe forty-five.

So it shouldn't surprise me the day Jules, strangely quiet and pensive all day long, looks over at me and says, "You really don't remember anything about the days you were out of it?"

I look up from my book and probably pull some sort of real goober-face. "No, I remember plenty. I did it for years."

"Not before we met. Your relapse."

My mouth falls open in a little O, and I think very, very carefully about what it is I want to say.

"Honey, I haven't given it a whole lot of thought. Other than as what it symbolized, I mean. To tell the truth, I don't know if I want to know what all I did. I doubt I'd be very proud of myself."

"But you'd have remembered if you'd done anything really, really terrible, right?"

"I don't know," I say honestly. "I still don't remember how I broke my leg."

"Oh. Right." She's twirling loose strands of her hair around her index and second fingers, pulling the locks so taut I have to wonder if it hurts.

I ask her if she's okay, and she flippantly says 'yes' and goes back to her own reading. I stand up to head out onto the front porch to smoke a cigarette, and feel a momentary sense of relief at not being grilled. I don't know what's gotten into her, but something's off, no matter what it is she's saying.

So I ask her again when I come back inside. She double-taps the corner of her tablet to place an electronic bookmark and sets it aside.

"I'd just been thinking about something, and I'm sure it's stupid. But I was thinking about you and that girlfriend of your brother's...."

My throat goes dry.

"… and I guess I just figured that maybe if you'd been so out of your mind as to, you know—do what you did then—that maybe you had been those days too, and you just don't remember it."

I run my knuckles along my jaw, trying not to clench it hard enough to break teeth.

"Jules, I'd never, ever cheat on you, if that's what you're thinking."

Her silence and the way she looks down at her lap confirms that that'd been *exactly* what she was thinking.

"I don't get where this came from," I tell her. "Why would you think I'd do that?"

"I know you wouldn't," she says, pointing at me. "But you've said that when you drink, you aren't really, you know… you."

Frustrated, I rub my hands on my face and shake my head. "This seems really unfair, Jules. Like you're accusing me of being unfaithful when you know how much I love you. And I don't think I deserve it."

"I'm sorry," she says with a faint sigh. "It just had been something I've been wondering about. I know it's not fair. Can we forget it?"

"Sure," I say, although I know I won't be able to, and neither will she.

Even more distressingly, I have no idea whether or not she's possibly right.

***

It's Anja's birthday, and the five of us are going out to celebrate. Jules is working late, but we're going some place literally down the street from our house, so we all decided it made the most sense to meet here and walk over there together. I'm used to having the place to myself, but there's something different about today I can't quite put my finger on. I went to AA earlier, I jogged, I finished a book I'd really been enjoying. But something is really, really bothering me.

We haven't talked about Jules questioning me about my relapse days, like we said we wouldn't. I know I'm not the only one thinking about them, though. It probably says a lot about me, and a lot about the asshole I am when I'm drinking, that I still can't answer her initial question—no part of sober-me would even look twice at another woman. Why would I, when I have literally the most gorgeous, amazing girlfriend I could ever hope for?

But I get what's bothering Jules, because the same thing is bothering me—I don't remember what happened. The whole terrible clump of days is lost to my memory in quite literally the worst blackout I've ever had. But something in my gut tells me if I had done that, even thought about doing *that*, I *would* remember. I'd beat my own ass over it. I'd remember every terrible moment and know what a scumbag I was. My gut, of course, has never been all that reliable, but I want so much to believe that about myself.

I take a long, hot shower to shake out the cobwebs in my head and get myself together. I step out, put a razor to my cheeks to shear away a couple of days' worth of stubble, then get dressed. Jules has already laid out the dress she's wearing along with a pair of impossibly high, sexy heels. I don't have the versatile wardrobe she does. All I have are the same few button-down shirts I had at Christmas. *First new paycheck I get, I'm getting myself some new clothes,* I decide, if only to look a little more like a guy Jules would date.

I'm buttoning the shirt I decide looks the least bad up to my throat and start looking for where my ties might have been stashed when I see it. Simple white button-down. Breathable cotton. Crisp from starch, even though the last person who would have starched it did so well over a year ago. Tucked under the collar is the ugliest tie on the face of the planet: the tie Mac loved wearing to drive Dylan and me insane on

Thanksgiving because he thought it was the funniest thing in the world how much we hated it.

I yank Mac's shirt off its hanger and press it against my face. I move the fabric around and around, taking deep, not-so-steady inhales as I go.

No... no....

I'd been at an AA meeting when Jules had unpacked the last few of my boxes. She'd texted me that she'd saved one for us to unpack together to officially make the place ours. It'd been the obligatory junk box—I hadn't even thought about the box that had lived under my futon. I wasn't even the one who carried it out of my old place or into this one. It had been amongst a couple of things Lukas had asked me where I wanted dropped off. I'd said the storage closet, and forgotten about it. Apparently, Jules hadn't.

I search the house for the rest of the box's contents. The cookbooks that had been in with the shirt are on the squat bookshelf in the corner of the kitchen. I can't believe I haven't noticed them there before right now. The photo albums made it onto the shelf above her desk along with some of her own. She'd tried to mix our stuff together seamlessly, make it all belong together like it was always meant to. But not *this* stuff. This stuff... No. It shouldn't be any where near our stuff. This stuff is special.

Anja's voice lets me know I'm no longer alone in the house. "I could do your makeup before we go," she says, obviously to Jules.

"You stay away from my face with your chemicals, woman. It's your birthday, not your wedding day," Jules replies.

I step into the living room, still shaking. All four of them are there, but I only see Jules.

"You... You hung this shirt up?" My eyes feel like they're about to bug out of my head as I hold the offending garment up to her.

She quirks her head as she looks over Mac's shirt in my hands and nods. "Yeah, it was getting creased. My iron crapped out on me or I'd have smoothed them out. It probably won't look so bad if you want to wear it tonight, but that tie is ugly as sin. I meant to ask you what possessed you to ever buy it in the first place."

I'd asked the same question of Mac years ago.

"I told you about this tie. I told you who it belonged to *that day*. Weren't you listening? How… how could you do this?" I hiss at her. My voice doesn't sound like my own.

"Hey, what's wrong?" Anja asks, stepping between the pair of us like she's still my sponsor. I step around her to get closer to my girlfriend.

"How could you do that, Jules?" I ask again. My voice is even more strangled.

Her eyes are huge in response and shock. She's looking at me like she doesn't know me.

"I thought it was just—"

"This was Mac's!" I scream. "I kept it in that box so it would still smell like *him*! And now it smells like *us*! It smells like your shampoo and my cigarettes and your fucking good-for-the-environment candles, and it doesn't smell like *him* anymore!"

"I-I'm sorry! I didn't know!" she yelps. I only half-see Mattias and Lukas stepping up next to her, their eyes challenging me to scream at her again.

But I can't stop. I can't stop, or I honestly would. "You did this with all of my stuff. You moved it all in like it's as much yours as it is mine. But it's not, got it? I might be mooching off you and useless to you for anything but a clean house and a decent lay but this shit is still mine, and I should have made the call about what to do with it. You should have asked me before you unpacked this stuff! *It smelled like him!* It used to smell like him and it doesn't anymore!"

"I'm sorry," she cries. "Ez, please, don't be—"

I throw the shirt down at her feet and my jaw clenches tighter and tighter. Then I feel pressure against my chest—Lukas's forearm presses me against the wall and Mattias's voice, ominous and threatening, booms in my ears. It takes me a long second to process how much being restrained by them hurts.

"Take a walk, Ezra," Mattias says.

I resist the urge to punch him in his smug fucking face.

"Fuck you. You don't live here."

"You're being a prick to my sister, and that doesn't fly in any house, period. Take. A fucking. Walk," Lukas practically picks me up by my collar and shoves me towards the door.

I narrow my eyes at all of them. Mattias and Lukas glare back like they're considering kicking my ass, as tears stream down Jules' face. Anja's eyes are darting frantically around the entire scene. I decide I don't give a shit and palm my cigarettes and slam the door behind me as I take off.

A storm is rolling in—the air feels electric and there's a musky, pre-rain scent to everything. I glare at the sidewalk as I stalk my way up the opposite way of the restaurant. I hadn't even thought to bring a coat, and the sleeves of my dress shirt aren't doing much to block the brisk wind that's whipping past. Maybe I should break out into a run, let endorphins cool my temper. My dress socks send my feet slipping in my shoes when I try. I stick to walking. That's how Anja catches up with me.

"Ezra, wait!"

"Leave me alone, Anja."

"No." Her heels clatter on the sidewalk as she catches up to me and grabs my arm at the elbow.

I jerk it away.

"I don't want to fucking talk right now," I snap.

She grabs my arm again. Her nails sink into my forearm through my shirt, a squeeze of their sharp pressure is all it takes to bring me to a stop and spin me towards her. "Fine. You don't have to talk to me," she says. "You just have to let me stay with you."

"God damn it, Anja…."

"No. No, a temper tantrum is not going to send you spiraling again, not when I can help. That's what this is, isn't it?"

A temper tantrum. I would never hit a woman, and especially not my best friend, but I definitely want to lash out when I'm being compared to a four-year-old.

"That belonged to my *dad*," I say, my voice breaking. "It smelled like him. It smelled like the terrible Castile soap he used and baby powder and the hot tea he always drank. It smelled like *him* and it was all I had left of him and it's *gone*."

"Scent doesn't last on clothing forever," Anja says sadly. "It can't possibly. You know that."

"If she'd left it in the fucking box, it might have."

"Where? Where you'd never smell it anyway?"

"You don't get it."

"What it is for a parent to be dead? No, you're right, I don't. My parents are still alive and just won't speak to me. Like hell I don't get what it is to lose them. And it's not like Jules and Mat and Luk have ever lost a father or anything. It's not like they know how much that hurts. She said she's sorry. She didn't mean to do it. Now snap out of it."

It does snap me out of it. Almost. Mostly. My shoulders slump and my heart stops pounding in my ears and when she opens her arms to hug me, I let her.

"Mother*fucker*," I say, my face buried in her hair. "Why do I do this? Why do I fuck everything up?"

She pulls away to look me in the eyes. "We're alcoholics, my friend. That's what we do sometimes."

The simplest answers are always the right ones, and the right ones seem like they're the hardest to swallow. This one is the one that makes me burst into tears, leading her to comfort me like she's comforting one of the little kids in her class. We find a place to sit down and she strokes my back to calm me down.

"We don't have to go back," Anja offers as a few fat drops of rain sink into our clothes. "Jules might need a little more time, too."

"You should," I say, nodding towards the direction of the house. "It's your birthday. You should spend it with your family."

"I am spending my birthday with my family, you dope. Now where are we going?"

"Not here."

"All right then," she says. We turn for my car and she links arms with me. "Not here it is."

**

"It's not like it's late," Anja reminds me for the fourth time since we sat down at the restaurant. "You sure you don't want to call Ryan? Get him to join us?"

"We're going running together in Wash Park tomorrow," I say. "I'll talk to him about this then."

When you're kicking yourself for freaking out at your girlfriend, who was only trying to be helpful and didn't mean any harm, and feeling every bit the asshole you probably are, nothing sounds appealing. But it's still Anja's birthday, and I'd already taken her away from her husband and family. We went to a movie she'd wanted to see that she couldn't convince Mattias to go to, we milled about a kitchen supply store, but we hadn't talked about my meltdown until we were both too hungry to ignore our growling stomachs any longer. Obviously nowhere lets you smoke inside anymore, but seated out on the heated patio as we are, we can both sneak long pulls off of Anja's vapor pen—I don't get the appeal of the device personally, but Anja made the switch while we weren't talking and won't come with me to smoke outside anymore because of it.

I know both our eyes poured a little too lovingly over the wine list before we each settled on iced tea. We have an appetizer on the way, but Anja isn't letting me off the hook any longer about what's really going on.

"The other day she asked about the relapse days. She wanted to know if I might have *been* with anyone while I was out of it."

She shifts uncomfortably at my admission. "That's a fair question, considering."

"I keep telling myself that no way would I have ever cheated on her," I say, finally giving voice to my own fears. "But I don't remember. Why the fuck don't I remember what I did?"

"You were so out of your right mind as to walk around with a broken leg bone," she says. "I know how it is to be that plastered."

"I didn't used to black out. Before. I have an eerily good memory of a lot of the stupid shit I did. It's fuzzy, but it's there. This not knowing is strange for me."

"It's been weeks, Ez," she says. "I have to wonder if you don't remember what all went on those days by now, if you ever will."

She drums her fingers on the tabletop and spins her phone around in a circle. Both of our cells have been quiet ever since we left. I figured Mattias would have texted Anja by now, wondering where she was, but if he has and I didn't realize it, she hasn't said so. "You were really angry at her for something that isn't ultimately that big a deal. Is that all that was upsetting you? That and her doubting you? I don't really think she means to be suspicious of you, I just think she still doesn't understand all the way."

"She's been with me for a while now," I say, exasperated. "I don't know how else to make her understand what a piece of shit I could be when I was drunk."

"Maybe you did, finally. Maybe that's why she asked the uncomfortable question. She's hyper-monogamous, you know that much, right? Even if it was just a kiss you remembered with someone else those days, she wouldn't forgive it, no matter what state you were in."

That feels unfair, but I know it isn't. I wouldn't forgive a drunken kiss if it were her doing it, either.

"I know I wouldn't have cheated on her," I say again. "But I can't prove it. And I'm worried her doubting me is a step towards something way more shitty."

"Look, I think the shirt was just a catalyst. I know you miss your dad more than I can understand—it's not surprising you relapsed on the anniversary of the day he died. But I think it was symptomatic of something else going on. And I think you need to figure out what that is—with or without me or Ryan or your group leader or whoever's help you're willing to ask for. Yes, you're in recovery, and that's hard on relationships. I snapped at Mat really unfairly a lot when I was in my early days, and I know it hurt his feelings. Jules is strong enough to take it, but you need to prove to her that it's going to get better if she sticks it out. A couple of good months and then a really nasty breakdown isn't going to inspire a lot of confidence in you."

It's hard to hear, but she's right. I'm set to open my mouth and reply when her phone trills. She picks it up and screws up her eyebrows reading it.

"Mattias?" I guess.

"Yeah. He and Lukas are heading home from your place now. He, uh… He said it might be a good idea for you to give her a little longer before you head home. I guess she's pretty mad you stormed off."

This doesn't surprise me. I know she hates it when I take off—she's told me that countless times before. And I know I hurt her, although I'm beginning to wonder whether I really underestimated just how badly.

"You can stay in our guest room...." Anja offers, but I shake my head.

"I'm gonna guess I'm not exactly Mattias's favorite person right now," I say, remembering how he stepped in between Jules and me, how furious he and Lukas were as they stared me down. They might be my friends, they might call me 'brother,' but they really will do anything they can to protect their sister. It's alarming that I became someone they needed to protect her from. "I'll call Constance and crash there. I think I've still got some clothes there, actually."

"Tell me you're going to be all right and not do anything irrational," Anja says. "I know this feels bad, but it's just a fight. If Mat and I could make it through everything we did, you and Jules have got to be able to, too."

"It was a fight I caused. One I picked. I hate thinking I hurt her in any way. I hate that I don't know what else I would have said or done if you guys hadn't been there to defuse me."

"You wouldn't have gone overboard. You were just upset."

"I don't know that."

"*Believe* it," she tells me.

But I don't. I'm seriously beginning to get scared that I don't.

***

It's too difficult to sleep without Jules in bed next to me—it's even worse when I think that not only is she not in bed with me, she's angry with me. I deserve her anger. I creep out of the guest room at Constance's house around two in the morning to make myself some tea to try and trick my body and brain into being tired. All it does is make me think more about what a mess I've made.

I don't know if I actually woke her, but Constance comes down not too long afterwards. I hadn't wanted to regale her with the story in front of Gemma, but now I find the words pouring out of me as soon as she sits down. When I've recounted the entire disaster, she grips my fingers hard with hers. "I'm sure she'll forgive you," she says, smiling at me and folding her hand over my forearm. "Women have a great gift for forgiveness."

"She didn't want me to come home tonight," I say. "I'm not so sure about forgiveness."

"It was one fight. Just one."

"It wasn't even a fight about the shirt, not really," I say. "I sort of wonder if I picked it because I wanted to prove her suspicions right, that I can't be trusted. That I'm too fucked up for her."

"Oh, darling, you know that isn't true," Constance says.

"She'll get sick of me walking out every time we so much as disagree on something sooner or later."

"Maybe. That's how things go sometimes, though."

I wonder if taking relationship advice from a woman whose addiction drove away perhaps the most loving man on the planet and lost custody of two of her kids to boot may not be the best of plans. From the way she falls silent, it seems like she's thinking it too.

"I can't shake the idea that she deserves better than this, Mom," I say. "She deserves better than me. I'm going to be so fucked up for so much longer and... I don't want to put her through this. I don't want to hurt her because I snap and take it out on her when she doesn't deserve it. I hate hurting her."

"You gave her the option to walk away, Ezra," she says.

"I wish she'd taken it."

The sentence hits me hard. I don't even realize what I've said until it's already floating in the air, impossible to take back. Do I seriously wish Jules had left me, given up on me? How can I possibly say that when it hurts so much just to breathe without her?

"I think Juliana is a wonderful person. And it's clear she

loves you very much. I'm not the best of examples of stable relationships, of course, but I can see you have something special. But I also know that feeling of not wanting to hurt someone you love. You may not believe it, but I felt that way about Mac. And about you and Dylan. I know I had a funny way of showing it."Even after it came up forever ago at that dinner at Mama A's, we still haven't discussed Mac or Dylan. We haven't talked about my growing up, the wicked things she'd say to us. The closest we ever got was that one night at the Almeidas'. Maybe I haven't wanted to watch her cry, because I know that's bound to happen when we really hash that sort of stuff out. Maybe I haven't wanted to cry in front of her myself. But knowing how drunk Mom always was, how not in control of her own faculties and what she was saying and doing, it surprises me that she'd ever have admitted to herself that the way she was treating us was wrong.

"You know, something has always bothered me, Mom."

"What's that, sweetheart?"

"You couldn't have been any less of an addict by the time Gemma came along. I mean, if anything, you'd have been worse off, right?"

"I suppose that's about right, yes."

"So… why would you get sober for her and not for me and Dylan?"

Constance studies her hands for a long time, and I wonder if my question is entirely unfair. But when I say it's bothered me, I really mean it. And as hurtful as it might be, I want an answer.

"I promise you, Ezra, it's not the simple answer you might be looking for. It's not that I didn't love you two enough or that I love Gemma more. It's just that I wasn't ready. And I think you know as well as I do that being ready is as big a part of this as any."

It makes sense what she says, but I don't like the answer

any more than if she'd told me it was because she didn't love me and my brother enough. It still fucking hurts.

I decide to be diplomatic. "I don't know what to say about that, Mom."

"You don't need to say anything. In the end, I chose drinking over my family, and that was terrible. The only good thing I did—maybe the only good thing I was capable of doing as a mother at that point in my life—was not fighting Mac when he took you two and left. I think you had a better childhood because of it."

I could say something snarky to that. I could say that, yeah, clearly I turned out so fantastic. An alcoholic by my mid-twenties, failing a recovery attempt, unemployed and mooching off my girlfriend and thanking her by being a temperamental asshole. I'm a real winner.

"I know the feeling of wanting better for someone than you can give them, Ezra." Mom swallows back the last of her tea and gets up to put her mug in the dishwasher. "Don't do anything rash, but think about it seriously. You'll know what the best thing to do is when it comes to you."

We say goodnight again, and I make myself another cup of much weaker tea, and stare at the cup for so long that the liquid turns cold. I don't sleep at all. I can't turn my brain off. As I toss and turn, I think about Jules, about us, about all the times we've said we want forever with each other. I desperately want forever with her. But as my brain spins, I find myself wondering if forever is good enough—for either of us.

***

I wait on purpose to return home until after Jules is off work. Having the day lets me get my head on straight. I go for my run with Ryan, I go to group, I smoke the better part of a pack of cigarettes and think everything through. I hit traffic on the way up, which only prolongs my thinking time. And the more I think, the more I certain I become.

I mull through my head the sort of things someone in my position ought to do before going home. I'm pretty sure flowers, chocolate, and at least one bottle of expensive wine are all supposed to be givens. But I know Juliana, and all three of those things would be hollow, insincere gestures that don't mean anything. Maybe another time not this close to my relapse, a bottle of wine wouldn't be the worst thing to offer. But then what time isn't close to my relapse? It may have been three days ago for how quickly and slowly these months have gone by.

I resign myself to the notion that nothing is going to help, find a parking spot, and head for our house. It's not surprising the front door is locked, but I drop my keys when the blade doesn't fit correctly in the lock on the first try. I think for a second that maybe she changed the locks. I try again and it turns smoothly in the cylinder. At least I have that much going for me. An empty bottle of what had been white wine is on the coffee table. There aren't any glasses, and my mind immediately goes to her drinking it straight from the bottle. It's distressing and also makes me want to gag, but that's the nature of white wine for me. No matter the severity of one of my cravings, the thought of white wine always makes me want to gag. I wonder if I ever told Jules that. Or maybe her choice in a bottle of wine had absolutely nothing to do with me.

She's reclined on the chaise, her tablet in her lap. Her finger runs along the screen every few seconds, her eyes flit across the words of whatever it is she's reading. Her shoulders are stiff and her spine is ramrod straight, a sure sign that she's noticed me come in even though she hasn't looked up. So yes, she's flagrantly ignoring me. And no, I don't exactly blame her.

I open my mouth, but the word 'Hey' dies on my lips. I duck into the bedroom instead. If she wants to ignore me, I can ignore her right back. It's not the most noble thing I've ever done, that's for sure.

I plug my phone into the charger on my side of the bed, then sit down and lie back on my pillows. Technically they're her pillows. Mine were old and a little ratty and didn't make the move with me. This is just the side of the bed I sleep on. I close my eyes and wonder if I could drift off for a few minutes before we face one another, but it's a pipe dream. My brain is still churning far too fast.

It might be just a few minutes and might be a whole other hour before she comes in and curls onto the bed next to me. Her legs are tucked underneath her chin. I'm sure if I tried kissing her or even just reaching for her, I'd get one of her feet to my chest. That isn't why I don't try, though.

"You can't come home twenty-four hours after a fight and go straight to the bedroom like you're expecting makeup sex, you know." There's anger in her voice even though I know that she doesn't want to be angry with me. I know her tone too well.

"I had absolutely zero expectation that you were going to walk in here and have sex with me," I say.

"So then are we going to talk about last night or just pretend it never happened?"

"Of course we're going to talk. I figured I'd let you decide to stop ignoring me first."

"I'm not ignoring you now." She sits up and straightens her legs out in front her so there's still a defensive perimeter around her. I deserve that sort of treatment.

I've been rehearsing what I've wanted to say for hours, but my tongue feels limp and heavy in my mouth. But thinking about what I want to say to explain myself and actually looking into those eyes of hers—damn those eyes of hers—are two completely separate things. She looks at me, her face expectant, and all I can do is stare back, my lips pursed and silent. *Way to be chickenshit, Mackenzie.*

"I get why you were mad. I'd probably have done the same

thing if that had been one of my dad's shirts. I get that you miss him. It's normal to miss him. But I didn't fucking deserve that, Ez. For the first time since I've been with you, you made me feel like dirt, and I didn't deserve that. Wouldn't you say I'm pretty justified being pissed?"

"I would," I say when my tongue starts working again.

"So are you going to say anything that will make me feel like you actually love me and feel bad about what you did, or do I just have to read between the lines and guess that that's how you feel?"

"I feel like an asshole, Jules. I *was* a massive asshole. And I am so, so sorry."

She relaxes a little, even shifts closer to me. "That's a start."

She reaches out like she's going to lace her fingers in with mine. I sit up and scoot away, because this is going to be so much easier if she doesn't touch me.

"You're right, Jules. You didn't deserve that. You didn't, Mattias and Lukas didn't deserve to witness it. Anja didn't deserve to have a crummy birthday because I was moody and needed a timeout with a chaperone. You all deserve so much better than all of my bullshit."

Her eyes narrow to slits, but she doesn't disagree with me.

"I was totally out of line. And I am really so sorry. But I can't promise you that I'm never going to be like that again. Or that I won't get even worse. It's getting more and more obvious that this isn't something I want to put you through anymore, regardless of how much I love you. And I do love you. I love you so much that it's killing me. And I do enough that should kill me all on my own."

"No," she says, barely waiting for me to finish my sentence. She gets it; I can tell by the way her face changes. "No, you don't get to offer me another out because you were mean and yelled at me. I already told you I don't want an out. Remember?"

"The out isn't for you, Jules," I tell her. "It's for me."

A breeze could knock her over. Fresh tears well in her eyes. Some well in mine, too.

"You deserve stability. And you deserve someone who can get up and go to work every morning without worrying about whether or not he's going to fall to pieces and set himself back at the slightest provocation. Don't you get how much better you deserve than me? How not good enough I am for you right now? I'm not good for anyone right now, and I think that's the problem."

"Ez, no...." Her voice is thick and and her eyes are dewy with tears I know she must be trying desperately to keep at bay.

"You deserve someone you can completely trust, honey."

"I do trust you."

"I think we both know that isn't quite the truth."

Her jaw trembles and she looks at me with so much sadness, so much pain etched on her face it makes my heart wrench. She has got to know what I'm about to say, and all I want is to say nothing and shield her from whatever pain this is going to cause. But I have to say it, because in the end, she's too important to me to keep doing this to her.

"I think I should move out. I think we should call this off, at least for now. At least until I get my head on a little straighter. I love you, but I don't know if we can do this right now. I'm so sorry," I say in a way I hope sounds final.

"No, this isn't... This isn't fair. This isn't what you're supposed to say right now."

"It *isn't* fair. But it's what's best, for you and for me. I want to do something right for once. I want to do right by you, and as much as I hate it, I think this is the right thing."

"How is it right if we're not together? How is that fair? I love you, I told you I love you. I told you I want forever."

"And I don't know if I can give you forever, Jules. I can give you a single day at a time. And you deserve better than that."

I can see the moment the weight of my words hit us both. It's like a pendulum has swung between us and severed the cord tying us to one another. If there is more to say, neither of us knows how. She begins to cry in earnest. I do, too. It's torture watching her cry. I'm reluctant to try to hold her, but when I do offer her my arms, she falls into them. Our bodies shake and we each take turns sobbing louder than the other. 'I'm sorry' and 'I love you' and 'I hate this' play over and over on our lips.

But it's over. It's really over.

***

She helps me pack a suitcase. I'll come back for the rest of my stuff when she's at work, because I know neither of us wants to relive this moment over and over again. The tears stopped several minutes ago. I know I'm doing more harm than good prolonging this any further, so I need to get going, and soon.

"You'll really be all right at Constances's?" she asks.

"Yeah, I think I will be. She and Gemma are all the family I have left. I should really get to know them better."

"They aren't the only family you have. And you know that wasn't what I was asking."

"I'll manage. There are plenty of places out there that I can apply."

"A little white lie won't kill you, you know. You don't have to be quite so honest in interviews."

"I'll keep that in mind."

We mostly clear out my drawers, but before we run out of room in the suitcase, we move to the closet. Her fingers linger over Mac's shirt and tie and her lip trembles like she might start to cry again.

"If I had known, I never would have…."

There's more to this than that, and we both know it. I loop

my fingers around her wrist to pull it away from the shirt, then tug it off the hanger and toss it in with my t-shirts. I'm guessing she won't want to see it while I'm still getting everything cleared out.

I'm zipping the bag up when I finally notice she's wearing one of my shirts. It's a long-sleeved thermal I've had forever. The cobalt blue color really doesn't suit her skin tone, but when we're home and lazing about, she steals it to curl up with. She's always cold, even in the heat of summer. She notices me looking at it, and moves to pull it off over her head. I shake my head to stop her.

"I don't need it. It's June—what am I gonna do with a thermal all summer?"

She folds her arms over her chest, like she's trying to hug the fabric. Her 'thank you' is almost lost for how quiet it is.

"I'll get everything out of here as soon as I can, I promise. Anything else like that," I nod again at the shirt, "you want, you can have. Just scoot it over to your side of the closet or fold it up."

"I can't have what I want," she says. It breaks my heart, because I can't, either. To break the moment, she clears her throat bravely and asks, "What are you going to do after you find a job and all that?"

"I dunno," I say truthfully. "Miss you, probably."

"Yeah, me too."

She inserts herself into my arms and holds onto my waist like I'm a life preserver. There's a finality in this embrace. I don't know when I'm going to see her again, but then, that's the entire point of a breakup, isn't it? It hits me like a painful, sudden heart attack: *this is our forever.* We're crying and miserable. This is our forever, because this is what's best.

"I always thought we'd end up like Anja and Mattias," she murmurs.

"Me too. I'm sorry we ended up being Ezra and Jules," I

reply.

She pulls away and brushes her fingertips under her eyes. "I need to run to the store. Will you… You won't be here when I get back, will you?"

"No. I'm gonna get my stuff from the bathroom and head out."

"Good. It's better that way. For me."

She doesn't leave like she says she's going to. Instead she leans towards me, and I cup her face with my hands. Years from now, when I think of the last time I kissed Juliana Almeida, I'll remember how her lips tasted of saltwater, how her eyes and her cheeks were puffy, how her mouth trembled under mine. And even though I had broken her heart, she still put her hand on my chest and said, "My family is your family. Don't you dare forget that. If you need to not see me for a while, that's fine, but they're *your* family, too. They need you as much as you need them."

I promise her I won't give them up. I think she knows as well as I do that I'd lose it if I lost all of them and her, too. When she turns and leaves, I know that so much of my own happiness is going with her, but that this is the best, the only way.

I walk out the door a few minutes later. The drive to Constance's is slow-motion and surreal. At some point I get a message sent to Anja that says, "I need to talk to you." She meets me in Constance's driveway, and before I can get the words out, she's hugging me and telling me how sorry she is.

She comes inside and holds my hand while I tell Constance what I've done and ask if I can stay with her for a while. My mother says yes, but then both she and Anja go silent, like neither of them know exactly what to say next.

As it happens, I don't want them to say anything.

***

Mattias: Dude, are you okay? I know Anja is with you right now but call me if you need anything.

Lukas: Just heard. I'm sorry, bro.

Voicemail: Mama A — 'Ezra, sweetie… please call me. Juliana just told me and… oh, sweetheart, I'm devastated for you both. Please call me, I just want to know you're doing all right."

Mattias: You're our friend. Please don't forget that.

Lukas: She's my sister, I know I said that, but we aren't choosing sides. She doesn't want us to. Call me when you feel up to it.

Mattias: Call me when you can.

Voicemail: Mama A — "You're still our family. You're one of my boys, always. Call me soon."

I can't face them knowing what I did to Jules, knowing how much she's hurting because of me. Anja comes by often now that she's out of school for the summer, and there isn't anything I can do to stop her. It's good to have her around, but as for the rest of them, I tell them to give me a month. A month feels like it ought to be enough time to get myself a little more composed, and hopefully not feel like I'm suffocating every time I think about Jules and how badly I miss her. I'm not sure I'll ever feel like I'm taking full breaths again.

Anja tells me Jules is all right, from what she can tell—not great, but getting by, like me. I tell her I'm not ready to hear anything more than that. She respects my wishes, and we find other things to talk about. My impending 'graduation' from my recovery group. Gemma, and how she's sort of my breath of fresh air, the little bit of salvation in this mess that at least I have a sibling again, and one who adores me to boot. The couple of private clients I have lined up, mostly thanks to Mom and some of the people at AA. The couple of false starts she and Mattias have had trying to start a family of their own.

Life goes on. It hurts. But I get through the days, and leave the most intense moments of my longing to when I'm alone at night. I wonder how I'll ever sleep in a bed Jules isn't in, because I haven't slept more than barely dozing in all the nights since.

A little under my requested month later, Anja's over hanging out with me, and hands me her vapor pen to take a drag off of. The nicotine juice inside is flavored like raspberry, and it makes me think of Juliana's favorite lip balm. I decline subsequent drags in favor of a proper cigarette and try not to blow the smoke in her direction.

"You're really coming to dinner this Wednesday, right?" she asks.

"I really am. I promised Mama A."

"Good. Having you there will diffuse things a little, I think. Mattias made the mistake of telling her about—" she looks significantly down at her stomach "—you know, and now all I hear about are these herbs she wants Jules to get from—"

I don't mean to wince, but Anja has been really, really good at not saying her name while we're hanging out. I already know Jules isn't going to be at this week's dinner, but it's been hard enough steeling myself for seeing her pictures on the walls, knowing I'm someplace that she shares, too, and is avoiding because of me.

"Sorry, Ez."

"It's all right. What about herbs?"

"I guess there's some herbs that only grow in Brazil that Mama used to take when she was growing up, and she swears they make you, like, super-fertile."

I study my cigarette as my defense against any sort of tell that this next sentence will hurt to say. "What would Ju— Juliana have to do with that?"

Anja sighs and blows a vapor cloud between her teeth. "She's… Well. She's down there. Right now, actually."

I look at her blankly, expectantly.

"She had some frequent-flyer miles saved up and needed to use them before they expired, and Mat and Luk hadn't been down there since before their dad died." (I know about the frequent-flier miles already—she and I were thinking about taking a trip as long as I was out of work and needed a distraction. We hadn't settled on where) "They thought Jules could use some company. Anyway, this was just this past week, and they were all meant to be back tomorrow afternoon... Are you sure you want to hear this?"

"Just tell me, Anja."

"She didn't tell the guys as much, but while they were there, she went to her old boss and asked to be relocated back down there. Mama and I... Well, we've been up at your old place getting her stuff packed up for her for the last several days. We sent off her last box yesterday."

My heart thuds hollowly. "Oh God... I chased her off."

"No! Ez, don't think like that," she says, but I can tell she doesn't believe I'm supposed to think any other way. "Mat said that she said that... Well, without you to come back to, it didn't feel like she had as much to lose back here."

"She has her entire family."

"She also has a house where everything reminds her of you, Ez. That's been really hard for her. She's been wanting to move, at least out of that house, since you took your last box."

It's not only hard to breathe, it actually *hurts* to breathe. When did Juliana become my only source of oxygen?

"How is that not chasing her off?" I ask.

"She needed a clean break as much as you did. I can't say I blame her. I think it's probably the best thing for her, though."

I nod my head and use the end of my cigarette to light another. Anja loops her arm around my waist and rests her head on my shoulder.

"Remind me again?" I squeak.

"This was hard," she tells me. "This was maybe the hardest decision you've made since you decided to get sober. But, Ezra, it was the right one. For both of you."

It's a rehearsed line, one she's been feeding me as steadily as nicotine the last few weeks.

"Then why do I still feel so empty? Why do I still feel like I want to curl up and die?"

"Because you love her. You wouldn't be you if you just stopped loving her at the drop of a hat."

She'll tell me this again and again if I ask her to, and I probably will. I know it will take what will feel like a lifetime to start believing her.

CHAPTER SEVENTEEN

I'm in the kitchen when Marta comes out from my treatment room, which up until a few weeks ago, was simply Constance's den. I'm not sure how her HOA might feel about me running a massage business out of her house, but Mom doesn't seem to care much, now that I'm working and making my own money again after so many months.

I hand Marta a bottle of water and survey how her shoulders have dropped. "How're you feeling?" I ask.

She beams at me, rolling her neck from side to side. Clearly it's not as stiff as it was when we started today. She stretches long for a moment, then begins to thumb through her purse. "Excellent. You're magic."

"I don't know about that, but I'm glad you're feeling better."

She pulls out her checkbook to pay me, but she doesn't have a pen. As I fish around the junk drawer to find one for her, she scans through her phone, probably checking the messages that vibrated through during her session.

"Severe snow alert tonight, can you believe it? Winter came so early this year...." she says as I hand her the only ballpoint I can find that isn't turquoise or neon green.

I think back to last year, to the early October storm that threatened to ruin Anja's wedding day, and think that this isn't so bad.

"Crazy," I say, only because Marta is clearly expecting an answer. "When did you want to come back?"

"Are you open this time next month?"

I scan through my calendar on my phone. "Sure am. Put you in?"

"Yes please. Oh... And would you be willing to work on my daughter when she's home for Christmas? She's been in a few car accidents and her neck is an even bigger mess than mine."

"Of course. Do you want to book it with me now?"

"Oh... I thought I'd give her your number and have her call. She hasn't decided whether or not she wants to drive or fly in yet. She's about your age; I'm sure you know all about that sort of indecision."

I grit my teeth and try to smile pleasantly. An extra session is still an extra session, even if it's obviously a thinly veiled meet-up scheme.

"Absolutely," I say, like I don't suspect a thing. "You can tell her to text me, too."

She practically claps with enthusiasm, maybe thinking I've been taken in by her blindingly transparent plan. To be fair, Marta is an attractive-enough woman, so if her daughter takes after her at all, it wouldn't be the worst setup in the world— once you set aside all the ethical issues of dating a client.

Not to mention that it's been months, actual *seasons*, since I ended things with Juliana, and I'm still not over her.

I walk her to the front door and watch her get into her car. The snow has begun to fall, but not hard. I turn back in the house and pull the linens off my table and stuff them into the washer. I have plenty of time to sit and relax before I have to pick up Gemma from ballet practice. I crack a window, light a cigarette, and prepare to make a cup of something warm when my own phone vibrates on the kitchen counter. I smile when I see who it is.

"Are you calling to yell at me too, Anja? Mama A did a pretty good job the other day of it…."

"You're damn right I am," she says, her voice all squeaky with obvious mock-irritation with me. "You have missed too many dinners, sir, and it ends this week. You're coming tomorrow, no matter how bad the snow gets."

"I'm sorry! I didn't think that I'd be this busy this month. I miss dinners with you guys, too." Working freelance like I am means I have to take any and every appointment I can get. And for some reason, all my clients seem to love coming to me on Wednesday afternoons. Anja's right when she says its been too long since I've seen her. We were meeting up at least three times a week, all of us, up until recently. I even missed her and Mattias' anniversary, which I swear I had no intention of doing. Maybe if I'd been with them celebrating, it would have meant fewer hours sitting alone, thinking about the first days Juliana was in my life for that brief, precious time before I ruined everything.

"So come tomorrow. You can crash there if the snow is bad. Hell, we'll put tire chains on your car for the drive back to the west side if we have to. I'm beginning to think you're avoiding all of us except Luk."

"Don't be dramatic. We have mutually antisocial schedules."

"I'll send him over to pick you up, then, since you're all of a sudden besties. We're thinking of moving dinners to mine and Mattias's place—does that work for you? It's at least a little closer to the highway."

"Yeah, of course. And I'll drive myself, thanks. Just make sure you and Mattias remember I'm coming over this time so I don't walk in on you guys trying to make a baby on the kitchen counter. *Again*."

"*Ass*. You didn't knock."

"I called you not ten minutes before I opened the door to tell you where I was."

"Yeah, but I didn't hear the ringer."

"I know. Because you and your husband were trying to make a baby on the kitchen counter. I at least had some idea of how you look naked from knowing you so long. I think Lukas is still traumatized."

"Oh my God, stop it!"

"Lucky me, I got to talk it over with my shrink… who did Lukas have to talk to about that trauma?" Technically, Linds isn't a shrink. She's a counselor. A grief counselor, if you want to get specific.

"Oh my freaking God, I'm about to un-invite you. Do you want to come over or not?"

"Yes, of course I do. But I wouldn't be me unless I was giving you a hard time, now would I?"

"No, I suppose you wouldn't—oh, I've got another call. I'm counting on you for tomorrow, all right?"

"Absolutely. See you then."

I make a large pot of hot chocolate and pour some into a thermos to take to Gemma. There's a tiny part of me that wants to call Anja back and cancel, but I don't dare. It's just the weather, I tell myself. I fell in love with Juliana in the snow, and I'll miss her every time it snows from now until I finally get over her. Maybe there's some sort of psychological term Linds knows that I don't.

I wish I could say I got better as soon as I started focusing on me instead of on my relationship with Juliana—but that'd be a bald-faced lie. I was a moody, insufferable bastard for a long time after I moved in with Constance and Gemma. For all the understanding Mom tried to have for me, after a few too many utter-shit meltdowns in front of Gemma, Mom gave me an ultimatum: find another way to deal with the crap going on in my head or find another place to live. Through a friend in AA, she got me Linds' phone number. I resisted it at first, because the last thing I wanted to be, in addition to being a twenty-something drunk living with my mother, was being crazy. Technically, I'm not—*crazy*, that is—but I do have a lovely little thing called a dual-diagnosis. Alcoholism and grief-related anxiety, to be exact. It all boils down to missing Mac, missing what our relationship lacked the last couple of years because of how I had to hide my drinking from him. When I tried to get sober without dealing with that grief, I failed. Now that I am talking about it, this second crack at sobriety is easier, or that's what I tell myself. Getting sober is still shitty. But at least I don't think and breathe missing my father as well as wanting a drink. As an added bonus, I barely go to AA anymore. I usually get what I need out of therapy twice a week and meeting with Ryan at the gym to lift weights and play basketball. I go with Mom to AA here and there, but I don't find I miss it or feel like I need it. I still hold my sobriety chips as sacred talismans, and I still murmur the Serenity Prayer in place of the Lord's Prayer at the church Mom and I started going to. I don't exactly think I believe in God, but I like the punk-rock, tattooed, recovering alcoholic pastor more than I like stuffy church basements and bad coffee and donuts.

So as reluctant as I am to be reminded of Juliana, I can't not go to dinner tomorrow. Not going would drive a wedge I don't want between the Almeidas and me. I miss them every time I don't see them for a while, and it's always good to go back, like being welcomed home—but it's different. It's strange without Juliana there. It hurts seeing her pictures, hearing her name mentioned, and knowing I have no reason beyond my own morbid curiosity to see how she's doing, meaning I have to keep my mouth shut. Maybe being at Anja and Mattias's will be easier, if I can manage to avert my eyes from the large group shot of the five of us from the wedding they have stuck over their mantel.

I finish my cocoa, put my mug in the dishwasher, and grab my coat. My car is plastered with snow when I step out onto the street. I lean in to get the engine running and grab my snow scraper. I dust off headlights, windshield, side windows, and move towards the back window. It's there I freeze in my tracks, because written in the snow are the words:

Can't you see I never stopped loving you?

***

The number I have dialed is out of service. My call cannot be completed. Check the number and try your call again.

I know the number is out of service. When your ex moves back to Brazil, her number gets disconnected or reassigned. You find that out when you longingly press the 'send' icon on your phone when you're thinking about her late at night and that's the outgoing message you hear. You don't have to be drunk to be desperate enough to make the call. I should know. I've been sober again for months.

There are alternative ways I can take this mysterious message, depending on how much I want to suspend my own personal disbelief. For example, I can just assume that the message wasn't intended for me. I do not have the only dark blue sedan on my street. There are plenty of others parked there on any given day. It could have been a mistake, pure and simple. Some other lover leaving a message in the gathered snow for someone who is not me. Maybe it was some secret admirer, hoping to leave a message less creepy and more romantic. It's a strange coincidence of wording and circumstance, but stranger things have happened.

Added to that, I'm still not sure Juliana even saw that note I left on the car-share vehicle all those months ago. She'd likely have mentioned it while we were together. Like when she said she loved me in the hospital after my relapse. The first time she told me she loved me, she used the phrase I wrote in the snow on that car-share's back window. But I was also hopped up on Dilaudid and Antabuse and too many emotions from too terrible a day at the end of a three-day bender, so I don't really know what I heard.

As I'm trying to figure out the cryptic message left on my snowy car, I get a message from a strange number that I realize is Marta's daughter. I'm impressed by how quickly my client got to work trying to set me up, but I still ignore it. I should never have discussed personal matters with Marta. Then she'd have had no idea I'm single, but not so recently single as to be opposed to the idea of being set up with someone else. Then maybe she wouldn't have tried to hint that she'd like to set me up with her daughter, who I'm sure is lovely but, at the end of the day, isn't Juliana. And it doesn't matter that I haven't seen or heard from her since last June when we called things off— I've come to the very sobering realization since our breakup that I am never not going to love Juliana Almeida.

This is what even thinking about this girl does to me. Nothing floating through my brain makes sense right now. Even just entertaining the notion of her being home, of her driving to my side of town and leaving me a message on my car that I would recognize… It strikes me stupid. I'm a mess. Juliana makes me a complete idiot. I loved being an idiot for her when we were together. Now it just hurts.

I've never been so glad to get one of Gemma's bear hugs and sloppy kisses when I pick her up from dance. She chats my ear off while I drive her home and make us macaroni and cheese for dinner. She's settled in with her homework by the time Mom gets home, and between helping her and cleaning up the mess I've made of the kitchen, I'm busy enough to keep my mind off the drink I so desperately want. I keep drafting a text to Ryan to tell him what happened, but I can't phrase it in any way that doesn't sound like me wanting it to mean more than it might. It might be a message better sent to Anja, really, but I don't send her one, either.

But still… I have a feeling that the solution of an incredible coincidence and mix-up of dark cars on a snowy street is not the answer here. Whether I want to or not—and I do want—and whether I'm ready and might never be, I'm going to be seeing Juliana again—sooner rather than later.

**

The snow isn't as bad as Marta's weather app indicated it would be, but I'm glad I don't have appointments to keep. I go to an early-morning meeting, because this is definitely an occasion that calls for it. I draft a long email to Ryan explaining the whole saga, but I don't get a reply. I call and bump my next appointment with Linds up by a day. When I can't stall leaving for Anja and Mattias's any longer, I grab an overnight bag in case I don't feel like driving back after dark sets in. I text Anja when I'm on my way, and ask her if there's anything she wants to tell me before I get there. If Juliana is in town, Anja will know—but when it's come to the fallout from the breakup, she's keeping silent on what Juliana is up to so as not to upset me. She doesn't reply before I'm on the highway, and I puff away on a cigarette as I drive. I'm still doing my best to ignore the niggling feeling in my stomach that something else is up, which sits heavier and heavier as my phone chimes in the front pocket of my overnight bag. I'm not risking totaling my car and killing myself to check a text message in this weather and this traffic.

I've pulled into their driveway and am reaching for my phone when I see Anja rush out her front door. She isn't wearing a coat in spite of the weather, and she rushes towards me when I get out of my car, but not in the way I expected her to greet me. She looks frantic and worried. I don't need to look at the phone to know the messages I have waiting for me are from her.

"I don't know if you should be here tonight, Ez," she says, forgoing any sort of welcoming hug when I step out of my car.

"Um... I just drove almost an hour to get here. Even on not-snowy, no-traffic evenings, I don't exactly live nearby, remember?"

"I know, I'm sorry. It's just... Oh, fuck it. Jules is back home. I didn't know when I talked to you yesterday, but she's staying with Mama A, and Lukas brought her over. She came in on something of a whim and she's... Shit. I can't tell you. But I don't know if tonight is the night you should find out."

My blood sluices cold in my veins, but I try to keep my shit together. I've wanted the validation the note on my car was what I thought it was since I saw it last night, but I also wanted to be in control of how and where I saw Juliana for the first time since we broke up. I can't keep my face straight enough and Anja figures me out.

"Did you know she was here? She told me she hadn't called you yet, but did she actually?" she asks.

"She didn't call." I suck in a breath of cold air through my nostrils and try again to get my nerves in check. "If she came tonight when you'd, I assume, told her we had plans, then I guess she wants to see me?"

Anja looks flustered. "I'm not sure Lukas gave her a choice."

"What? Why?"

"I really don't know if tonight is the night," Anja says again.

"It's fine with me," I say, even though it's anything but fine. "Look, I had to see her again at some point, right? I'll stay out here and if she'll come out real quick, we'll get the awkward part out of the way in private."

Anja shakes her head. "Ez...."

"It's okay, Anja, really. If it still feels awkward, I'll head home so you can all spend some time with her while she's back in town and I'll see you guys next week or whenever. But we're grown-ups, right? We can be civil and polite to one another." I'm trying to convince myself of this as much as I'm trying to convince her.

"Ezra, I'm telling you, this might not be the best way to…."

She's cut off by the squeak of the front door. That's what initially draws my attention, even though Juliana could get my attention if she were silent and appeared out of thin air. She'll never lose that indescribable way she can draw me to her, that thing about her that drew me to her at the very first moment I met her. She invades my every sense all over again, and I'm actually delirious looking at her.

She sighs and sort of half-waves to me. "Hi, Ezra," she says.

I'm about to wave back, and then I notice everything that's different about her. Her face is fuller than I'd last seen. Her breasts are heavier and her gait is saddled. It's the sort of gait a woman has when she's….

"I wanted to tell you," Anja murmurs. "I was trying to warn you without telling you because it wasn't my place to say anything."

Anja is right. The only person who should be telling me that Juliana is pregnant is Juliana.

***

I can't stop staring at her stomach.

I've seen plenty of pregnant women in my life—I got certified in prenatal massage when one of my favorite spa clients got pregnant three years ago. But I've never known one so personally and intimately as I know Juliana. I've always thought of it as endlessly fascinating—a spine forming organs and a brain and flesh until it's actually a tiny human. An amalgam of two people, however imperfect and flawed they might be, transmuted into a small creature that gets a fresh start. Alcoholics are very, very interested in fresh starts.

Anja leaves us alone and I stagger up onto the porch. Juliana leans against the railing and watches me staring at her belly. The question hangs between us unasked, unconfirmed.

"When are you due?" It's the most sensitive way I can think of to get the confirmation I need.

"End of February."

This can only mean one thing. A million thoughts battle in my brain at once, but not one of them makes it past my lips.

"I've wanted to tell you," she says, her voice nervous. "I drafted emails, half-dialed your number. I even wrote out a postcard that I tore up before I put a stamp on it 'cause I'd actually written, 'Hey, by the way, I'm pregnant and it's yours.' I was so far away. And I was hurt. And honestly… I didn't know what I was going to do."

My mouth is dry. Maybe more than I have any other moment since my relapse all those months ago, I want a drink.

"When did you… How did you…?"

"I *didn't* know when we were still together, if that's what you're wondering. I didn't find out until after I moved back to Sao Paolo. I figured I was late because of the stress of the move and tired because I was sad over the breakup, but I wasn't sick at all so I didn't even put two and two together. I didn't find out for sure until I was a couple months in. And then I just didn't know how to tell you."

"You were on the Pill."

"I guess there's something to Mama's theory of the women in my family being super-fertile."

"I guess so."

"I'm sorry. I know I messed this up."

"Yeah, well, coming back here after you started showing certainly is one way of telling a guy you're having his kid." I'm a lot meaner than I intend to be, and wasn't that exactly why I left her to begin with? To keep her from the dark, craving, asshole version of myself? But then, I'm not reacting this way only because I'm still dark, craving, and an asshole. I think I sort of have the right to be a little pissed over this. "So... congratulations."

She throws her hands up and rolls her eyes. Sure, *I'm* being sarcastic and kind of petty, but I don't know where *she* gets off being exasperated. She wasn't blindsided with this like I was.

"I was *always* going tell you. But you were the one who wanted space and distance in order to avoid screwing me up while you fixed yourself. I wanted to respect that. But cut me a little slack, huh? Because this wasn't how I ever intended for this sort of thing to happen. Being single and pregnant and hopelessly in love with the father—with a guy who didn't want me anymore—is about the worst way I can imagine doing this."

As soon as she says the words, I can see her face change. I can't tell if she wants to pluck the words out of the air and take them back, or shove them down my throat. I'm not sure it would hurt as much if she actually punched me in the gut.

"I don't know what to say," I say. "I never meant to ruin you."

"That's just it, Ezra," she snaps. "You didn't. You wouldn't have. I wouldn't have let you. And this—" her hands fly to her belly "—didn't either. But that didn't stop me from being scared out of my mind!"

There are words on the tip of my tongue that I have to force myself to bite back. They're the sorts of things you can't take back once you say them. They're the sorts of words I broke up with her to protect her from, to protect me from feeling rotten about later. And there is a just-rational-enough part of my brain that knows how unfair they are. So I take a lesson I should have learned ages ago and keep my mouth shut.

It strikes me that she isn't wearing a coat. I shrug mine off my shoulders and go to her. She allows me to wrap it around her, but we keep a careful distance between us. My forearms brush against her. She's actually radiating warmth. Pregnant women tend to do that, as I recall. She smells the same, only more intoxicating. Even when we're furious and snapping at one another, everything about her is enticing. Perfect, even when she's flawed. I realize now she's a lot more flawed than I've ever given her credit for being. She always seemed so together in comparison with my own mess that she struck me as perfect. But now that I see her as scared and vulnerable and decidedly *not* together, I feel the pang in my stomach all over again that is the pang of wanting her. I want someone just as fucked-up as I am. Instead of saying as much, because how would that possibly go over, I go back to staring at her stomach.

"Look, I don't want anything from you you aren't able to give me. You don't have to choose this. If you can't handle it, you can't handle it." She clasps her belly protectively. "I'll respect whatever you decide. And I won't think any less of you one way or another." I think she means it to be freeing for me. A way to liberate me of culpability if I decide I can't have anything to do with her or…. She's giving me permission to continue using the out I crafted for myself, even though the stakes are higher and harder to swallow. She's endlessly noble, my Juliana, even when it means sacrificing so much at her own detriment.

"When are you… You're going back to Sao Paolo, or are you…?"

"I took a leave of absence. My maternity leave will kick in soon anyway—it's longer down there. But I don't know what I'm going to do after the baby comes. I don't know if I want to go back. I haven't decided anything yet."

After the baby comes. After our *baby comes.* Because even if I chicken out, it's still the baby she and I made together.

"So you might stay." There's a hopeful edge in my voice that obviously confuses her.

"Mama wants to help, of course. Mattias and Lukas are

pretty pissed I kept this from them for so long, if that's comforting for you at all, but they'll help too. I don't know if I can do this all by myself, at least not at first. So yeah, I think I need to be close to home. I think that'd be best. And it gives you the option to be involved. If you want to be, that is."

There hasn't been a moment since I last walked out of the house in LoHi that I haven't wanted Juliana in any and every way. And maybe there was some tiny part of me that always thought that if I ever had kids, I'd have them with her. But this isn't something I'd ever have bargained for. This is so much bigger, so much more real, and it's one more thing I could screw up so, so easily. And it wouldn't just be her I'm screwing up anymore.

"Can I... Is it unreasonable for me to ask for some time to... just figure this out?"

"No. I expected time. I can give you time," she says graciously.

I look nervously towards the house, half-expecting Anja, Mattias, and Lukas' faces to be pressed against some window watching us. They aren't, but it doesn't really set my mind at ease at all.

"I think I should take off. Seems like it's a night for an Almeida reunion...."

"You've always been an honorary Almeida, you know, Ezra. Even before this—although I guess, by blood at least, this really makes you part of us now."

My eyes drop away from her stomach to the ground. "I always wished I had Almeida blood. My Mackenzie blood is pretty fucked up. It seems almost unfair to wish it on a...." I don't know why I can't say the word.

She shrugs the coat back off to give it back, but I shake my head. I'm eerily not cold. Frantic, sure, but not cold. I turn to march down the three little steps to my car, but I have to check one more thing before I go.

"You didn't tell anyone until you came back? Really? Not even Mama?"

She shakes her head. "I wanted you to be the first to know. I figured I owed you that. That didn't happen, I realize, and I'm sorry. But I wasn't going to ask you to come pick me up from the airport."

"I would have done it in a heartbeat."

"I know. That's why I didn't ask."

I look at her belly again, but I'm not staring.

"Do you know yet if it's a... what gender it is?"

"Yes. But does it matter right now?"

"No. I suppose not."

"I won't rush you, but please figure out what you need to sooner rather than later, Ez, okay? 'Cause what you decide is going to change a lot of things and February doesn't feel that far away when it's snowing."

I fell in love with Juliana on a day it snowed. On another, she's asking me to choose to be a father or not. It was only a year ago—how can so much happen in so short a time?

"I'll think as fast as I can," I tell her. "Tell them I'll be back, though. Regardless of what I decide. I'll be back even if it's just to say...." I don't want to say the word 'goodbye.' But if I choose to walk away from Jules and this—our—baby, I'll be walking away from the entire family for good. I'm not going to get to choose one or the other any longer.

"They'd never expect anything less, Ez."

She lets herself back in the house as I slide back behind the wheel of my car. My tires spin as I pull out of the driveway and head down the street. My mind goes the speed my car can't safely travel in the snow, and I know I won't be able to slow it down. Maybe not ever.

CHAPTER EIGHTEEN

Lukas: Dude, I'm sorry to spring it on you like that.

Anja: Are you okay?

Mattias: Call us if you need to talk about this. We're all pretty pissed at her, too.

Lukas: I wasn't going to let her chicken out of telling you any longer.

Anja: I'm sorry again I didn't tell you.

Mattias: For whatever it's worth—I think you'd be a kick-ass dad.

My friends are magical. But I don't drive back or take them up on talking. Sometimes the only way to really suss something through is to think about it on your own.

***

I drive slowly, without purpose or direction. The snow is still coming down, and it's taking more oomph from my windshield wipers to keep it clear. My defogger can barely keep up with how high I have the heat cranked versus the cold outside. I find myself really missing my old place, as rundown as it was, because at least it would have been a place to brood by myself where I wouldn't be expected to sit in just one place. I'm not quite ready yet to go home and tell Mom what's happened. I think that will make it a little too real, a little too tangible. I drive past about a dozen bars and notice them all. I give myself exactly one minute to be proud of myself for not swinging into one and drinking myself into oblivion. It's an achievement for me, even if it's just a tiny one.

It hits me all over again: Juliana is having a baby. Juliana is having *my* baby. Even though I know it's a real and true statement, it feels so foreign. It feels a lot like remembering that I'll never see or hear Mac again. And I'd be lying if I said anything but this: I don't know if I can handle it.

It's not my addiction or my recovery, as much as those are the easy, convenient excuses. Maybe the truth isn't all that much better. But, damn it, it's all I have to work with. I don't know how to be a father in a world my own father isn't in.

When I thought about it in the past, it was something nebulous and intangible. Once, right out of massage school, a girl I'd been seeing had had a scare, but it was quickly resolved as an incorrectly taken test. Ever since, it wasn't something that was any sort of imminent threat, so why concern myself with it? Now that it's not nebulous and is very, very tangible, I'm scared out of my mind. Because in a world without Mac, who am I going to ask questions of when I get confused or start screwing up? Juliana will have Mama A, but both of our fathers are dead—so who do I get *my* sage advice from? Who tells me what to do when whatever instincts people are supposed to have when it comes to their kid fail me? How am I going to deal with him or her when I have no one to turn to?

I worry so much about this because, honestly, most of my memories of Mac don't feel real anymore. Half of it is the natural progression of someone's memory—your childhood years becoming duller and more vague, which is normal, I know. But the other stuff, the memories that should be the freshest in my mind because they happened more recently, are all fucked up. I feel like I've already begun to forget Mac, because I spent the last few years avoiding spending a lot of time with him so he wouldn't see how bad my drinking had gotten. The time I did have with him was hazy in the way my drunken memories all seem to be. So how the hell can I try to be a father myself when I barely remember the one I had?

I'll bet Dylan remembers everything. He has a great memory. But whatever he remembers, whatever words of wisdom our father told him and not me, or us both that I don't remember, is off-limits. *He's* off-limits to me now. And the more I think about it, the more I realize that he'll be off-limits to my kid, too. And that's really sucky to realize. It strikes me that I have, at best, half a family to support and love this kid. Juliana has Mama A, her brothers, *and* Anja. How do Mom and Gemma compete with that? How do *I* compete with that? Linds is going to have a fucking field day with me next time I go in to see her, I swear to God.

My car starts to skid as my thoughts continue to race, and I throw the parking brake on. Only then do I realize where I am. I must have gone into some forgotten sort of autopilot, and driven myself some place that used to be reliable and safe. The place the man I've been dwelling over called home before he died.

Mac's old house isn't much to look at from the front, though it's got a certain charm with a fresh layer of snow on it. He'd done a ton of work on the inside after we moved in. Mostly little things like painting and replacing doorknobs and handles on things at first, but later, when he had more money, the appliances and the counter tops. He even made the two little rooms Dylan and I each ended up with into one massive room by knocking down a central wall. By then we were fifteen and hated the idea of sharing a room, but it grew on us. Mac said it would build character and a bond between us. I suppose he wasn't entirely wrong about the character part, in a way.

My car idles in front of it until I see the light in the living room snap off. It's getting late, so whoever lives there now must be heading to bed. I wonder if he or she is married. Maybe has a kid or two of their own, whose toys clutter up that massive room like my junk did for the longest time. Maybe their partner hates the kitchen, the work of keeping the stainless steel appliances wiped clean of fingerprints. Maybe they both love it. Maybe they don't so much cook as much as they 'experiment,' like Mac always did. Maybe they hung up a pot rack in the same place Mac did.

Maybe... maybe....

It strikes me that of all things I don't remember, I do still remember Mac's phone number. It was a simple pattern of threes, zeros, sevens, and nines that in my head will always be his, even though his voice will never again be on the other end of it. That still hurts—hurts the way it did the first day I realized it. I used to be able to drink away the hurt. Now I have to breathe that pain in and out until it subsides. Maybe it's one of those things that never will.

I flicked the windshield wipers off while I idled, and it's gotten cold enough that the snow has started freezing. Before I have to get out and scrape and increase the odds of some hyper-vigilant neighbor calling the cops on the weird guy in the idling car, I turn the wipers on full blast and release the e-brake. This is never going to be the place for answers. At least, not anymore.

"Please tell me what to do," I whisper anyway as I drive off, like maybe Mac hopped in my passenger seat when I wasn't looking. "Mac, what the hell am I gonna do?"

Fairmount Cemetery, where Mac's buried, is only a few miles away. Despite the late hour and snow, I'm tempted to drive there. Maybe if I stand at his grave long enough, some corporeal version of him will appear out of nowhere and point me in the right direction. I used to think people who talked to headstones were nuts, but I can see now where they're coming from if they have the same fleeting thought as me. It could work. Maybe I'll catch a mysterious witching hour and I won't just be talking to the falling snow.

The thought is every bit as ridiculous to me as it probably is to anyone else, but I cling to it all the same.

My phone trills a minute later. I want to ignore it, but I at least check who it is. I expect Anja, maybe Lukas—it's my mom. I push the button to turn on speaker and answer with a gruff, "Hey, Mom."

"Sweetheart, are you okay? Are you on your way home?"

"I… I don't know."

"Anja called me. She told me you didn't stay there after all because… Ezra, is Juliana really pregnant?"

"Yeah. She is."

Mom pauses. The silence is thick and telling. Then, "You should come on home so we can talk. Or go back to Anja's and talk to her."

"No offense, Mom, but I'm not really ready to talk about this with you. Not yet."

"What about with Ryan? He's over on that side of town, why don't you…."

"Mom, I don't need to be fixed or babysat right now. I just need time to think."

I try not to get terse with her, especially not after everything she's done for me the last few months. But dear God, do I ever need her to just back the fuck off.

"Ezra, I think this is something really big and really scary and you can't stew on it on your own. You need to talk to someone. This is a huge decision. I'm just trying to help."

"I know, Mom. But I can't talk to you right now."

"Why not?"

"I'm driving. I need to focus. The weather's bad. I'll be home later, all right? Don't wait up. I'll see you and Gem in the morning."

"Are you sure? Sweetie, I…."

"I'm okay, Mom. I'm not going to do anything stupid. I promise."

She finally lets me go, and I surrender my body to autopilot again. When I come to, I'm at a bar. All my hard work to avoid a place like this, and my car is idling in a spot right in front. So much for my promise to Constance.

It's cold. My car is running on fumes. That's why I go in, or so I try to rationalize. It's cold outside, warm in there. I sit down—the place is almost empty, it being well past the hour any functional adult would have paid their tab and gone home to bed, so I get served right away. I order a plain Coke, nothing in it. There's a couple of tough-looking guys playing pool in the corner, an older woman at the other end pulling off a vapor pen when the bartender isn't looking. What I don't do is order a drink. My self-preservation astounds me.

The bartender asks if I want any food before the kitchen closes and I shake my head. I sip the soda, the bubbles rolling across my tongue, and drain it so fast I give myself a brain-freeze. I stare at the empty glass until the bartender refills it. I must look crazy enough that he doesn't question me. I find a fixed mark to stare at. I'm probably the quiet, vaguely creepy guy at the bar, but my brain is anything but quiet.

You couldn't be a father if you tried. You'll fuck it up, like you fuck up everything, one half says.

Juliana needs you. She needs you to pull your head out of your ass and be there for her, argues the other.

You're too selfish to do that, aren't you?

You could be as good a dad as Mac was.

You'd never be as good a dad as Mac was.

"Shut up," I say to myself, pressing my palms hard on the sides of my head. Doing that has caught the attention of the woman at the far end of the bar. Yep. Definitely the crazy guy at the bar.

I don't realize how much time goes by until the tough guys finish their game of pool and leave. The bartender asks if I want anything else for last call. The woman mutters something to the bartender I can't hear, and a second later, a single glass of whiskey appears in front of me.

"From her," he says, and jerks his thumb at the woman with the vapor pen.

My mouth waters. My brain continues to scream so loud I'm shocked no one outside my head can hear it.

I grip both glasses in my hands. Then I toss back the soda, push the whiskey back towards the bartender, and throw a twenty dollar bill on the counter. When the bartender reaches for it, I say, "No change, thanks. And don't charge her for that."

I don't look the woman in the eye before I stalk out of the bar. I don't even dust off my windows before I rev my engine and drive off. I can navigate my way towards the closest gas station mostly by muscle memory of the area, and fill up my car with shaking hands. They tremble a little less from alcohol deprivation as I pump my gas and more from the cold that I'm only now really feeling with this much distance from the bar. I remember I gave my coat to Juliana, and I fish out the sweatshirt I brought to sleep in and throw it on before I get back in the car.

The cemetery is gated. I have to park off the street and walk up and down the fence line, looking for a gap large enough to squeeze through. An apartment complex shares a part of the fence, and it's easy to hop over a low patch there. It takes a minute to get my bearings, but the yellow glow of night snowfall lights everything beyond the gates enough that I manage to stumble my way down the unshoveled walkways without slipping. I get turned around twice, and have to duck down once to avoid the glare of headlights near the street so I'm not seen. But I find Mac all the same. Half-drunk as I might have been, I buried him. He's always been right where I could find him—it's just that I've only now thought to come and look.

I sink to my knees in front of his headstone and dust off the snow to see the engraving. My jeans are soaked instantly, but the cold is gone again, replaced by something else.

If I'd taken that shot of whiskey, it'd be that deceptive warmth that drinking gives off, even as it's dilating your blood vessels and making you colder. But I didn't take that drink. This is something else entirely. I settle in, content to talk to him for a long, long time, to make up for all the talks we never had, all the visits I haven't paid since he's been gone. Except it takes me forever to form the first few words.

"Hi, Mac... *Dad*. Hi, Dad."

***

It's early, maybe too early, when I trudge up the pathway to the front door at Mama A's and ring the doorbell. They must be disoriented at having an early-morning visitor, considering the sun isn't even up yet. I ring it twice more because I'm soaked and cold and kind of in a hurry to be let inside where it's warm after spending more hours than I realized I had at the cemetery. Juliana pulls the door open, huffy, tired, and beautiful.

"I move a little slower these days." She's bleary-eyed and her shoulders are sagging, maybe from carrying all her weight up front. She's wearing that cobalt blue thermal shirt. It was always too big on her back then, but now, with her belly distended as it is, it rides up past her belly button. I want to ask her how often she's worn it since we've been apart, but that sort of small talk isn't why I'm here. I like that she's wearing it.

I like the way her hair is kinked around her face when it's tousled from sleep, too. A rush of longing surges through me before the gauntlet—the one I spent all night thinking about, talking to dead people at cemeteries, talking to myself at a bar like I've lost my damn mind—falls.

"I'm not marrying you because it's the 'honorable thing' to do," I blurt out before I can stop myself. "Honestly, I don't think it's all that honorable anymore. It's the twenty-first century, and it's not like I defiled you. If Mattias and Lukas want to come after me with pitchforks, let them. But I'm not marrying you just because you're pregnant."

She blinks rapidly and shakes her hair out of her face. "Get in here; it's freezing out there. Are your pants all wet? Where the hell have you been all night?" She looks me up and down, and I swear she even sniffs me. "Ez, please tell me you didn't...."

"No. I'm stone-cold sober. And, um, cold. Very cold."

"Get the hell in here already then, you idiot."

She stands aside and shuts the door behind me, but I'm the one who decides on the kitchen as our destination. There's almost always water and grounds in Mama A's coffee maker, so a quick push of a button is all it takes for a pot to start brewing. I'm running on zero sleep and lots of questions, so it doesn't really occur to me until after I hear it percolating that coffee is one of those things pregnant women aren't supposed to have.

She hoists herself onto a barstool at the island and I lean against the stove while the coffee brews. She rubs her sleepy eyes with the palms of her hands and leans forward. "I didn't ever expect you to marry me because it's the honorable thing," she says. "No matter how much I still want you, Ezra Mackenzie, I wouldn't say yes if that's why you were doing it. I'd only want you to propose if your heart was in it. And I've stopped pretending that you'd change your mind and start wanting me again."

"Are you fucking kidding me?" I ask, agape. I shiver in earnest. "I *never* stopped wanting you. I've wanted you from the day I met you. I'll probably want you until the day I die. I called it off because I was scared of how much I wanted you. I wasn't any good for me so I knew I wasn't any good for you. It broke my heart to say goodbye to you. Please tell me you've at least suspected that all this time."

She smiles a misty sort of smile. It's so lovely it's everything I can do to not surge across the island and kiss her.

"I'm still no good for you," I say instead. "I want you so bad it hurts. But I'm rotten for you. Look what I did to you. I may not have defiled you, but I sure as shit fucked you up. That was what I was trying to prevent and I did it anyway."

Her face drops. "You didn't fuck me up. You didn't ruin me, or my life. Birth control pills aren't foolproof, and we both know it." She storms out of the room and I think for a second maybe she's storming off for good, going up the stairs to shut me out. But she's back a second later with a throw blanket and a spare hoodie that lives near the front door in case anyone ever needs it draped over her arm. She shoves both at me. "Get the hell out of those wet clothes before you catch hypothermia, if you haven't already."

I peel my jeans, shirt, and socks off, pull the hoodie over my head, and wrap the blanket around my waist. She takes my clothes from me to throw in the dryer and our fingertips brush. There's a familiar electricity in that tiny, brief connection that I know she feels, too. While she tromps to the laundry room, I help myself to a cup of coffee and sip, letting the caffeine and warmth curl through my body.

We're silent for a while when she comes back. "I just want to be honest with you," I say. "You're talking to a guy who has no idea about what and how it is to be a father—"

"No one knows how to be a parent, Ezra, for fuck's sake," she snaps. "*No one.* Do you think our parents, any of them, knew the first thing about what they were doing when we came along? If you think they had it all figured out, you're deluding yourself. People who actually plan for this don't even know what they're doing. Don't use that excuse on me. You're better than that."

"Can I finish my sentence, please?"

She purses her lips, sits back, and crosses her arms. Instead of over her breasts, they wrap over her belly now, and I wonder who it is she's really protecting—herself, or the baby.

"What I was saying was: you're talking to a guy who doesn't know how to be a father. But the one thing he has going for him was that, once upon a time, he had a really good father. I was thinking about that last night after I left Anja and Mat's house. I drove around and thought about it. I thought about Mac and what kind of guy he was. I don't remember everything, and I'll never forgive myself for forgetting as much as I have, but what I remember about Mac was how wonderful he was. I guess that's normal, you know, when someone's gone, only remembering the good stuff. He was just so giving, you know? Everything he did, he did for me and Dylan. He gave us everything he could without spoiling us. He was proud of us, even when I didn't deserve his pride. But it hit me at last that if I have nothing else to offer you and this child, then at least I can offer you that. I had Mac. Maybe I'll be able to figure it out even half as well as he did."

Her lips part, like she's going to say something else. I don't let her.

"I'm in," I tell her. "I want this baby with you. I'm in for him or her. I want you, too, of course I do. I don't know if we're ready for that again, and maybe we won't ever be. But I want this baby with you, and I'll do everything I can to make his or her life as wonderful as Mac made mine. Us we'll figure out later. If you're okay with that, at least."

She nods, and sighs the way someone does when they're

trying to keep themselves from crying. "You can stop saying 'his *or* her.' I know what it is, remember?"

My heart gallops in my chest. "You gonna tell me now?"

She purses her lips. "You're really in? You don't need another few days to think about it? One night wasn't a lot of thinking time."

"I haven't thought about anything else since I left Anja and Mat's place. It was enough. I'm sure."

I circle around the island and search for her fingers with mine. My hands are still cold, or maybe they just feel that way with how she's radiating warmth. "I also didn't say hello to you last night, not really. So: Hello, Juliana."

"Hi, Ezra," she says, and our fingers twine together. Her bottom lip trembles. Her top is red from running her bottom lip across the Cupid's bow. I watch her for the familiar wink/bat with her eyes that I've missed so. It surges like a bullet through my heart when she does it finally, especially since I can tell it was automatic, not intentional.

"I missed you so much," I say, because I did. I want to kiss her. I don't, but I want to.

"I m-missed you, too. Now shut up before I really start to cry." She leans forward, expecting I'll catch her in my arms and hold her. And of course I will. It's all I've wanted to do since the last time I'd touched her.

My arms wrap around her shoulders, despite the mass of her stomach getting between us, I hold her to me and marvel that she still fits in my arms like we were molded for one another. She squeezes back, maybe harder than she intends to. I hold her close and wonder if maybe that last salt water kiss all those months ago wasn't really the last time I'll have kissed her. God, I hope not.

"Tell me what we're having?" I ought to brace myself for impact, because no matter what she says, my life is bound to change in one more way. It ought to scare me, just the tiniest bit. Instead I welcome it as thoroughly as I welcomed her into my arms.

She grins up at me, the exact sort of gorgeous smile I never thought I'd see her shine in my direction again. It slays me just like it always has. When she stands on her tiptoes and whispers three words in my ear, my face nearly splits in two.

CHAPTER NINETEEN

It's an unseasonably warm day. They happen in Colorado from time to time, but February is a strange time for one *this* warm. If I had the time or energy to go for a jog, I might have seen people in t-shirts, maybe even having picnic lunches or trying to use the grill pits in the park. A day like today usually means only one thing—another snowstorm is coming up. It's been a dark, snowy winter, and I've loved every second of it. The storm is coming, though, and it might just be a dusting or maybe one that'll shut the state down, like we had around Christmastime. But more than likely, tomorrow won't be a day to sit out on this little balcony of mine with my vapor pen (I still don't like the thing, still miss my regular cigarettes—but it's better for Juliana and the baby this way) and a cup of strong coffee. Tomorrow Mama A and my mom and a myriad of siblings will be tucked into their own snowed-in houses instead of here. Today is a good day to sit and enjoy, as long as I can.

I'm better off out of the way. Juliana ought to have some time with her family for a change—this place is closer to Constance's place than Mama A's, so it's a drive for everyone else to get here. I swill back my now-almost-cold coffee and pull on the vapor pen—the juice could use a top-off.

When Anja steps out onto the balcony with me, she has a real cigarette in her hand. "Have anything I can use as an ashtray?"

"Here, this'll work." I hand her my almost-empty coffee cup, and she places it between her feet when she sits down next to me.

"I like this place," she says, looking up at the house behind us. "It seems like it fits you guys."

"Yeah, I like it, too." I like that there's a finished basement I can see my clients in once things are a little less hectic and I can actually get the space decorated. I like the jacuzzi tub in the master bathroom. I like that a townhouse kitchen, while neither big or luxurious, is at least bigger and more functional than an apartment galley kitchen. And I really, really like my view of the mountains, one of the perks of living on the west side of the city.

"I thought you were supposed to be quitting?" I ask her, nodding towards the cigarette that's curling smoke around her face.

"I will when the stick turns blue," she says with a shrug. I'm not going to judge her—smokers get it, even though I'm sure ardent non-smokers would be calling for her head.

We spend time enjoying what neither of us have been getting that all often—silence—and don't talk about the things that are confusing. Like why Juliana and I are living together, but we aren't *together*. And why she and Mattias are starting to get concerned that they've been trying to get pregnant for nearly a year, and still haven't had any luck. I wonder if they're jealous of me and Juliana, who didn't even have to try. But then, we're such a spectacular mess in comparison to their functionality that jealousy would be ridiculous. They're together. They have each other. We're still figuring us out.

"So I have something for you," Anja says. She straightens

her leg and buries her hand in her front pocket, but what she withdraws she keeps hidden in a tight fist. "I decided that you earned this, even if you're still barely going to meetings."

I hold out my open hand and she drops a tiny thing into the center of my palm. It catches the waning afternoon sun, and my breath catches in my throat.

It's not just another aluminum chip—a one-year token is treated as a little more special than the ones handed out for the month milestones. It's lacquered and sturdy, and the '1 year' emblem glints in the waning sunlight.

"Anja... This is way too early. Way, way too early."

"That's the one I had for you last year. It's not official, of course, since I'm not your sponsor anymore. Ryan'll get another on the actual anniversary. But you've been trying so hard. You've been doing so well. Early or not, going to meetings or not, you've earned it."

There's a lump in my throat that's almost impossible to swallow over. "Have I really?"

"After everything you've been through the last two years? All of it, and you're here, sober, and have all of this...?" she says, holding her hands up for emphasis. "You could have spiraled out of control a hundred more times, but you haven't. You've stayed sober. That's an incredible achievement, Ez. I'm proud of you."

I rub the token between my thumb and forefinger, and, for a second, miss the bumpy texture of the other chips under my skin. But my lips pull up into a smile and I reach across the space between the two chairs and grab Anja's hand by the wrist so her cigarette doesn't burn me. "Thank you. For this. And for not giving up on me."

"I told you I'd never give up on you. And I meant it."

"I know you did. But thank you again."

I pop the token in my own front pocket and she shifts and moves her chair closer to mine. She loops her arm through the crook of my elbow and rests her head on my shoulder. She smokes a second cigarette as we stay there like that, silent and grateful. For a split second, it feels like we're in high school again, even though those days couldn't be farther away. And that's probably best.

Mattias taps on the sliding glass door and pokes his head out. "Time to head out, baby. Anything else you need before we go, Ez?"

I shake my head and stand to give them both a proper hug. Lukas slips out with them, but it takes an extra few seconds to get my mother and Mama A on their way. I close and lock the front door behind them and draw the blinds, lest the setting sun on our western exposure blind Jules, collapsed as she is in the chaise.

I drop onto the footstool, pick her feet up, and set them in my lap. I pull on her toes and bury my knuckle in the arch of her left foot. She moans gratefully in response. "I seriously thought for a second we were going to have to move your stuff out of the second bedroom and move Mama in instead."

"She's just excited, that's all. The novelty will wear off sooner or later, like it did for Gemma."

"Comparing my fifty-something mother to your eight-year-old sister is hardly flattering."

"Yeah, but it's apt."

"It is." She chuckles.

God, I want to lean across and kiss her. It's happened once or twice. Never passionate and lingering, just a brush of my lips against her cheek, her jaw, or the corner of her mouth. There's more than enough pressure behind her lips that convinces me she wants more, she'd so happily take more if I gave it to her, but I still can't. I always chicken out, back off, and just hold her instead. For now, this is all I can give her. Hence our things in the separate bedrooms, even if we've been innocently sharing a bed for the last several nights. Maybe I can give her more soon.

Maybe it'll still take a while. Add it to the list of things I still don't know.

There are much bigger things we need to keep in mind, anyway.

She wiggles a throw pillow out from behind her back and stuffs it between her shoulder and head. "Think I'll wake up and have a horrible kink in my neck if I sleep right here?"

"How long do you really think you'll end up sleeping for?" I say, my eyebrow raised.

"Touché."

I knead her other foot while she dozes for a few minutes. I swipe my fingertips over her ankles before I push her feet off my lap entirely and stand. She whimpers at me, sounding more tired than pathetic.

"Just running upstairs for a minute. I'll be back down in a second."

"M'kay," she says with a yawn. She smiles up at me wistfully when I lean down and peck the top of her head. It's such a waste of a kiss when it could have found her mouth, but it's still something.

In my room, I set the new token on top of my dresser next to my keys and the rest of my chips. Then, before I can think twice about it, I palm a few of the tokens, ones from earlier months well and truly behind me, and turn toe. I figure Jules is bound to have a box of envelopes in her desk. I know I don't need to ask to take one, to borrow a pen from another drawer. Unless he's moved, I remember Dylan's address off the top of my head. Funny that would be something I'd remember when so many other things are lost in the drunken abyss of my memory, but there it is. I scrawl his name and address, but write only my return address in the top corner. He'll probably recognize my handwriting, but maybe if he doesn't see my name, he'll give this a chance.

I should stuff a note in as well, but I have no idea what to write. An apology would be obvious, of course, but my apologies never seem to sit well with Dylan. And besides, it's probably too little, too late. I don't know if I want this, the spirit of this, to be a simple apology. I just want him to know I'm trying. Deep down, as fucked up as I am and I always will be, I'm trying so damn hard to get better. I'll make it to a year sober this time, and hopefully, two, three, and the rest of my life. I still might slip up and have to start over somewhere along the line, and God help me if I do because I've got too much to lose by screwing up. That's what I want Dylan to know.

Stuck on Juliana's desk, propped under her lamp, are two different ultrasound stills. She had others taken in Sao Paolo before she came back, but I'd been there for these ones. We've decided to frame them, put them in a shadow box or something for posterity, but I feel like Jules would understand I need one of them for this. I slip the photo and my chips into the envelope, lick it closed, and hunt for a stamp.

I'm interrupted before I find one.

I pick my way down the stairs carefully, arms laden as they are, and smile when Jules looks up at me.

"Hi, baby," Jules sing-songs. It's the first time our daughter has been in my arms all day, so Jules doesn't reach for her like she might otherwise. She's at least gotten to feed her a couple of times in between the swooping, circling arms of her grandmothers and uncles. "Was she fussing?"

"Just a little. Fell asleep again when I picked her up, though."

The baby sleeps astonishingly well, which means that we've gotten some rest here and there, too. We're still not unpacked fully from moving into this place, since most of our time awake has been occupied with the baby instead of settling in. That's why everyone was over just a bit ago—our bedrooms are finally unpacked and organized, the kitchen is stocked with food and clean dishes. It's a home now, for us and for her. We can actually start getting into some sort of pattern, some sort of schedule, my family and I.

The word 'family' trips me up. I have a family, even though Jules and I are still walking this strange line together. But together, we have a baby. A daughter. And yeah, I'm probably being a typical bright-eyed, wrapped-around-a-little finger new dad to a baby girl when I say that she's pretty much perfect. But she really is. She's perfect, just like I've always believed her mother to be. Someday I'll see her flaws as she grows and possibly becomes more like me than like Jules, but what I've realized about family is how deeply in love with them you always are, no matter their flaws. Maybe that's why I hope Dylan will forgive me some day sooner rather than later—deep down, I'm sure my brother still loves me, even if he doesn't like me.

"Scoot over?" I ask Jules. I pull the throw blanket off the back of the couch and hand it to her as she shifts to make room for me to settle down next to her. The baby shifts against my chest, making impossibly cute squeaking noises before she settles back and falls into an even deeper sleep. She's soft and warm and has that crazy-addicting baby smell that just slays me. Jules curls her legs up into my lap and places her palm on the baby's back. I tuck my free arm around Jules's shoulder and pull her closer. Like the baby, she is asleep in a matter of seconds.

The living room gets vibrantly bright for a moment, then begins to dim as the sun disappears behind the mountains. A wind picks up outside. I assume it's the first rush of cold air that'll bring the clouds over the mountains down into the city. As if on cue, our heat kicks on with a gentle whoosh. White noise is almost as good as silence. And I like silence. It lets me think.

I wish Mac were here to meet his granddaughter. I'm sure he'd be crazy for her. I'm sure he'd be proud of me for rising to the occasion and not shying away. I'll never be as good a dad to my daughter as he was to me, but damn it all if I'm not going to try.

In all likelihood, Dylan will scrawl 'Return to Sender' on the envelope with my chips and the ultrasound picture in it. It might take years for him to find out he has a niece, even longer for him to forgive me enough to ever know her. For all I know, he's had or is expecting a kid himself. It'd be important to Mac if and when we both have kids that they know one another. That, eventually, we bury the hatchet and at least learn to be civil to one another. Maybe one day he'll learn to forgive Constance, as I have. Maybe he'll get to know Gemma and maybe we can all be a new family. I'm not holding my breath. But it's a nice thing to hope for. I'm hopeful for a lot of things these days.

I wiggle one of my arms free and turn on the lamp next to me. Juliana shifts like she's trying to block out the light, and I kiss her forehead at her hairline. One day, hopefully not so far off, there won't be any more wasted kisses between us. I'm getting there. It's a slow process. She's patient, and I'm grateful. I want to do right by her. For both of these girls, curled up on me like I'm their rock, their everything.

Maybe I am. I'd like to think I am. I know for sure they're *my* everything.

This is what I know: my name is Ezra Mackenzie. I turned twenty-seven last November. Last week, I held Juliana Almeida's hand as our daughter entered the world.

And in that moment, she saved my life.

THE END

Thank you for reading! Catch book two of the IF IT'S BROKE novels coming soon from City Owl Press!

And be sure to find Kristin Rouse across social media.

Twitter: @krousewrites

Facebook: www.facebook.com/krousewrites/

Tumblr: krousewrites.tumblr.com

Please sign up for the City Owl Press newsletter for chances to win special subscriber-only contests and giveaways as well as receiving information on upcoming releases and special excerpts.

All reviews are welcome and appreciated. Please consider leaving one on your favorite social media and book buying sites.

For books in the world of romance and speculative fiction that embody Innovation, Creativity, and Affordability, check out City Owl Press at www.cityowlpress.com.

ACKNOWLEDGMENTS

I've been a writer ever since I could rub two words together, but it wasn't until I found a tribe of writers, readers, and fans in my little corner of the Internet that I really felt like the stories in my head might be worth telling. It was in that little corner that I found the incredible CPs—Diana Gallagher, Lindsey Ouimet, and Sarah May—who did so much to make this story better. My incredible early readers—Heather, Mandy, Jenn, Rike, and Any—cheered me on endlessly. Jennifer Ibarra, Natalia Jaster, and Stacey Lund were the first to make me brave. Elizabeth Davis, Megan Fowler, Kimberly Gardner, and Steph Kroll kept me brave. I wish I had the space and time to give the rest of you beautiful weirdos your entitled due, but in its place, please accept all my thanks and love.

Mary Cain, you are truly the best editor I could have ever hoped to work with, and I am so grateful every day you took a chance on me and my writing. Thank you will never be enough, and I hope this is only the beginning of a long and beautiful friendship (with limited uses of the word 'just'. Wink wink). Tina Moss, you and the entire City Owl team are incredible and I am so fortunate to be a part of this publishing family.

If you ever find yourselves in Denver and come across Sojourner's Coffee and Tea, Stella's Coffee Haus, or Comrade Brewing Company, do yourselves a favor and buy yourselves many, many beverages there, because this book would not exist without their delicious crafts.

Finally, to all the people I get to call my family by blood, by marriage, and by choice: thanks for loving me, flaws and all, and making me the person I am. To my best friend, the love of my life, and my partner in mutual weirdness, Richard Rouse— thanks for choosing forever with me.

ABOUT THE AUTHOR

After a lifetime of falling in love with all aspects of the written word, KRISTIN ROUSE became an avid reader and, eventually, a writer of "kissing books". She believes in writing *where* she knows as opposed to strictly *what* she knows—that said, she's lived all over the world, so this doesn't exactly limit her story settings. She currently lives in Denver with her husband, and can be found on a yoga mat or at a local coffee house with her laptop in equal measure.

Twitter: @krousewrites

Facebook: www.facebook.com/krousewrites/

Tumblr: krousewrites.tumblr.com

ABOUT THE PUBLISHER

CITY OWL PRESS is a cutting edge indie publishing company, bringing the world of romance and speculative fiction to discerning readers.

www.cityowlpress.com